THE SCHOOL RUN

To Ada and Brian
with best wishes

Bob Yondoto

20. 3. 003

THE SCHOOL RUN

BY

BOB GONDOLO

Blackie & Co
Publishers Ltd

A BLACKIE & CO PUBLISHERS PAPERBACK

© Copyright 2003
Bob Gondolo

The right of Bob Gondolo to be identified as the author of
this work has been asserted by him in accordance with the
Copyright, Designs and Patents Act 1988

First published in 2003

A CIP catalogue record for this title is
available from the British Library

ISBN 1 903138 71 X

**BLACKIE & CO PUBLISHERS LTD
107-111 FLEET ST
LONDON EC4A 2AB
AND PO BOX 30
ELY CB7 4WU**

Dedication

This book is dedicated to M and B.

*To Maggie, for turning my longhand, sometimes
unintelligible pages into a readable manuscript.
To Bettina, for leading me onto, and along,
the lengthy path to publication.*

A champagne cork bobbed playfully along the side of a motor yacht, it nudged the smooth white fibreglass hull as though trying to rejoin the party at which it had recently been popped. In company with a Diet Pepsi can, it would travel the boat's overall 40 feet length before drifting off into the calm marina night. Inside the hull, lights were bright and the music loud as some forty people sipped champagne, crammed, sardine fashion, into every luxurious corner of Jack Delaney's new boat. Elegant fingers managed to support a filter tip, smoked salmon nibbles, and sip from a tall stemmed glass whilst balanced on a navigation table.

'Lovely finish Jack. Love this suede everywhere, navy blue, very smart I must say, hope nobody spills Martini down it Sweetie.'

'They'd better not,' replied the host, squeezing between packed bodies. 'It's cost me an arm and both legs, I can do without cleaning bills. Anyone want topping up, what about you Sidney, old horse, can't have our Secretary running dry can we? There you go, hold still.'

'What's in this?'

'Don't even think about it Sidders, just lay back and enjoy it.'

The boat tilted slightly causing all drinks to slop dangerously close to spilling over. 'Oops,' croaked the rusty voice of Treasurer Tully Masters. 'Another mob coming over the gangway, standby to repel boarders.'

'They'll have to stay on deck,' suggested Fiona from the navigation table. 'If we get anymore down here it'll be positively immoral!'

'That's what I love about these floating get-togethers, darling,' came the cool voice of the Commodore's wife, Liz Blake. 'One just couldn't be stand-offish if one tried!'

'I know but I just wish I could work out whose hand is on my leg'.

'Ah yes,' owned up Paul Rogers from underneath the table. 'It's me just trying to stand up.'

'What for?'

'Well actually I was going to pop along to the heads.'

'Sorry.' cut in Jack. 'The heads aren't operational yet. Sid's lads have still got to finish off the plumbing. You'll have to go ashore or use the 'porta potty' chemical job up for'ard for now.' Fiona laughed, 'You're the end Jack you really are. Fancy inviting us all to your boat warming and then telling us we can't use the loo, you know what I'm like after two or three glasses of your champagne punch, goes straight through me; all it needs is for Tully to sing that song of his about the Nuns and I'll probably wet myself and that's the truth.'

'Well in that case,' shouted the host, 'You'd better get off my chart table, that's the North Sea you're sitting on and we don't want that to get wet now do we?'

A chorus of laughter almost drowned the music until, in a lull, Sid's voice ventured. 'Did I hear you say you'd bought a chart of the North Sea Jack? You don't actually mean you're going to risk taking this spanking new boat out to sea do you?'

'Not until you've finished putting in the loo's he won't,' said another voice.

'And, after all, the heads is the most important place on the boat, at least it is for Fiona as she is always pumping out her bilge.'

'Avast you pontoon dwellers,' roared the public address sized output of the Commodore's voice. 'Turn that music down for a bit... I think it's about time we raised our glasses to this new addition to the Milehaven cruising fleet. Our Flag Officer, Mr. Jack Delaney, as you all know is a sailor of considerable experience... both ashore and afloat. True he ran aground in the past a few times like the rest of us. Short cutting across Nore Sands at low tide and maybe putting to sea in a boat more suited to the Norfolk Broads than the English Channel, but this is a good sea boat and I know she'll do him proud. With two Volvo turbo diesels and a good planing hull she'll

2

push along nicely in most conditions.

As a club we will of course always fall into two groups, those who go for the comfortable life with nice beamy displacement hulls content to make twelve knots (like Tully and his big single Perkins diesel) and those who want to get up on the plane and skim over the surface with twin turbo diesels at 40 knots. Well, as you can see, if you want to go to sea on a Greyhound special you'll have to sacrifice a little space which is why we're all wedged in here rather cosily. Perhaps that's an argument for holding our next soirée on Tully's 'Grande Banks' then we could all sit around in that nice wide saloon. I'm actually quite amazed how many of us have managed to squeeze on board tonight. (Perhaps we can get into the Guinness Book of Records!)

Whilst on the subject of space, this club doesn't have the exclusive rights over the Marina. We are allocated a guaranteed number of pontoon berths for our members, leaving the rest for the public and of course visiting vessels. At the moment we've used up that allocation and with a waiting list of six anyone now accepted for membership will either have to tie alongside one of you or take a mooring outside on the riverbank for now (and with a six knot current and a tidal range of over fifteen feet, that's not going to be very comfortable). I know having someone tied up alongside is not ideal but do try and help if you can.'

Only those within ten feet of the Commodore could actually hear what he was saying and, even then, he was fighting a losing battle against the effects of Jack's punch, Glen Miller and ongoing conversations. Smokers outside on the upper deck were once removed from the congenial claustrophobia below, whilst two higher still on the flying bridge were simply shapes against a starlit sky. The falling star of a butt-end flicked into the night describing a perfect arc until it dropped into black water where the bobbing cork and tin had made their way. A lighter flared and for a second lit the face of Sidney Arthur. 'Sounds like the Skipper is saying a few words, still I'm sure we've heard it all before.'

'Yes,' replied the sort of husky voice that breeds affairs, 'I'm sure. Here, light this for me will you'. He took the cigarette holding it tip to tip until a glow united them; then breaking the silence of inhalation said, 'Best place to be is up here above it all, unless you're at sea in a force seven that is, then you get thrown around a bit, but I like to be on top of things.'

'I'd noticed.'

'You know what I mean, down in the wheelhouse I feel sort of shut away from things. Out here it's different, you sense the power, and it's like riding a huge horse. The moment you ease the throttle forward she rises above the water, then you hear the whine of the turbos as they push you over twenty knots...nothing like it I can tell you sweetheart. It's the ultimate buzz!'

'Better than sex?'

'Different but certainly less complicated. You can enjoy it without feeling guilty.'

'You do feel guilty then. I know you pretend to be Jack the lad, but you're not!'

'Sometimes, I suppose, well it's different for you isn't it I mean you're separated and I'm married with three kids. God help us. It's having to pretend the whole time that gets me down. You know having to play happy families.'

'Well, at least you have the excuse of running your own company. SA Marine gets you out at all hours, doesn't it?'

'Yes it does, but then I've always been able to do that. You forget I was an emergency plumber for five years. Some of the housewives who called me out in the night wanted much more than their leaking tanks sorted out!'

'Oh! It's all coming out now isn't it, no wonder you did so well.'

'Yep, must say I didn't do too badly at all. I overcharged the rich old ducks and serviced the widows. Don't know why I

4

gave it up now I come to think about it. It was a great life, but then I suppose I wanted the high life.'

'Now you've got it, up here on this smart new flying bridge.'

'But it's not mine, is it? It belongs to Jack, King of the one-armed bandits, (there's mega bucks in clubs and amusement arcades. It's coming out of his ears!')

'You're doing OK with SA Marine. You employ three fitters and me. You have a full order book and your own business premises which can't be bad can it!'

'As long as it lasts.'

'Don't be such a pessimist. You're under contract to fit water systems to every new cruiser on their production line, aren't you? And they are doing very nicely, so stop worrying. Anyway as I do the books I'd be the first one to see anything wrong with our profit and loss.'

'It's not our business life that concerns me it's where we're going in our love life.'

'What do you mean? There's nothing wrong with us. In fact we've got it made as far as I can see.'

'Well I'm looking a little further ahead. OK, yes at the moment all is well. We're together at the office and I keep a boat here which Janet and the children are hardly ever on, which suits us fine as we have somewhere to sleep together whenever we want to.'

She put her finger on his lips gently, 'But I heard you saying to Rodney that you might consider changing your boat for a new one like this. Now if I were Janet even if I didn't like boats, nothing would stop me from coming over here every weekend, just to pose on such a nice new one, and look filthy rich. Do you really fancy changing? There's not much wrong with yours is there?'

Sid hesitated sometime before replying, 'Yeah, quite a lot really, at least as far as this club is concerned. The thing is I've got to keep up with the others, mine's over ten years old. The technology's dated, and it's only got a single engine.'

'Is that a big deal?'

'Oh yes, it makes me into a second class citizen.'

'How's that for heavens sake?'

'Well basically I don't fit into either group. I'm too slow for the first lot and the wrong type for the second. I mean they're more like a caravan club!'

'Oh you mean old Rodney's scheme for separating everybody into fast boats and slow cruisers on our club outings. You're not worried on that score are you?'

'Well Rodney's got a bee in his bonnet about forming a special high-speed power boat section called The Greyhounds. You know actually painting them all grey like warships. I think he's potty but I'm the Club Secretary after all, so I should set a good example by up-grading my sea-going hardware. I do hear what you're saying about Janet though, she's kept nicely out of the way so far and we don't want her over here at weekends spoiling things for us that's for sure. So, my love, there's a perfect answer if you think about it.'

'What's that when it's out?'

'Well she is scared stiff of the sea - right! Doesn't even like big slow boats.'

'Yes that's true, she's made that quite clear.'

'So I trade mine in for a sleek powerboat like this. Join the Greyhounds and she'll never come out on that, so you can be my crew, can't you? That way Rodney is happy and we get a perfect excuse for being on our own whenever we like. Neat eh?'

'Not bad big boy,' hummed the husky tone of Tina. 'Even if we do have to take on a battle-ship grey paint job, but of course I'll get a new galley and loo, sorry I mean 'Heads,' Skipper, not to mention that gorgeous fore cabin with the double berth for us to roll about on. This is beginning to sound quite interesting. You're not such a bad boss after all, Sidney Arthur.'

'There's just one snag,' mused the big time plumber soberly. 'The Greyhounds have a crew of three and we don't want a chaperone do we, honey bun?'

'Too true, so how do we get round that one Skipper?'

'We divide all the jobs between us. I'll take on Engineer, Coxswain and Master whilst you act as Radio Officer, Galley slave and Deckhand. Think you can cope with all that?'

'Aye, aye, sir, but what about navigation, that's far too high tech for your Secretary/PA!'

'Comes under Yacht Master, so that's OK. I think we'd better go below again we're missing out on the food. I can smell it. I saw a big dish of coronation chicken in the galley. The gannets will see it off in no time at all.'

'Too true,' agreed the voice which could make the most mundane statement sound like an invitation to bed. 'I'd hate to end the evening with damp crisps and left over sausage rolls'.

In the average marina, boating activity had its highs and lows with summer at the peak, and winter when shutters rattled in bitter winds and boats were hauled out on the hard for anti-fouling and repair. But Milehaven was not average and as a major yacht club, generated interest that was something more than casual family entertainment.

On most days of the year there was a general air of purpose, with boats in use and the clubhouse graced with conversation and the clink of glasses. As Steward Kenneth Miles was often heard to say, 'There's no need for a PA system, if someone's missing - just look in the bar.' It was a long room but contained and cosy with low level lighting, mellow brickwork and exposed beams taken from the old boathouse, now long demolished. It was a long-standing custom of the club that those proposed for membership should attend as guests for several evenings before the committee gave their application due consideration. Much beer would be consumed on evenings such as these before Sid as secretary rang the big

7

ships bell for silence and gave a formal call to order.

'Gentlemen we have strangers on the gangway, splice the main brace.' At this moment Kenneth, always the perfect Steward, would appear bearing a silver tray laden with silver tots of vodka. These would be plucked off and held aloft by all and sundry until Sidney declared the Toast "Milehaven." This was echoed in chorus by the assembled company who then downed the tots in one. At this point Rodney Blake rose at his table in the corner as the lusty chorus died, to face the members. 'The committee and myself always ask all candidates for membership to join us in the Wardroom for a drink because we believe that it's the best place to get to know someone whilst leaning on a bar with a glass in their hand 'In vino veritas' one might say, and tonight we welcome Keith Parks and Brian Mansell. Whilst I hope they will have formed some impressions already, I'd just like to say a few words about us in general.

Firstly, Milehaven is what you make it. To some it's a family thing, somewhere they can bring the kids at the weekend to mess about on the boat. (I can name several boats which rarely leave their moorings) which is fine, the marina is a nice place to spend a day after all. And of course the public is made very welcome at anytime – it's good for local business trade. Milehaven Motor Yacht Club flies the Blue Ensign. It is entitled to do this because of its war service, not my own involvement with Coastal Forces I hasten to add, but its own direct contribution when three of its wooden motor boats made the crossing to Dunkirk to assist in the evacuation of British Forces. Only one of those boats returned. 'The Sea Swan' which you'll probably have noticed, preserved up on blocks at the marina entrance. It's there as a reminder of our traditions, we're proud of the flag we fly and are anxious to ensure that all our boats honour it by their example as they cruise around our coastal waters. A lot is expected of us, which is why we need to vet all candidates for membership with more care than perhaps many other clubs around. Basically candidates need to be the owners of a safe, seaworthy vessel and themselves a qualified Skipper with reasonable sea time experience under all conditions.

Once accepted as a member of MMYC, your boat will fly the Blue Ensign and our club pennant whilst at sea and observe our code of seamanship. Outside of that, as I've just said it's up to you, come and go as you please on your own or choose to take an active part in club activities.... (On the water as well as in the bar!) We enter competitions with other clubs; organize trials and events which can involve all members of the family all year round. Like most cruising clubs we also like to cruise in company. This offers many advantages. It's safer should anything go wrong as we usually keep in visual touch as well as in radio contact. It's more fun as we have a great time socially when we eventually get together ashore. Now, in order to keep together, it's easier to cruise in two groups, separating the heavier deep draught or displacement vessels (which are slower of course) from the fast planing boats. I lead the faster boats and Tully the wide boys as we call them. It seems to work out well and encourages everybody to venture further afield in their cruising... it all comes down to the old 'safety in numbers' syndrome really I suppose.

Now there's a third group of members who like to play together, at present five in number. We call them 'The Greyhounds.' Identical Sea Beaver 36 'specials' powered by twin V-eight turbo diesels producing a top speed of around 36 knots at sea. I've been accused by some of trying to create a private navy. Whilst this is nonsense as there are no weapons or militant intent, I must concede there are some similarities to warships in that these boats are grey, spartan in profile and powerful in performance. So what are they doing here? I'll answer your question before it's asked. The Greyhounds are here because I believe there was a need to provide a boating

9

challenge for a more serious section of our membership, something which would stretch their seamanship skills to the limit in exactly the same way cave divers risk their lives underground, and civilian parachutists jump out of airplanes. You see the spirit I encountered whilst in command of gunboats during the Second World War was something I can never forget and a quality worth passing on to others privileged enough to go to sea in expensive small boats. The whole thing started because I had my last new boat painted grey and fitted out like a warship, cutting out all unnecessary weight, shorter in length and with more powerful engines so I could relive the feeling of being on my old naval MGB again. Someone here saw it and wanted to do the same. The yachting press featured our two boats and it's grown from there'.

'I can see the attraction,' cut in Brian Mansell 'To have a firm purpose instead of just pottering around offshore on fine weekends, bit hard on the family though isn't it, adopting the active service life? No time for sunbathing on deck or water skiing. I'm not sure mine would go for that. They associate motor yachts with cruising in calm waters at a leisurely 12 knots. Gin and tonic on the hour and five star meals ashore in the evenings, not hanging on by their teeth in a North Sea gale for hours. Plus I imagine these special Sea Beavers set you back a bob or two!'

Rodney held up his hands. 'Yes you're right of course, it's not a family thing, but nor is crewing racing yachts offshore especially in events like the Fastnet, or climbing in the Alps as a group for that matter. As for expensive - yes it's that too. Our specials cost around £65,000 more than the normal Beaver Marine range simply because they're custom made for us, although in actual fact many of the plush fittings have been cut out. Beaver Marine were quite surprised when I told them what I wanted. They hadn't produced anything like this, other than for HM Customs and the Coastguard. In family motoring terms we'd still be classified as social domestic and pleasure but in reality we've got a bit more bite to us.'

'This Greyhound group of yours sound a bit like a seagoing version of the Red Arrows,' suggested Keith Parks...'Is that a fair comparison?'

'It's flattering and perhaps optimistic,' replied the Commodore. 'But to achieve that standard of formation work needs real professional dedication and possibly far more sea time than we can hope to put in as a group. Certainly though that sort of precision when manoeuvring is one of our aims, possibly leading to performances at sea festivals and regattas in the future. You sound as though you might be interested Keith. We could always use enthusiasm, that's the main ingredient.'

Keith smiled, 'Oh it's an interesting and very unusual concept, I must admit, there's no doubt about it. If one could use one's own boat, fine, but to have to make a change, that's a big commitment. Not however out of the question,' he reflected, 'If one were to buy it on the company as a management training facility, for instance, it might be tax deductible. After all I send my management people on leadership and initiative courses all the time.'

'That's something we've never thought of ourselves actually,' chipped in Rodney. 'We could run training cruises for sea cadets and other groups. I mean the sailing people do it all the time with sail training on ships like the 'Winston Churchill.' Thank you for the thought, Keith. It's nice when new boys come up with fresh ideas. We'll give it some thought. Now I think that deserves a round of drinks. Steward would you like to take the orders?'

Sidney Arthur had been in the pink in the days when as a self-employed jobbing plumber he was paid in cash. It was menial work but basic and carefree, sweating over copper joints bending pipes and sorting out the sexual fantasies of frustrated urban housewives in the working afternoon. But then a chance ball cock replacement in the lavatory of a boat manufacturer led to contract work fitting out the glass fibre shells of power cruisers with fresh water systems. Sid gained in status immediately and in six months he had a glass sided office with rented working space within a spacious boat shed. He also had a secretary, three employees and a substantial working overdraft. He was now a man of substance. Only now on paper and not in his back pocket.

On the premise that success breeds success, he was astute enough to know he must now look to his image and that would of course take money. Fortunately the bank, which had been happy to provide his working overdraft, also produced a gold card to steer him on the path to affluence. Three years, one BMW and one Greyhound special power cruiser later, he had progressed from being in the pink and was now firmly in the red. This was not entirely due to the acquisition of worldly goods but simply sustaining the life style to which he had now become accustomed. Membership of the Golf Club, the Chamber of Commerce, Freemasons, and of course Milehaven Motor Yacht Club were necessary to anyone who aspired to the higher realms of the business world, weren't they?

Janet Arthur understood this for her husband had explained it so many times, a high profile and credibility in the market place had to be maintained. You couldn't stand still. You had to constantly push forward in business or you could end up dead in the water (which was no place for a plumber) and her Sid was a Director. She was so proud of him and all he'd done. They'd got a gold card now too, she'd told the ladies of the social club (many times) at Bingo and at the meat raffle on Fridays... Mind you he'd had to work for all he'd got Sid had, out all hours, half the nights sometimes, even weekends, but it was worth it and they didn't lack for anything, Sid always saw to that. He never minded all the things she ordered on the catalogue. She'd like to see a bit more of him, but you couldn't have everything now could you. He knew generally what was best for the family... except for this new boat. There was nothing wrong with the old one that she could see and they didn't use it much anyway... as a family... She'd have to talk to him again about it. Janet never challenged Sid directly for to her he was very much the man of the house, but she did have a way of scratching her left ear that effectively signified doubt or non-agreement.

There was a long standing arrangement of their meeting two friends for lunch at the social club on Saturdays and Sid's transition from artisan to business class usually provided food for conversation around a plastic table bearing pints of lager, bitter lemons and plates of ham, eggs and chips.

'Been out on that boat of yours lately?' inquired kitchen fitter Dave, waving a fork lift of chips. 'It's alright for some isn't it!'

'I don't get much time,' replied Sid defensively. 'Too much work on really. Got to keep things moving at the works especially with the season coming on, and there's the wages bill always to pay every week.'

'Stop - you're breaking me heart,' laughed the chip lifter waving another delivery in mid air. 'You've got them doing it for you now you're the gaffer. All you need to do is to check their time-sheets isn't it?'

'He works very hard my Sid does,' cut in Janet. 'Just like he's always done never mind him being the boss. We hardly ever see him now or the boat for that matter. That spends all its time tied up at the marina... doesn't it, Sid?'

Rubbing her ear gently she continued, 'But he's thinking of buying a new one now would you believe!'

Dave lowered his fork momentarily. 'Hey is that a fact? You rich pig, bigger and better I suppose for your corporate entertaining, and still more room for us. Now perhaps we'll get to the Channel Islands; remember that cruise you've always been promising us... Come on tell us what it's like then and when we can come down for the boat warming.'

Sidney took a long pull on his lager before saying, 'It's actually smaller than 'Plumbline' and different.'

'Smaller than your Fairline Forty?' Disappointment was apparent in the tone. 'But more luxurious inside eh? More of a sport boat, sort of Sunseeker type perhaps?'

'No I'm afraid not, it's a Sea Beaver Special.'

'What's that? Sounds like some sort of fishing boat but you don't fish.'

'It's a dedicated no-nonsense sea boat, slim, high speed. Looks like a pilot boat or customs launch.'

Doesn't sound like lots of weekend fun... why d'you want a boat like that, me ol' mate? We've had some great times together on Plumbline.'

'I've been asked to join the Milehaven Greyhounds and all the boats have to be of exactly the same specification. It's as simple as that!' He explained Rodney Blake's new scheme as Dave shook his head slowly.

'Sounds as though you're taking your boating very seriously then Sidney.'

'Well let's just say it's a challenge I want to take up.'

'What about crew? It doesn't sound much of a family sort of thing.'

'Oh there's always spare bods who want some sea-time but don't own a boat at the club who would only be too pleased to crew with me.'

'Well, you wouldn't get me going out on it the way Sid's described it anyway,' laughed Janet. 'I'm not too keen on deep water it frightens me to death but I'm sure Sid won't lack for crew, there's always Tina at a pinch.'

Her husband paused, breaded scampi suspended in front of a ready-open mouth. Was this an innocent comment or did she know something? He decided on a disarming if ambiguous little smile followed by extended scampi mastication to gain thinking time. 'He's lucky to have such a devoted secretary,' she continued, waving her fork rather close to Dave's left ear. 'Real treasure that girl, works all hours, at the works, at the club.... as a volunteer, that is she doesn't get a penny, does it all for love. It's more than I would do. Efficient, well I don't know how she manages to keep on top of things day-after-day, Sid'll tell you how she does it.' Her husband felt his face colouring-up as he scattered garden peas across the table causing a timely diversion. 'Oh! Sid, you always do it don't you. Here let me.' She joined the others in pea recovery and the moment of danger passed, to linger only in a mind which had seen reality laid bare seemingly for all to see. But Sid Arthur was a veteran of talking his way out of things and, composure recovered, he proceeded now to justify the need to buy a new boat (which lacked space to entertain friends or in fact provide the accepted luxuries associated with cruising yachts.)

'It's alright for some,' observed Dave smacking the sauce bottle until it splat great globules of viscose red across his lunch. 'I wish I had that sort of dosh!'

Sid smiled his 'I'm in control' smile. 'No problem, son, it's all a question of liquidity control. First it's part exchange, and I trade in 'Plumbline' that drops the anti by about 40%, then the balance comes out of the company capital. I buy it on SA Marine you see.'

'How do you justify that to the Tax Man?'

'Easy, don't forget we design fresh water systems for cruisers, so we need a vessel as a floating test bed don't we!'

'D'you think you'll get away with it?'

'Accountant reckons it's OK and the bank don't care what I use the loan for as long as I keep up the interest payments.'

'So Sidney, doesn't look as though we'll be having many boozy weekends on Plumbline Two.'

Dave's elbow nudged Janet at waist level vigorously, 'you and the kids will have to come away with us in the caravan

when he's out with his greyhounds on operations eh? You
want to watch him, luv, next thing it'll be a sailor's farewell
when he gets a wife in every port! Oh! dear, oh! dear, poor
Sidney, I suppose your movements will be classified
information soon won't they. Oh! dear,' he laughed.
Sid reached across the table, 'I'll get another round in before
you choke yourself to death. Sup up Gloria, same again?'

Tradewind looked out of place in the marina, old varnished
wood against the polished fibreglass, a traditional motor-
sailor. Its dowdy, dumpy lines owed more to those of a
cornish crab boat. Unlike most other owners John Crowther
lived aboard all year round. Having sold his house where he
lived in retirement until his wife died. He planned to cruise
worldwide when his boat had been refitted (after years of
disuse up the pre-marina creek). Being always on the
moorings he had become the Ex Officio guardian of pontoons.
With the true sailor's ability to jury-rig, (the seaman's DIY) he
could be seen on deck most days splicing painting even
welding. People stopped to chat to him, brought their boating
problems to his shed-like wheelhouse, and listened to his
merchant navy tales. Some came by coach just for the day and
would crouch down to photograph 'Tradewind' with Bosun,
his shaggy dog sitting on the bow as it did for hours like some
classic figurehead. Inside, below deck it could be best
described as snug in kindest terms, at worst as cluttered, dark
and claustrophobic but to John and Bosun it was home.
Somewhere secure that fitted like a well-worn shoe, a place
where everything they needed was more or less in reach. No
more silent, empty rooms to stand in and feel the hurt that was
the absence of her voice. No greenhouse with her cuttings still
in rows of pots which he had never planted out. It didn't make
much sense that the house and garden he'd loved so much
when Angela was part of it had so quickly become something
cold, almost sinister, that he could hardly wait to leave. Bosun

16

hadn't been much comfort either. He'd just stand for hours staring at the seat beneath the Cedar tree where she'd so often sit reading in the afternoons, as if he could see something unseen by his master. John knew he'd have to sell the house before its pressing silence drove him to distraction, but the prospect of some top flat or a cottage in a cul-de-sac seemed really like the end of things. To simply get away each day, out where he could see the sky and feel the sun was the answer. He'd get in the car with the dog and drive down to the river. They'd walk for what seemed miles along the towpath to where Milehaven Creek turned sharply inland. At low tide its bed was all black ooze, rank smelling and beloved of seabirds with just a straggle of boats dispersed at crazy angles at the edge of what brackish water still remained. That's where he first saw 'Tradewind' looking very much the worse for wear. She was lying over on her side as though left for dead, her keel and deep displacement hull livid green with slime, all upper works concealed beneath an old tarpaulin cover. Yet even in those distant days of gross neglect, exposed to all the ravages of wind and tide before the coming of the new Marina, the vessel displayed great strength and dignity. Even the dog that dared approach her demonstrated a sense of possession by passing water over her propeller. Now after all this time the boat was his, to live on, eat, sleep and work on, tied up safely to a pontoon with all mod cons.   John reached for his old Peterson pipe, packed a bowl slowly with his favourite sweet smelling tobacco, tamped it down and lit up carefully. He looked around the saloon through a haze of exhaled smoke in quiet contemplation. Apart from Bosun he was actually alone; that hadn't changed but somehow it was different. It was as if her spirit had decided to join him on board the boat so they could share a new life together, leaving all the shadows of the greenhouse and the garden seat behind. He patted Bosun's back down on the floor beside him softly. 'Right my old son, we'll make a start stripping down that

17

engine first thing after breakfast tomorrow.'

There was a haze of smoke in Jack Delaney's office too but not the tang of pipe tobacco. It came from a loosely rolled joint of cannabis protruding from the mouth of Alfie Morello which flapped up and down as he spoke, which was most of the time.

'Do you have to sprawl all over my desk Alfie, there's plenty of chairs in here and for God's sake open a window - that weed of yours is killing my throat!'

The addressed shrugged his shoulders sulkily. 'If you had one yourself you wouldn't notice. You need to chill out man. Don't get so wound up.'

'Wound up am I, well I damn well need to be. You're so spaced out most of the time you need a route map to find yourself. Have you fixed that machine yet?' His scruffy employee turned his grubby hand palm upwards. 'Needs a new return spring.'

'Well! Bloody well go and get one. We can't have a fruit machine that pops out a jackpot every two hours, no wonder the punters are queuing up to use it. The odds must be in our favour Alfie, get it!, that's what the machines are there for. It may say amusement arcade outside but what it really means is abusement, separating the mugs from their dosh as efficiently and frequently as possible. No wonder I need a chain of these dives to make any decent profit. God! It's a hard life trying to make an honest living and no mistake. Ah there's Fenton arriving. Go and give him a hand to bring the stuff in quickly before he gets a ticket.' Fenton Gesler didn't look like an accountant clad as he was in soft leather jacket and stretch jeans, but then he didn't act like one on most occasions.

'There you are, Fenton, come on in,' He ushered the Gesler chic through the electronic whirlpool of the arcade where a thousand flashing lights and computer generated voices clamoured for attention. Lines of slot-feed addicts stood heads bent forward, shoulders hunched, pulling handles, ever

18

hopeful of the win which would fill the tray again with coins to refeed the machines ad infinitum. A rear door sealed off the phoney world and they stepped into the functional simplicity of Jack Delaney's office.

'Sorry I'm late Jack there was a lot to go over and well your books ain't the simplest in the world to bring to order.'

Jack held up his hands. 'Point taken, ours is a complex business, it's difficult to keep tabs on everything at times... coffee?'

Fenton shook his head, 'No thanks I'll get caffeine shakes if I have any more today. I've been sorting out a reinvestment plan for a client of mine, Charlie Nagle, and his partner.'

Jack laughed, 'You mean you've been laundering a little doubtful dosh for the Bayswater Boys. What is it - protection or insurance scam this time?'

'We haven't had this conversation Jack, you'll ruin my street cred if you're not careful. Now let's get down to business. Frankly I'm just a little concerned about your profit levels.'

'Do you mean the arcades or the clubs?'

'Both really. Don't misunderstand me. In normal trading terms things are fine, even allowing for the usual fiddling by casual staff, everything is acceptable. But, compared to similar operations I'm dealing with, you're losing out old son.'

'How's that then?'

Fenton lit up a cigarette and inhaled before answering. 'Well let's say there's a lot of action going on in and around that you get no percentage of... and it's lucrative action... you must be aware of it. Is it that you are turning a blind eye?'

'I think I know what you're going on about. It's the pushers isn't it?'

Fenton nodded 'Yes, it's the pushers Jack, pubs, clubs arcades, it's the market place you know that as well as I do.'

'Of course I do, that little runt Alfie is one. I've seen him at it many times.'

19

'And you've done nothing about it, with all that cash changing hands?'

'What can I do? If I challenge him he'll deny it and I've no proof and if I sack him the next one will probably be doing the same thing.'

'Yes I can see that, but you know what they say don't you. If you can't break 'em, join 'em. Get a bit of the action. Has that never occurred to you?'

'What me become a pusher, that's not my style Fenton, No way!'

'Of course not, I don't mean push the stuff I mean supply it. Control the pushers, that's where the money is and it's big money.'

'Oh! I see now, the Bayswater Boys, the money you're laundering, it's from drugs and you're part of it. I'd no idea. God you're taking a risk. Your fees are big enough, aren't they, without getting involved in that scene as well? You could end up inside.'

'Listen Jack, I'm an accountant not a gambler. I add things up, and end up with a balance. They just cut me in for handling the money, which is quite complicated, I can tell you, but I'm not fully involved because everything is on a 'need to know' basis, that's the way they work. It's just like a normal accounts job in many ways. To the outside world I'm doing a normal job, I deal with normal average people, nothing flamboyant or special, hauliers, shipping agents. I've just got on with things in my normal way. The only difference is I'm making something like ten times more than my usual fee.'

He stopped suddenly. 'I don't know why I'm telling you all this. I've never talked about it before, not to anyone. You could shop me Jack if you wanted to.'

Jack chose to ignore this statement.

'What made you think I would be interested in drug trafficking or that I would have the ability to do so without putting myself in danger?'

'I've known you long enough to know what you want out of life and what you've got to offer,' explained the accountant, and actually I don't think you would be capable of carrying it off.'

'You don't?'

'That's right... not on your own, but you and I could together, we've got everything necessary to do the job. We're complementary to each other.'

'Go on I'm listening.'

'Well the Baywater Boys have supplied me with all the background contacts necessary for payments on their behalf to the Growers, Refiners, and Shippers. So I should know where to go for the best deals, and who to trust to get it over here in prime condition. But, more importantly, they know me. Distribution, however, is another matter. I couldn't sort that out myself, but you could by Christ, you've just been talking about it. You are standing in the middle of the market place, Jack, surrounded by people like Alfie and for every one you know about there will be four or five doing it behind your back in your clubs and arcades. They could be doing it for you and me if we got together. Don't you see, we are supply and demand, the basis of all trade and commerce?'

Jack Delaney stood up to face a window, which looked out upon a blank brick wall. 'I don't know, Fenton, it's a frightening world and one I've always kept away from, partly because I don't want to end up oozing blood down some dark alley and partly because I've seen what drugs can do to people. You've considered that surely?'

'Of course I have, I've gone over the ground many times but I've got one foot in already don't forget, have had for sometime now, so it's not the same for me. But in moral terms of course you're not exactly on the outside Jack. I mean you run two nightclubs where sex and drugs are all part of the same scene and a string of amusement arcades where, as we've discussed, pushers operate on a regular basis. Frankly, to be squeaky clean you'd need to sell up and get into kitchen furniture or something and I'd need to get on the chartered audit circuit. Look somebody will always supply if we don't and the users have free choice don't forget, nobody is forced to be a user are they? I mean we don't use it, we're not addicts are we?'

'That's your third cigarette since you've been here Fenton!'

'It's only a social habit not an addiction. I can stop it anytime I want to.'

'OK what about the Bayswater Boys are they going to cut up rough if they find out you're importing on your own account in competition I mean, as far as I know it could be them who are already supplying the pushers in my club (the ones I'm not supposed to know about.)

'Ah!' exclaimed Fenton. 'That would be down to me. I would be looking after security and making sure that my producers overseas never disclose they are selling to me, and also that the pushers never know who is actually supplying them.'

'You seem to have thought of everything. Seems as though, Mr. Gesler, you had prepared for this meeting with me. I mean apart from depressing me with my profit figures.'

'No, Jack honestly, I'd never given it a thought as far as you were concerned but it did occur to me several times that all the knowledge I've gleaned from handling the Bayswater money could perhaps be put to better use on my own account.'

'So what's stopped you then, not your conscience from what you've just said?'

'No. I've got over that stage, the truth is I know it could be done but I just haven't had the bottle to go it alone. That's about the size of it really. Now today, talking to you, I've realised that you would be perfect as a partner.'

'Partners in crime eh. That's a thought now, isn't it, and I've always thought you were clean as a whistle.... except of course you've shown me a few tricks in tax and vat evasion over the years. I hear what you're saying Fenton and I know the stakes are high but I must say the risks are high as well. As far as I can see those who've pulled off a big hit, like the Great Train Robbers have drawn attention to themselves by flashing great wads of cash around, paying for everything in readies'

'That's right, they just haven't the intelligence to handle it so they start flashing it around instead of stashing it somewhere while the heat's on - unlike the Bayswater Boys who employ me to squirrel it away, safely invested offshore in nice respectable stocks and bonds. Do you know the Cayman Islands have more banks than pubs? There are laundering facilities all over the place if you know where to look...and of course if you have a respectable face like me. I've been doing it for years for some of the nicest people; names in public life you'd never guess were in the game. I think I'm talking too much but then I trust you Mr. Jack... you've got an honest face too!'

'I have, well I don't know about that. I think we need a drink don't you?'

He took two glasses from a corner cabinet. 'We'll finish off the single malt...for starters anyway. Now let's run over how you see things then (hypothetically of course you understand.) So you would buy in the refined product using your Colombian contacts with capital put up front by the both of us' Fenton nodded. 'And investment capital, but I have a friend who could help out in that connection.'

'What about importation that's where the risk is? Isn't it?'

'The Cartel ship it from Colombia into Amsterdam and it's from there that things can get difficult. We've come unstuck on that leg on too many occasions. Mostly on lorries overland and through the tunnel. The custom boys have really got it sorted now that's the problem. We've tried individual carriers too, you've heard the stories of course, swallowed in condoms, or shoved up every available orifice of the body or sewn into garments, all good dramatic stuff, but not in the sort of quantities we need to move. We're talking bulk here to turn over big money Jack, kilos. Yes and before you ask we have tried air and sea. Light aircraft with no filed flight plan can be tracked on radar and searched on landing, as can yachts moving offshore. The stuff is getting through OK but not without some difficulty I have to tell you' He lit a cigarette and drew long and slow on it before observing 'You've got a boat haven't you? I seem to remember'

'I've just bought a new one actually, it was time for a change'

'Bigger and better I suppose'

'Different really, more powerful, state of the art navigation and communications. It's a new class. We've got five at Milehaven. Sort of long range power cruisers.' Jack shot a glance sideways at Fenton 'Hey, you're not suggesting!'

'That you might take care of the last leg, well I must say the boat you've just described does sound remarkably well suited to the task'

'No way, not drug running I couldn't, it's far too risky. I've seen the custom boys at work at close quarters. They're good, damned good at finding things. Christ you've just said so yourself. They'll pick out a lone cruiser on radar and in no time they're on you at thirty knots and alongside. I've sat there shitting bricks when we had a locker full of booze and fags. But drugs well that's something else again isn't it...a very different ball game indeed.'

'Yes you're right it is. It's the ultimate profit jackpot, but not something to take on lightly and I've no business talking to you like I have. Forgive me I got a bit carried away. I came here to go through your books so let's do it'. Fenton stood up and went over to the desk and started to thumb through the accounts. 'I can keep your tax and vat down to the acceptable minimum as usual no problems. Forget what I've just said about our getting together Jack if you know what's good for you. Know what I mean. As far as you're concerned I'm still a straight accountant when I have to be and a friend who has your best interests at heart. I'll just go away and get your final accounts prepared.'

'Hey look at this we're in the navy now!' Sid stretched out to pass the pink A5 sheet across to Tina. 'It's a memo from our Leader (get this) To all Greyhound Commanders' She looked and laughed 'He's joking surely, isn't he!'
'No not Rodney. He's taking this all very seriously who else would say something like...As we now have five operational grey boats I should like us all to get together for our first briefing. This will take place on Saturday 5th June at 10.30am aboard Grey Lady... Not exactly chatty is it...I suppose I had better reply ASAP, mind you it would be good to familiarize myself with all this high tech stuff first.' He indicated with a sweep of his hand the complexity of instrumentation which took up most of the wheelhouse and navigation area of his new boat. 'It's more like a cyber cafe than a sea boat'
'I must agree' said the husky voice. 'Perhaps we should spend a little more time checking things out than in bed here in the master cabin. How did you explain away spending last night on board here yet again?'
'No problem I just said I was finishing off an order late in the evening and it was simpler just to bunk down here on the boat, also I had to be here early as we were moving all the moorings around this morning'
'Yes I suppose that sounds quite reasonable doesn't it. He's got a cheek our Rodney, getting everyone to move around on the pontoons just so all the Greyhounds can be tied up together. That chap on his own, you know, on Tradewind that old motor-sailor. He won't be very pleased, with an engine out of action he'll have to heave his boat around by hand'
Sid was looking out of the wheelhouse window to where four other slim grey hulls lay. 'No you're right he won't be very

25

chuffed. But I tell you what, we shall be a very smart bunch all tied up together for inspection so to speak'
'And you'll look smarter when you get some clothes on Mr. Boss. If someone comes up the gangway you'll have some explaining to do, especially if it's Janet'
'You can talk my girl...God you've got a lovely pair of buttocks. Tell you what, stay there and I'll bring coffee and toast. No point in wasting too much time in technicalities'

The saloon on Grey Lady was smart but spartan as of course to be expected in a man with such an active service mentality. It had an air of purpose endorsed now by the bearing of its owner who stood looking round with obvious satisfaction. 'I'm very pleased you all have managed to make it this morning gentlemen. We are now a group of five operational Greyhounds at last. Here is the list as it stands.
No.1 Grey Lady - myself leading
No.2 Jackpot - Jack Delaney our Flag Officer
No.3 Plumb Crazy - Sidney Arthur - Our Hon Sec
No.4 First Draft - Keith Parks our new member
No.5 Pegasus 11 - Major Miles Foxwell -Our long standing member. Welcome to our new member Keith and to you others who have swapped your original boats for these wonderful Greyhounds. And thanks are due to all the members who have cooperated in the shift around which has enabled us five to be berthed all together as we see them this morning. We will get together with all crews before going out on our first sortie, but in this instance I thought it best for us to meet as Skippers. While Liz is sorting out some coffee in the Galley I'd just like to go over the projected programme for our working period as I'm sure you're all as keen as I am to get on with the job of becoming a first crack unit of powerboats ever to be formed in this country. The Royal Yacht Squadron promotes and upholds the highest standards of sailing in the UK. We propose to do the same for power

boating. They fly the White Ensign in common with the Royal Navy itself. We have the honour to fly the Blue Ensign in common with the Royal Navy Reserve and Trinity House. All other clubs in common with the British Merchant Navy fly the Red Ensign. The plain fact gentlemen is that anyone can fly the red duster. Anything that floats however unseaworthy, disreputable or sinister may go about its business flying this flag. This devalues it and insults our ocean going merchant ships. I tell you this so you will always understand that the MMYC as a club in general is flying the flag of the RN Reserve and its Greyhounds group is going to ensure that it will always live up to the honour' he paused, in the manner of a practised public speaker to let this fact enjoy its proper prominence before continuing in earnest terms 'I know just how much it has cost each one of you not only in financial terms, but in dedication to an ideal to achieve what we're setting out to do, but I promise to share with you a great sense of achievement in its end and perhaps even more importantly the sense of comradeship experienced by myself and all the crews of little ships in the wartime Royal Navy's Coastal Forces. Now down to detail, most of you will be familiar with the technicalities of your boat, and I imagine impressed with the superb state of the art quality of the instrumentation. There's no excuse for navigators getting lost even in the worst of weather conditions, unless of course you are unfortunate enough to experience complete power failure. In that case it will all be down to good old-fashioned navigation skills again. Dead reckoning gentlemen will never die. Not if you want to stay in one piece that is. GPS and all that goes with electronic navigation is a modern luxury. The sea going necessity is being able to produce a good estimated position on an Admiralty paper chart as and when circumstances demand it. Now for all realistic purposes our field of operations will be coastal off-shore most of the time around the Channel and North Sea . We're talking buoy hopping mostly with all waypoints plugged into our projected track before we leave our moorings and all chart plotters set up in accordance with the pre-operational briefing. This of course assumes a solo passage but we five will on most occasions be cruising in company in line ahead or 'V' formation. Now in this situation I as Leader will be navigating, with you others simply keeping station (like our opposite numbers in the RAF Red Arrows) our skill will be learning to carry out all manoeuvres as one single entity. Something that can only be achieved with constant practice. We shall have to spend some time just getting used to moving in close proximity at speed well before contemplating anything more complicated. We did a lot of it in Coastal Forces, it's all a question of split second timing and accurate changes of course. Now the key to this lies in perfect communications. To achieve this we will work on channel four VHF in constant open two-way mode via headphones and throat mikes. I will monitor open channel sixteen separately in the normal way on our groups behalf. So once switched on to group link state having cleared the sea lock, keep channel four open at all times with no idle chatter (like the others members get involved in when at sea) radio silence is essential unless it's important or relevant to what we're doing. The last thing we want is five of us talking at once. If you have a query quote your number and position which will be as follows. Grey Lady will lead in the arrowhead position addressed as "Leader". Numbers two and three to port will be "red two and red three" with numbers four and five to starboard "green four and green five" So if Jack in Jackpot has a query he'll say simply "Red two to Leader", then air his query. Any questions at this stage?'

Jack raised his arm 'What happens if we all speak at once?'

'Good point, you're all linked the whole time so if someone else is on air, hold until they are clear'

'Can we talk to one another' asked Sidney 'Or must we keep

radio silence at all times?'

'Everything must come through Leader unless of course you're about to collide then shout a warning like "Red one alert, alert".

'Or something similar' whispered Sidney.

'Obscenities are definitely not allowed at any time - we leave that sort of language to the fishing boats. They are certainly a prime example of the abuse of two-way radio. Whilst on this point I'm sure there have been occasions where we used VHF RT like a public phone box whilst at sea and this is one area where we can set a good example to anyone who happens to hear us over channel four. We are going to set a fine example to all those who use the sea....in every way from now on...not only by the things we do but by the way we look, no dirty paint work, no fenders or lines hanging over the side whilst at sea. Which reminds me, yes I.D. numbers. Being virtually identical in profile and colour we can't tell one from another so we need identification. I suggest we follow the Royal Navy style by having numbers on the bow. Say a letter G for greyhound followed by our running number. So Grey Lady will be G1 and Jackpot G2 and so on. All in agreement? Good. I'll arrange for the work to be done ASAP. Just one more point. It would be nice if we could all wear something similar to give the whole thing a touch of class. I was thinking on the lines of grey jump suits with Greyhound as a logo and possibly grey caps to match. Anyway we can discuss this later. And talking of discussing things you may feel you have just been conscripted into the navy but let me hasten to assure you we are just a group of like minded friends who want a bit of excitement in their boating lives and all decisions as to what we get up to will be discussed and arrived at democratically. Basically I want us to enjoy what we're about to do, if in doing so we can set a few standards for those at sea for pleasure or just to travel from A to B so much the better... Now where the hell is that coffee?'

Jenny Sutcliffe had no difficulty in locating the subject of her visit to Milehaven marina at all. They stood out like sore thumbs from the jumble of white boats of all shapes and sizes. Five slim grey hulls all moored together in line astern, silent and somehow sinister in this light holiday situation. Each one painted with a large number on its side one to five. 'So these were the Greyhounds. Well that looks a good shot'. She crouched down on the smart new pontoon and framed the group with her fingers and frowned... 'mm... Yep.. That will need to be a wide-angle job to get them all in'. With a dexterity shown only by a press photographer her slim fingers probed the large camera case and eased out the 28mm lens replacing the long telephoto on her Nikon SLR. The flash fired three times and then she moved in closer, camera slung at the ready. 'Let's have a peep at Number One shall we'. The name on the wheelhouse said Grey Lady. It looked shut up but she gave a shout from the gangway 'Hello...anyone aboard...hello!' Everything was closed down and the deck as neat and tidy as a boat show exhibit. Every line coiled neatly like it had never been used. She called again but there was no reply. 'OK Grey Lady, let's have a look at you' Jenny said to herself. The flash and the motor wind-on sequence was the only sound as the local newshound covered every angle of the sleeping boats. 'Good that's a wrap, that'll do nicely' She carefully repacked her camera bag and slung it over her shoulder. There was still nobody around as she made her way back along the pontoon, only a scruffy old dog looking down idly at her from what looked like an old fishing boat. They looked at each other silently for a moment until she said 'Hello dog are you guarding something?'
'He's not very talkative I'm afraid' said a voice behind her. She jumped visibly 'Oh I didn't see you there'
'Were you looking for someone?'

'Not exactly I'm from the Milehaven Messenger I've just been taking some shots of the grey boats over there. There was nobody around so I just went ahead. I had an appointment to do an interview with a Captain Rodney Blake but he doesn't seem to have shown up yet. Have you seen him around this morning?'

John Crowther leaned heavily on his elbows on the wooden guardrail a ball of oily cotton waste in one hand, which he raised to point towards the distant sea-lock. 'Saw him going off an hour or so ago towards the Keepers place, shouldn't think he'll be too long, not if he knew you were coming. Come aboard and wait for him if you like. You can see when he comes from here. I've just put the coffee pot on. Here let me give you a hand. The gangways a bit rickety, like everything else around here'. He extended his non-greasy hand as she negotiated the narrow gangplank watched warily by Bosun.

'Thank you if you're sure I'm not interrupting your work'

'Not at all, time's my own and I'm glad of a bit of an interruption actually. I get cramp working in my engine room for hours on end. I'm beginning to think I've bitten off more than I can chew with this job, stripping down this thing, I've only got a single engine but it's a big blighter, an old Perkins Diesel, they go on for ever of course. But it's difficult to get at it and I'm not as young as I was and that's half the problem if I care to admit it. Sit yourself down and I'll just wash my hands and then pour out the coffee' Bosun left his vigil on the bow and having decided that Jenny posed no immediate threat to security sat quietly now beside an old green leather bench practically obscured by papers and magazines.

'It's biscuits' explained his Master 'He knows he gets a shortbread when I take a break about this time of day. Loves 'em he does. Here we are then one cup of coffee coming up black or white for you?'

'Dark brown just to be difficult, no sugar thank you'

He passed her a sturdy stoneware mug 'Mind it's hot...so you're doing a feature on the grey boats then are you? I suppose they make a good story. They're certainly different I'll say that'

She smiled 'It's funny really we had a phone call from Rodney Blake saying he thought our readers would be interested to know all about them and what they hoped to achieve so the Editor asked me to cover the story. I've no real idea what the punch line is, except of course they all look like warships'

'I think you've got it in one. Most of us on the moorings are of the opinion that the Commodore is simply playing at battleships. It's a bit of a laugh really. Seems like he couldn't bear to retire from the navy, beached I think is the word. So he's trying to create a mini naval fleet here at Milehaven. He and the four others are extroverts, there's no denying that which I suppose is good in some ways from the point of promoting the Motor Yacht Club.' Jenny nodded in agreement 'Yes you would think Captain Blake's background had been in advertising rather than the navy. He's been to our office many times with his "press releases" usually concerning what he's been up to.'

'You mean he's good at self-promotion, I would agree with that. We've all had little flyers shoved across our gangways I'll show you the latest one'.

He rummaged in a drawer full of papers and found a crumpled pink sheet. 'Here we are, couldn't miss this memo could you. Listen to this "Greyhounds are getting ready to go" ...You've seen our Milehaven Grey Boats grow to five in number, now ready to commence their training schedule in the Channel and East Coast sea areas. Led by our Commodore Rodney Blake in Grey Lady they will learn to work as a single unit capable eventually of executing spectacular fleet manoeuvres similar in lateral sea borne terms to those carried out by the RAF's famous Red Arrows acrobatic team. Their presence in visits to holiday resorts both around the UK and on the Continent will not only publicise the work of the Royal National Lifeboat Association and Royal Yachting Association in their campaigns to improve safety at sea but in doing so enhance the reputation of the MMYC as worthy of the distinction of flying the British Blue Ensign. I know you will all wish our five crews every success in this new national venture'...

'How's that for a piece of sea going spin... not bad eh'

Jenny brushed aside a few long auburn hair strands from her face as she took the pink memo which bore a photograph of the smiling Commodore 'Well at least I know what it's all about now if I don't get to see him. It's very much our brave boys at the front bit, good flag waving stuff. Almost writes itself and I've got the shots covered already so that's OK...except the Commodore is almost bound to want a mug shot done isn't he!'

'You mean on the Bridge taking the salute' chuckled John

'Of course what else'

They both dissolved into spontaneous giggles then conscious of the intimacy of the moment Jenny changed the subject.

'You live on board here do you. All the time?'

'Yes, yes I do. I'm one of the few who do actually. It's very quiet Monday to Friday especially out of season. They all arrive on a Friday night for the weekend and it's bedlam on the pontoons, children, dogs, hoses, cases everywhere. Not that I mind, it's nice to see a bit of life. And on quiet days I've got plenty of work to do to keep myself busy on board here. She'd lived on her own for years this boat, lying neglected in the mud of Milehaven creek at the mercy of the tide. That was before they put the sea-lock in over there and built the new marina, I used to see her when I drove here to walk the dog. Sometimes she would be afloat at high water bobbing at her mooring lines... alive it seemed and then when the tide had gone out she'd be lying on her side in the black ooze, lifeless as the creek itself. Now she's got me to get her back in shape again which is how you find me this morning. Forgive me if I sound a little morbid. I didn't mean it that way in fact it's quite a cheerful story really. Tradewind and I were both washed up and now we're in the process of refloating ourselves with a little help from Bosun of course.'

She made as if to ask a question but he forestalled it. 'My wife died you see, leaving me in a largish house with just this shaggy mutt for company. I couldn't stand the silence of closed off rooms, knew I had to move but didn't want another house, then I found this derelict and well here we are.'

'You're working on making her seaworthy are you?'

He nodded. 'Yes I need her in good shape for deepwater cruising. At least the survey gave the hull a good report. I wouldn't chance an Atlantic crossing with a boat of this age unless I was sure she was up to the job'

'So how far will you be going'?

'Well I hope to make it to the Windward Islands at least, I'll make a further decision from there'

'I'm impressed Mr....I'm sorry I don't know your name'

'Crowther John Crowther, and you are?'

'Jenny Sutcliffe. How do you do' They both laughed

"Well Mr. Crowther'

'John please'

'Well I think I should be doing a story on you really what you've just told me has more human interest than half a dozen grey boats.'

'Oh there's bags of human interest on this marina, believe you me. Just sitting here quietly I see it all and hear it...see that boat over there on the next pontoon with the pink wheelhouse. That's Permanent Wave. Owned by Robin and George, hairdressers, gay hairdressers at that! They plan to sail up the Thames to Westminster so they say, as a Gay Rights protest and tie up along the Members' Terraces at the Houses of Parliament...it would make a wonderful story, wouldn't it?'

They are calling it the pink protest of the river queens'

She tossed back her hair, 'You're joking. What a hoot. I'd love to write up that one before it goes national'

'I'm sure they would only be too pleased to get the publicity. Leave it with me. I'll pop over and see them, ferret out some more details or better still arrange for you to meet up with them both and do an interview. Tell me are you a photographer or a reporter. I'm confused'

'Both' said Jenny 'We're talking small town journalism here. Pure local paper stuff. I also process the negs. Do the research and sometimes page make up on the Apple Mac as well'

'There you are, a true "Jack of all trades" or Jill should I say. Well I'm electrician, mechanic, sail maker, cook and bottle washer not to mention navigator, and vet around here so I guess that gives us something in common' He peered outside the small brass porthole. 'Well well looks like our Commodore is back on board'

'Can you see him'?

'No but his flag is flying from the Jackstay'

'That sounds rather ceremonial doesn't it'?

'Not really it's customary to hoist whatever ensign you fly as soon as you come aboard, and the blue one is flying now over on Grey Lady at this moment. So you'd better get along there if you want to catch his Lordship for a few words'

'Yes I better had' She stood up and reached for the canvas strap of her camera case. 'Well thanks for coffee and the chat. It saved me standing around looking suspicious' They shook hands across the dog and she gently scratched his shaggy head 'I'll let you know how I get on with the Admiral' she laughed, 'and I'll certainly follow up on the pink protest story. You'll be around will you if I need to make contact?'

'Oh yes I'll be here for sometime yet before I'm ready to cast off and head out to sea. Jock the lock keeper always knows where I'll be if by some chance Tradewind should be off her mooring. But without a working engine at the moment I ain't going nowhere fast as the Americans would say'

35

Jenny turned on the narrow gang plank pointed to the bare flagpole at the stern and smiling said 'Hey you're on board Skipper, so where's your ensign then?'

'In the flag locker with the other flags until I go to sea. Nice to have you on board. Happy hunting. Keep in touch.'

Elbows on the guard rail once again he watched her leggy stride along the pontoon towards the grey boats. She had an impulse to turn and wave but thought better of it in spite of sensing the attention of two pairs of eyes.

The grey boats merged into the more general grey of the dawn sea mist, which clung closely to marina water now silent and still. Number three however was rocking gently side to side causing tiny ripples to separate outwards. The disturbance of its balance wore just a pair of boxer shorts and stood beside the double berth in the master cabin shaking it. 'Come on come on wakey wakey sweetheart. It's six thirty, spread yourself about, I've made a nice cup of tea. It's now zero minus one hour, rise and shine.... well rise at least' The hump of duvet resolved itself gradually into something resembling human form with a tousled head and two hands which mutely grasped the offered mug. Then after staring at the digital clock ventured huskily 'Oh God it's only six thirty even Sea Bass sleep longer than this. What a way to spend a weekend. God Sid... that's too hot. Here, take it before I drop it'

'OK but don't forget it, I'm going to take a shower I'll only be a couple of minutes then I give you a shout. OK?'

'Yeah yeah' The duvet mound collapsed again as Tina savoured a few more moments at the edge of sleep while outside frothy effluent from Sid's shower splashed its pollution noisily overboard from the waste pipe. In 15 minutes number three had come alive in the whirring of its water pumps and fans and the atmospherics of its radio on open channel now in constant contact with the sea world at large. Breakfast in the saloon would have to be swift and simple given the hour and nature of the day. 'This is it at last' said Sid through a mouthful of buttered toast. 'Let's hope it goes off OK for all our sakes. Look I'm going to crank up all the systems after I've had a quick shave. Could you make up some bacon rolls for later on and then join me.' His partner in the running of the office and now as Greyhound crew nodded and staggered out of bed and into the galley.

'If you want to use the heads use them now darling, you know what you're like when you're excited at sea. Don't say I didn't warn you'

'Now is everything breakable secured properly and anything we don't need stowed away'

'Yes my Captain'

'And all safety equipment ready to hand. Very pistol, cartridges rockets flares, red smoke etc'

'Yes Commander'

'And all the upper decks cleared and ready for leaving harbour?

'Yes darling. Is that the lot now?'

'Should be, but don't forget you'll be on your own on deck as we leave. You'll have to take in the lines and fenders'

'I usually do don't I'

'Just pointing it out sweetheart'

'You're twitching Sidney, chill out. It'll be fine you'll see'

'Seven fifteen, only fifteen minutes to go. I can't see much activity outside'

'Yes there is, at least on our other four, they are all flying their ensigns, looks very smart too'

'Oh Christ I'd forgotten the bloody flag. Tina be a luv and hoist it quickly before his nibs notices will you. Rodney would have bollocked me over that.'

By seven thirty Sidney stood tensely at the wheel, headphones and throat mike in position, one eye on the bright colours of the computer screen, which displayed the comprehensive navigation plot. He jumped visibly at the crackling in his ears, and a crisp voice cut in. 'Grey Lady to all Grey boats. Go to channel four, action now'

He switched the VHF channel control to four as directed and after a pause the voice continued. 'Good morning Gentlemen, all boats confirm ready and standing by' Jack Delaney's rather laid back drawl came on 'Jack Delaney, Jackpot, Red One ready' Sidney cleared his throat Sidney Arthur, Plumb Crazy, Red Two ready' On confirmation of the other two boats the crisp commanding voice said starkly 'Start your engines cast off and follow me out in line astern. Grey Leader over'

'Here we go sweetheart' Sidney checked the preheat light then turned over the port engine. There was a shudder, then a roar as the big diesel fired up. The starboard engine coughed twice and then joined its brother in producing a sound that only twin engines on tickover can make. It was a pulse, which permeated everything causing two coffee mugs to jingle noisily in a dance of anticipation on the VHF cabinet. Sid slid open the wheelhouse window and shouted 'Let go for'ard line' to Tina who had practically disappeared in a cloud of blue smoke as the engines cleared their lungs. He watched Grey Lady swing away from the pontoons followed by the slim bow of Red One. Then gently using the twin screws he eased Red Two off her moorings taking the spring and stern lines as pivots 'OK let go aft'

Tina took in the lines, coiling them swiftly as she did so and by the time Red Two was clear of the marina basin and approaching the sea-lock all fenders and ropes were neatly stowed. She stayed standing on the bow as they stationed third in line and responded with a wave to the little knot of people who had turned out to see them off. The Lock Keeper cupped his hands as they slid past his red brick pump house. 'Bout time you took your dogs for a walk, don't get lost out there will you!' Tina snapped him off a smart salute whilst putting out her tongue. They were practically clear of the marina now, but with the high tide and the big lock gates wide-open Milehaven was still part of the sea and it would be until the next ebb tide tried to suck its water out and the gates closed off to stop it. Down river it was bleak indeed as high water slopped its muddy foam over banks populated only by feeding waterfowl. Gone in minutes were white buildings, pizza bars, cafes and car parks in cosy congestion. Replaced now by the breadth of the river, as it became a wide estuary stretching into infinity of silvery grey sea and mist.

'Close up and maintain line astern' came the curt voice of instruction. 'Leave two boat lengths in between and maintain radio silence'

'Not too keen on this radio silence bit' moaned Sid as Tina regained the security of the wheelhouse. 'We've always kept in touch with each other cruising in company, that's been half the fun, chatting amongst ourselves. I feel a bit cut off seeing Jack ahead but not being able to call him up'

'Well you shouldn't have joined Blake's navy then my boy. Rodney made it quite clear at his briefings how things were going to be if you remember...didn't he? Grey Lady the brain of the group, setting the course and speed, all the rest of us listen and watch very carefully and make every move together'

'I know that of course I do, I'll get used to it in time. It's just a bit strange at the moment that's all'

"Grey Leader to group' cut in the voice again 'Increase speed now to fifteen knots'

Sidney moved the two small throttle levers forward to match the indicated speed and they both felt the boat lift slightly in response.

'Now check your plots and you'll see we shall clear Sheerness in one minute and form our arrowhead formation for the first time. At the zero count Red One and Two will close up line abreast to port. Green One and Two to starboard'. The four boats increased speed to catch up on their Leader, two breaking to his left and two breaking right until they were moving in line abreast.

'Not bad for the first go ...OK...now drop back on the wings to form the vee formation, our standard cruising arrowhead. A bit ragged but not bad. Now we'll hold until we clear Maplin Sands. Your course should be 082 magnetic but listen as I sing out changes. Above all, watch the others to maintain a perfect arrowhead visually OK.'

'You look worried Sid' observed Tina from her position bending over the electronic chart plot screen.

'Too bloody right I am, at this stage sweetheart everything seems very close on either side. Hang on as we ride the wash' Tina grabbed the vertical steel pole at her side as the boat leapt across oncoming swells. The VHF repeater on the bulkhead cracked again. 'Grey Leader to all boats, standby to increase speed to thirty knots... on my count down'

'Christ' shouted Sid 'We'll probably take off' He eased the throttle levers further forward and lurching ahead the boats slim bow rose even higher out of the water on the plane.

'Look at the wake' Tina shouted above the increasing roar of the engine, which had now changed to a higher whine as the turbos cut in 'It's amazing isn't it?' They twisted around to look astern whilst holding on against the violent movement of the deck beneath them. The grey sea behind was now like a five lane highway stretching back into the mist.

'Watch your spacing Red One and Two' cut in the Leaders voice. You're all over the place, keep a boat length between your sides. Right next we'll try a gentle turn to starboard. On my countdown...Green One and Two slacken speed as pivots while Red One and Two increase speed. Now once again watch each others bow to keep in arrowhead formation.... standby'

The big Sikorsky Coastguard helicopter Bravo Tango Echo was on the outward leg of its patrol area. In five minutes it would cross the northern channel traffic zone and follow its course before turning in again towards the coast. It had been an uneventful vigil broken only by a rendezvous with a tanker to carry out a training exercise lowering a crewman onto its wide steel deck. A routine practice for the crew.

'Bit murky down there Lewis eh' stated the chief pilot as the winch man disengaged his tackle and closed the big side door. 'Could hardly see the bow when I was on deck Skipper mind you it must have been half a mile long'.

The second pilot stretched lazily 'God the sea can be boring on a morning like this when everything's the same overall grey, no beginning and no end. I think we'll go down a little on the inward leg, anything on the scope Curly?'

The addressed scratched his balding head as he checked the radar sweep.

'Strange, can't make it out'

'What?'

'Well I'm picking up a sort of cluster'

'It's probably a group of fishing boats'

'If so they're going around in circles at very high speed'

'Let me have a look'

'Oh yes you're right, let's head over that way and take a further look, weird isn't it!'

The helicopter slewed round onto the echo bearing, losing height as it did so. 'Range closing Skipper should have a visual anytime now'

'Can't see anything yet...nothing...wait a minute...good grief what's going on down there?'

'I can't see from this side. What is it?'

The pilot banked the chopper steeply giving a good view from the side windows 'That's better, well I don't know what to make of it. If we were over farmland I'd say they look like outsize crop circles' They peered down and in the clearing mist saw the surface of the sea below marked by a series of vast connected circles.

'Looks like a giant scalextric layout.'

'It's a huge wake' butted in the pilot 'but I can't see what's causing it at the moment. Let's drop down a bit lower for a better look.' The huge machine shuddered as it descended slowly towards the sea level. 'You're right Curly it's not one object it's a group of boats very close together. Five of them. Their individual wakes merging into one broad one. That's what looks so strange. They're definitely in some sort of 'v' formation, see that?'

'But why are they going around in circles at such high speeds right out here and close to the traffic zones?'

'Why indeed Curly, try and get them on channel sixteen will you?' The crew member replaced his helmet with its integral mike. 'Coastguard Helicopter Bravo Tango Echo to unidentified group of vessels below, Come in please' He repeated the message and after a couple of seconds a clear voice responded. 'Hello Coastguard this is Grey Lady, Quebec, Alpha, Leader of Milehaven Greyhound power boats display team ...over'

'Good morning Grey Lady. Why are your vessels going round in circles two miles off the northbound channel shipping traffic zone. Do you have a problem? over'

'No problem thank you Coastguard. Just exercising close formation. I'm aware of our position with respect to traffic zone.... over'

'Grey Lady report your position to North Foreland Radio ASAP and be advised large tanker 4 miles south east your position ...over'

'Understood, will transmit transit report and present position to North Foreland'.

'Thank you Grey Lady over and out'

The nose of the Sikorsky dipped as the helicopter switched out of auto hover and the huge rotor pulled up through the swirling mist.

'OK that'll do. Let's go home, lads I've seen everything today. I mean crossing the channel on a pedalo is one thing, but synchronised swimming in motorboats is something else again. Still makes an interesting entry for today's log. Performing greyhounds, my oh my'

Strange as it must have seemed to the crew of the helicopter reports of the grey boats would increasingly appear in the logs of coastal offshore patrols within striking distance of the Thames Estuary, the East Coast and far out into the North Sea, their close 'v' formation moving at high speed would be seen by ferries, container ships and deep draught super tankers. With sleek warship grey hulls and white numerals they would most times be mistaken for the Royal Navy exercising its coastal forces ML's and MTB's. The high profile Rodney Blake had hoped for was becoming a reality as time went by. Goodwill visits made to seaside resorts, Regattas even Cowes Week on the Isle of Wight. At Milehaven marina visitors now came to see the home base of the Greyhounds and were charged a 'pontoon fee'. Whilst this influx of visitors on high days, holidays and weekends was welcome by the nearby pubs, cafes and car parks, boat owners moored alongside were not so keen. Except of course George and Robin on Permanent Wave. They thought the extra exposure rather wonderful flying a large banner which said *'Give Gays A Hearing-Repeal Section 28'*

'It's beginning to look like Butlins on a Saturday. Look at that lot peering into everything, there's no privacy round here these days'. The dog looked around at his master's voice as if in agreement, then resumed its silent vigil on the bow. 'Time to put the coffee on, it's nearly eleven. She might turn up you never know Bosun'. The bottled gas popped and then hissed underneath the aluminium kettle with a reassuring flame as he reached up to the cupboard and took down two mugs. 'Heck that's got a crack in it. We'll have to replace it Bosun me lad. Got to look after our visitors. (If we have any). Might get bone china instead of stoneware for a change. Say something dog if it's only a growl...perhaps I'd be better off with a parrot. Only joking Bosun, only joking'. He chuckled clearing a space amongst the tangle of electrical wiring on the dining table. 'There's no room to swing a cat in here. Do you know that?'

It was sometime later when he knew she had arrived, just a gentle rocking of the boat and the thumping of the dogs tail on the cabin top overhead told him well before the gangway creaked and her voice called 'John...Hello are you there?'

'Down below, come on down, mind the steps'

He stood up soldering iron in hand as her legs appeared above him. Even trainers failed to kill their femininity as calves and then little dimples behind the knees became the fullness of a rounded thigh. It seemed an age before a hemline intervened and blue denim stopped his eye. 'Nice to see you, glad you made it after all.... I had a coffee earlier'. She noticed the two mugs side-by-side one half full, the other clean. 'But I'll make a fresh pot, unless you'd prefer a beer, I've got a four pack in the fridge' She smiled the smile that made him touch the soldering iron. 'Christ that's bloody hot still. It's such a mess down here I'm afraid. It was the last time you came. It's Bosun, he's so untidy. Never been boat trained that's his trouble'

The smile matured into a laugh. 'You and that dog. You're like a double act you two only he never says anything'

'Can't get a word in edgeways. Now I'll get you that drink. When you rang my mobile I wasn't sure you'd actually come over here'

'I had to come and tell you my news in person rather than just phone. You had a lot to do with it after all'. He watched as she put a plastic shoulder bag down on a locker top. It had the words 'Cool It' on the side.

'Keeping your film cool?'

She unzipped it and hauled out a champagne bottle by the neck. 'No just the bubbly. It was meant to be for elevenses but I'm a little late. We won't need the four pack'

'This is very unexpected, what's the occasion?'

'My change of status. When I first called to see you I was a staff reporter on the local rag as you know. Now I'm a freelance'.

Oh is that good?...congratulations...but where do I come into things?'

'The Greyhounds' story. You remember you filled in all the background for me that morning'

'Glad I was able to help. You took some shots on Grey Lady and interviewed Rodney Blake as I remember'

'Yes that's it, I put together a feature for the paper, it came out on the Thursday morning and on the following Monday my editor had a phone call from a London news agency asking if they could buy the rights for syndication, agreed a fee and it's gone national. So far it's appeared in three Daily's and one weekend magazine. You see up till then I'd been covering all the hack stuff you know, council meetings, fetes, local social stuff, not to mention all the local weddings and funerals. Have you got the glasses yet?'

'I'm afraid not, all the glassware from the house is in store still. I've never had call for champagne glasses on the boat before'.

'Right then, mugs it is, I'll be "Captain" and you can be "Mate" today. I'm sure Moet and Chandon wouldn't approve but I don't give a toss so here goes'

She aimed the neck and fired the cork skywards through the open hatch causing Bosun to leap swiftly to one side. Then flushing the residue of coffee from "Captain" she charged the heavy peasant stoneware with the wine of Kings in abuse of all known etiquette and held her mug aloft. 'Cheers, get that down if you can. It's like drinking liver salts isn't it! Now where was I... Oh yes, the feature, well having done so well out of the syndication our editor decided to let me handle major stories, features and some investigative work. But being a Scot he was not taking too many chances, so the deal he put up was I go on a good retainer for which I handle some of the nuts and bolt jobs and when an interesting assignment comes up I can handle it on a freelance basis, fee and expenses. It gets me into feature work, as long as I come up with the goods of course, that goes without saying. And I'll be expected to act as photographer, he made that quite clear, not that it bothers me I enjoy photography and this is not Fleet Street after all'...she drew breath quickly.... 'We might as well finish off the bottle. It'll only go flat. Here hold out your mug Mr. Mate and I'll top you up.'

'This is all wrong you know it's living here alone that does it. Here I am sitting in my dirty overalls swigging champagne with a lovely young lady and a journalist at that. I should have changed at least, but I really thought you weren't coming'.

'Chill out, your overalls have a certain rustic charm. Tell you what it's nearly lunch time. Can I invite myself to lunch? You can clear this workshop of a table, and then get changed if you want whilst I fix us something to eat... deal?'

He scooped up handfuls of switches plugs and wires and dropped them onto the old tin tray, which was serving as a base. 'No problem, actually I think I'm flogging a dead horse trying to revive this old radio. Technology has moved on and I'm going to have to update systems on here before I commit myself and Bosun to the open sea. As for lunch there's only the cowboys bunkhouse special, corned beef and baked beans. Oh, and a bit of bacon of course. Bit of a come down after the bubbly, even if we did drink it in stoneware mugs'.

She laughed 'Well my lunch would have been a burger and a black coffee anyway, so I wouldn't worry about it. I suppose you'll have to start stocking up for your epic voyage soon won't you. Lots of dried noodles and such like. Things are a lot easier these days but it's still a big sacrifice. You know, the smell of eggs and bacon for breakfast, fresh coffee, fillet steak and all that. Have you done anything like this before?'

'What been at sea for long periods. Yes I have but not single handed on a small boat, mostly tankers, big stuff 50.000 tons plus'.

'So you're an old sea dog then. I thought you might be. Not like all these Flash Harry's on their weekend gin palaces'

'How did you guess'?

'Oh I don't know they don't walk around in faded jeans, splice rope and have a shaggy dog by their sides. Their boats don't look lived in like this one. This looks part of the sea'

'My word you are perceptive aren't you. But then you are a journalist so that's not surprising I suppose. Actually I used to be quite formal at work whilst watch keeping at least. Here look at this taken about ten years ago'

He pulled the battered photo from a drawer and passed it across. She nodded 'Four rings eh a Captain no less, very smart I must say'.

'I got my Masters ticket ten years before that but had to wait that long for my first command. Daft system really, you spend most of your career working up to control of a ship then you end up ashore in a desk job. That's why I took early retirement'

'Why does that happen?'

'Why? Too many Captains not enough ships. There used to be a huge British Merchant fleet of ships. Now there are just a few large ships. Bulk carriers and super tankers. You could have a tanker of 100.000 tons worked by a crew of only thirteen. Whole business has been turned upside down. Look what's happened to our great ship yards dead mostly, except those building and repairing oil platforms, and my old Public School Pangbourne Naval College, most of its graduates don't end up in the navy now, they go in for banking and insurance'

'Well at least you've come back to the sea again'

'That's true on a Tankers bridge I would be 40 feet above it now I can almost lean over the side and touch it.'

Two hours, corned beef, bacon and a can of beans later they sat easily on the dusty cowhide of the saloon bench with the back end of Bosun poking out underneath. The stoneware mugs now rinsed and full of coffee once again. On the table beside an open packet of Rich Tea biscuits lay a scattering of photographs of life before Tradewind. His wife and the house they had shared, a fluffy doe eyed ball in a basket that was Bosun and a tall young man who could easily have been Jenny's brother. 'Big lad isn't he, looks like his Mother'

'How old is he?'

'Thirty five, they've got two children now...I'm a Grandfather'

'Well you don't look too bad on it. You realize of course I'm making notes on all of this for the article I'm going to write on you. It's the subtle way I do my interviews. Did I show you the clippings of the Greyhound articles? Don't think I did. Let's see, yes just read this one'. She held out a newspaper cutting showing a photograph of five powerboats in formation at speed on a choppy sea. Below the copy read:

'Are these the Red Arrows of the sea?' These five boats are the display team of Milehaven Motor Yacht Club, an elite group of powerboat enthusiasts based at Milehaven Marina on the Thames estuary. Trained and led by Captain Rodney Blake RN Rtd (an ex MTB Commander of Coastal Forces). The team has been formed to demonstrate in marine displays at holiday resorts around our coasts, fine boat handling and seamanship in the traditions of the RAF's Red Arrows.

Inset was a picture of Rodney Blake resplendent in Royal Naval uniform with a group of Officers on the Bridge of a Destroyer.

'That was taken a few years ago, he's put on a bit of weight since then'

She leant over his shoulder and he was conscious of her proximity. 'That's the one he wanted me to use. The rest of the copy goes on to talk about the boats themselves; you know the technical stuff, what good sea-boats they are, that sort of thing. Oh yes and he was dead keen that I should mention how proud they are to fly the Blue Ensign'

'He would wouldn't he, because he thinks of the Greyhounds as being part of the Naval Reserve and yet all boats on this marina are just as entitled to fly that flag. Even the ships cat could in a rubber dinghy. That's the way it really works'

Jenny shook with laughter and he felt her long hair brush his face, then she stood back with the clippings in her hand. 'Oh I know this article's not all that wonderful. But it's got some human interest in it. The great thing is it's got me credibility as something more than just the office hack. I know I'll still have to cover all the mundane stuff, but when something with a bit of bite comes along I shall be able to get a crack at it'

John looked a little embarrassed. 'I'm sorry I wasn't putting down what you had written, it's good stuff and you're quite right the opening is now there for you. What area would you like to cover? Anything in particular?'

She shrugged her shoulders 'Crime I think, I've spent quite a bit of time covering the Magistrates courts and that was interesting. Not the parking or speeding fines but the heavier stuff'

'What murders, GBH that sort of thing?'

'Yes but not just reporting, more the cutting edge work, ferreting out information on something almost ahead of any Police investigation but cooperating with them, do you know what I mean.'

'Yes you're talking about investigative journalism aren't you, dangerous stuff that especially if it involves the underworld. There are some very nasty people around who don't take too kindly to being investigated.'

'Yes I know, I take your point, but I've thought about the other possible areas and nothing else really grabs me. I mean I just can't get excited about domestic issues, gardening, cooking, and interior decoration. Although they all seem to be topical at the moment'

'There's always motoring, travel and of course the boating world. You've already got a foot in that door'

'I know but I keep coming back to crime, must be the dark side of my nature coming out. I just dream of uncovering the big one' She raised her long fingered hands above her head. 'I can see it now, the crime of the century with my by-line beneath the international expose' syndicated worldwide. How's that for fantasy'

'It could be a fact one day. I'm a great exponent of self-belief and at this moment Ms. Sutcliffe I believe another black coffee is in order as we've both got things to do this afternoon. I've got to get up the mast, fit a new radar reflector...what about you?'

She smiled the smile that made his pulse race. 'Me, now let me think, ah yes four o'clock. I must get back to the office soon.'

SA Marine had done very well. In five years it had repaid all the money Sid had put into it, saved from his fruitful years as a call out plumber. He had finally made the jump from spending his days bent over someone's leaking toilet to lying back in an executive recliner, not bad for a man who'd left school at fourteen with few qualifications. His office might not have been the last word in corporate prestige but it was functional, that was the best way to describe it and it was all his. He was the boss man. He gave the orders now and the others did the work, well most of it. He could still turn to and roll his sleeves up if the situation demanded it of course. Those skills would never be forgotten. Sid sipped his morning coffee reflectively, feet up on his metal desk looking out of the glass sided office to where three motor cruisers sat propped up in the middle of the hangar-like boat shed. Around them was strewn an array of work benches sheet metal, and racks of copper piping. The grimy concrete of the floor snaked with electrical cables extending power to each of the as yet, unfinished hulls. Bright lights streamed out of the port holes and the blare of pop music blended with the crash of hammers and the squeal of power drills echoed painfully within the cavern of the workplace. But this was music to Sid's ear, cost effective predictable production, the same operation repeated on each boat. Three plumbing fitters working non-stop, 8.30am to 4.30pm day after day, all paid piecework of course, no insurance, pensions or sick pay. It was money for old rope. SA Marine took on all other marine water systems work, conversions repairs and replacements, but this contract was bread and butter stuff. No doubt about it. He watched Tina going to each boat in turn collecting the days job sheets. She didn't miss a trick that girl, they never got away with anything, knew better than to try with her. He left her alone to run the charging and book work too. She knew more about the systems than he ever would, damned useful girl he thought to himself....in every way. She'd got a good business head on her shoulders. He'd have to listen to her a bit more, what was it she was saying the other night about preparing a proper business plan, a forecast, something the bank had asked for twice before. She felt perhaps they had got too many eggs in one basket. Could be.... he watched her walk across the floor, clipboard in hand and climb the four steps to their office.

'Hi Tina everything OK?'

She nodded. 'Yep fine, Jeff will finish up tomorrow so we can move another in. Steel sheets are getting low. Did you reorder this week?'

'All done, should get the delivery shortly. Have a coffee. I've just made a fresh pot...I've been thinking just now about your views on new business by the way. I think we should discuss them further'

'What was it I said, I've forgotten. I was probably just talking on my feet again' she replied with a chuckle.

'You said I shouldn't get complacent because we have a full order book. That too much income from one source could be a bad thing. Now I know I've said that we couldn't actually cope with any more work without either taking on someone else or letting Sea Sprite down by interrupting their production line. But I do realise that if their work dried up we would be in the shit big time. I mean we're practically on our overdraft limit and the steel people wouldn't extend our credit that's for sure. What doesn't help is the way Sea Sprite keeps us waiting for our money isn't it. I mean three months is a bit cheeky.'

'You're right, they cause our cash flow problems,' interrupted Tina taking her cup of coffee from Sid's outstretched hand. 'I'm always sending reminder statements but as you know they just ignore them. They just trot out the same old excuses, cheques in the post, computers gone down; we just need a second signature and the directors on holiday. Heard them all haven't we?'

'Certainly have almost every month, the problem is they know we won't push them too hard because we rely on their work. I suppose it comes down to your point of us having too many eggs in one basket doesn't it. I think perhaps we should do some trade advertising or perhaps even take a little trade stand at the next boat show. That would mean spending more than we could really afford but we've probably got to speculate to accumulate. Perhaps we could put a few ideas together'

'Good idea, we'll do that. But I think we should try and find out what is going on at Sea Sprite. I spoke to Jane in their accounts the other week and she said they're all worried about rumours of a take-over by Global Motors, the engine group. It's probably nothing, there's always a buzz of some sort going around' Sid sat up with a look of concern. 'You never know it's better to check these things out. I hadn't heard that one I must say'

'Sorry I didn't mention it because Jane's an awful gossip. Goes on all the time I think a lot of it's just in her head. Still I'll sound things out next time I'm on the phone'

However in the mail next day with three red notices on unpaid invoices was a white envelope bearing the distinctive Sea Sprite logo. Her delicate fingers plucked it out and waved it in front of the newspaper Sid was reading. 'Here we are talk of the devil, this could be our cheque, except it's usually in a little brown window job'

He took it, slit it open and withdrew the crisp A4 white sheet. It did contain the eagerly awaited cheque. Sid put this on one side and with foreboding went on to read the letter.

Enclosed please find our cheque to cover your invoice number.4561 with apologies for delay due to an internal problem with our computer system. In order to pre-empt rumours circulating in certain sections of the trade, our Board of Directors has decided to release the following statement.

A hostile bid has been made to the holders of Sea Sprite UK shares. If this offer is taken up it is likely that production of the Sea Sprite range of offshore cruisers will be taken over by a facility of the Global Motor Group. This will involve all aspects of production including the hull, engine and systems. Unfortunately this must include the fittings of water systems and holding tanks for both fresh and foul water, the service provided most satisfactorily by yourselves. Whilst naturally we hope the Global Motor bid will fail it was felt only fair that you should be advised of the possibility by us, rather than an outside source at some later stage. In any case our present contract terms will continue to apply until it expires. We shall of course keep you advised as matters progress.

Yours sincerely Ralph Holman   Technical Director

Sidney let the letter fall onto the desk staring up into the dark girders of the boat-shed roof.

'What's wrong'? Tina looked at him and picked up the cheque. 'What is it? They've paid haven't they? What have they said in the letter?'

'It's too late!. Too damned late. It's already happening' he said in a flat voice.

She reached forward picked up the letter and read it silently at first, then mumbled huskily 'Oh no they can't, the bastards. They can't just swallow everybody up. Perhaps they'll fail, the shareholders could reject the offer'

'Would you' said Sid. 'Would you turn down instant profit? I wouldn't, shareholders aren't loyal anymore it's just shares on bits of paper. All they want is rising dividends or a nice fat capital gain. You can't blame them; they don't see anything of what goes on in the companies they play with. The people whose lives they spoil, all the workers who get made redundant. It's all money money money Tina. We could go down the drain because of this'

She touched and lightly squeezed his shoulder still holding the letter in her hand. 'Hold on luv, we're not done yet, not by a long chalk. It hasn't happened yet, we are only being warned it could and our contract has still got over three months to run so we've still got time in hand. Tell you what we'll do. Acting on the basis of the worst-case scenario OK and assuming it is going to happen. We hit the road both you and I. This place can jog along on its own. The boys know what they're doing don't they. I'll get on the phone, call round to make appointments and keep at them until I get them. Then we can both follow up. No cold calls, that always looks like desperation. I'll start going through Yellow Pages and make

54

up a list of possibles and there's last years boat show catalogue that's got masses of boat yards and manufacturers listed in the back'

'What can we say. Please give us work, we've just lost our largest customer and in twelve weeks we are facing melt down. It's no good.'

'No of course not silly, don't be so pessimistic what we do is to go in strength as though we're doing them a favour. You forget I used to work in advertising. I'll put some words together. Something positive like *SA Marine the on-board water system specialists can now offer savings of up to 30% against all others with their hi-tech production techniques as used in British Nuclear Submarines*. How's that off the cuff?'

Sid shook his head in amazement. 'But that's not true, it's absolute bollocks'

'Of course it is sweetheart but it sounds good doesn't it. Anyway you can be pretty sure that the water systems on a sub will be similar to ours. You know copper pipes, stainless steel bits and pieces. What we've got to do is gain their attention for a couple of minutes'

Sid laughed 'You're an amazing woman Tina. You've got the mental muscle of a market trader do you know that. Streetwise, that's what you are. Takes me back to when I worked the call-out racket on all those flats in south east London. A couple of cold snaps in February and I'd made a killing, hundreds of pounds in one day. Believe me if you've got cold water pouring through your bedroom ceiling you don't stop to get a quote or argue the toss. I just got on with the job and socked them with my sundries and special parts menu. They whipped bundles of fivers from teapots and under beds. Cash nearly every time. No cheques or credit cards in them days, didn't know when I was well off'.

'At least you know you'll never be stuck for cash. You can always go back to the plumbing business again'

A look of sadness lingered like a shadow over Sidney's face.

'You don't understand do you my love. It's not just the money I'm worried about it's losing everything I've worked for. I'm a respected businessman now. I own a company. I'm Hon Sec at the MMYC, Freemason and my kids go to Private School. Sure I need a pile of cash to keep up my present way of life but it's my image that bothers me. I've just spent a fortune on the new boat because I thought I should be seen to be one of Rodney's poxy Greyhounds. I find it hard to keep up with some of those snobbish bastards as it is, imagine where I'd be if they found out I was a jobbing plumber. What about Janet, she'd go absolutely ballistic you know she would. She's told our neighbours I'm chairman of a group of companies working on Ministry of Defence contracts and now being concerned with the Greyhounds she thinks I'm attached to the SAS or Special Boat Group. She fantasizes. She can't help it. It's just her world. Plus it helps to explain why I'm hardly ever around the place I suppose. And speaking of not being at home, if the boat, the office and club were to disappear where would that leave us two. Up the creek without a houseboat I'd say at the very least'

'Chill out Sid. Do for goodness sake. It's not going to be that bad. We'll sort things out, believe me'

Tina was an attractive woman, physically, in her personality and most importantly in the present situation in the quality of her voice. She could hold a male audience captive on the phone even if reciting a passage from The Old Testament. Sidney knew this and was to a certain extent re-assured but knew from past experience that it was one thing to gain a buyers attention with a bold inviting claim and quite something else to convert this to the point where a contract was agreed and signed.

The fitters in their strong smelling fibreglass cocoons drilled and hammered on to the strains of Radio One quite unaware their livelihood was under threat as days went by and the jaws of Global Motors stood poised to snap up Sea Sprite Cruisers and with it in effect the big boathouse labelled SA Marine. They hardly noticed that Tina Garside was always on the phone and time sheets now lay uncollected on the benches amongst the copper piping. And the Gaffer was hardly there at all. Sid's wife Janet noticed the change however, in little things like the tuneless whistle he made when doing anything from shaving to polishing his shoes.. It suddenly stopped like a cats collar bell falling off and she no longer knew exactly where he was. 'You're the quiet one Sidney these days, overdoing it I shouldn't wonder. Spending all the hours God sends in that office as usual. I'm always saying you need to slow down a little. I expect Tina says the same, she knows you like I do, always on the go'

He was tempted to tell her the position but decided against it for nothing had actually happened yet, it just looked ominous. Ignorance was bliss and she was best left to enjoy it while she had it. How could she know just how unquiet his mind actually was? How desperately preoccupied he was with the business of self preservation or more correctly 'front preservation' This was the strange thing, Janet knew the old Sid, she'd chosen to marry him for God's sake and have his children. The old flux-and-solder Sid with his open leather tool bag and dirty white van. The Jack-the-lad Sid who knew every sink and flushing toilet on the Flanders Field Estate and most of its bedrooms too. But she didn't know the new Sid. The black tie dinner-suited, gold card, never drop an 'aitch' Sid. She could be proud of the image, throw it up in peoples faces, and bring what it represented up in every conversation to elevate her social standing. The new Sid was there for her to use all right, but just out of reach. His world had gone beyond dinner on a plastic tray in front of the TV. It was bar-tab drinks in the Wardroom and maybe Table-d'hôte in a cosy corner of the members lounge. The Wardroom was seeing more of him than usual. His bar tab growing into a lengthy list of doubles. Unlike some members however he was careful to retain his guard even when 'ratted' or soiled with the 'sauce' and never let his background show or old Sid slip through to show his face, although he did sense a kindred spirit in the voice of Jack Delaney which resonated somewhere in the bar behind.

'Usual Steward, make it a double, no ice' Sidney glanced in the mirror behind the rows of spirits and exotic cocktails and saw the reflection of the hand of MMYC's Flag Officer just before it descended on his shoulder. 'Hi Jack, long week no see'

'It's been a fraught one, been in London on business. Feet haven't touched the ground. It's nice to get out here and slow down for a bit. How are things with you?'

'Oh so so, can't grumble I suppose'

'You don't sound too certain me old mate'

Sidney found himself explaining the situation, his natural reticence weakened by Johnny Walker and the need to share his burden with someone other than Tina.

Jack listened in silence, then took Sid's tumbler saying 'Let me freshen your ice a little. I'll take the drinks over to that table in the corner. It's more private over there' The corner was shut off visually from the bar itself by a long wooden trough full of tropical house plants and enjoyed a panoramic view across the crowded moorings to the pump house and lock keepers cottage.

'There you are Sidney, sink your fangs into that. It was Canada Dry and not Soda Water wasn't it...Good... That's not good news over that Global Motors business I must say. Seems to be happening all over the show at the moment. Dog eating dog you might say. It's not always a bad thing being taken over but in your case when they've got in-house capabilities which cater for your external services, I can see how you are placed; and your other customers work can't cover the loss of business then?' Sidney shook his head. 'No chance I'm afraid. We've had all our eggs in one basket. They were giving us all the work we could handle. There's no time left to look around for other work even if we had the facilities, it would have meant taking on extra people'

'Oh I see it's the old shit or bust situation'

'Yep and we are about to bust by the look of it' Knocking back his drink Sid continued 'Still I mustn't keep going on about my problems'

'I wish I could help old mate but I haven't any contacts in your field being in the leisure and pleasure industry myself. I must say I'm not really sure what you do, other than you're around the corner from the marina here, and as you've just explained it's something to do with fitting out boats'

'Marine water systems, that's my field. I run a small company (or try to) we design and install complete fresh water and sewage systems to offshore and ocean going yachts of all shapes and sizes. Our fitting out building is the old sail loft and boat shed just up the river from here. We've got our own slipway, but we can send our fitters out to work on the larger vessels afloat elsewhere. I wish to God I'd concentrated more on that sort of work now I can tell you. But it's easy to be wise after the event isn't it. Here your glass looks sad, it's my turn to energise the ice, in fact I think we need new rocks'

It was some time before he returned having chatted to at least three people at the bar. Bearing recharged tinkling crystal tumblers he put them down between them. Jack raised his in salute 'Cheers Sidney here's to an upturn in your fortunes'

'I'll drink to that all right and so will my creditors and there's enough of them at the moment including Beaver Group Finance. I'll be paying off forever on my bloody Greyhound the way things are going. That's if I don't have to end up selling it and that won't be easy either. I mean who would want to buy something that looks like a warship'

'Amen to that Sidders I think you and I are in the same boat in a manner of speaking that is. In fact as you are into boats big time you must know your way around them inside and out, every nook and cranny eh!' He drained his glass until the ice hit his nose. 'In fact you're just the sort of bloke a school friend of mine should have been speaking to today instead of me. You'd have known the answers straight away. I never thought to ask you'

'Ask me what?'

'Well this chap I was at school with is writing a novel which involves smuggling some stuff into the UK on a yacht, nothing new in that of course and it's nearly always discovered when the boat is boarded by the customs. It's usually in the bilges, behind false panels in lockers you know pretty obvious stuff and he said to me, you've got a sea going boat, where would you stow it so they would never find it? I'd got no idea other than down behind the engine or under the cockpit floor but that's not very original is it?'

'What happened, did he come up with anything in the end?'

'No only perhaps to stow it in detachable pods beneath the hull either side of the keel, but that's a bit uncertain as you need to haul the boat out of the water to get at them or send a diver down over the side, all very noticeable and James Bondish stuff. But you're the expert, what would you do?'

Sid was flattered. He sat back rubbed his chin and said cagily, 'You get the next round and I'll have a think about it'

Jack returned grinning. 'Two whisky macs this time, I've had enough ice, never did like the stuff much. Have you solved our problem yet?'

'Not really, the thing to do perhaps is put yourself in the Inspectors' shoes'

'Go on'

'Well they can sum up the situation almost before they have come over the gangway. If it's a family boat out over a weekend they would probably ignore it but if it was further out to sea it'll get properly checked over which includes all cupboards, seat lockers and bedding. As you've already said they would probably take up the bilge boards, empty chain lockers and even check behind the double skin panels. Now unless they had a positive tip off the search would no doubt end there, but any completely sealed off compartment like fuel tanks would probably just be sounded for resonance'

'What's that exactly?'

'Well they would tap on the casing. If it's empty or full of liquid there's a resonant echo but if it's full of soft packets it will sound dull in response. We fit systems incorporating several holding tanks. For fresh water used in drinking and washing and also for foul water that's sewage flushed down the toilets, now a sewage holding tank is something nobody is going to want to examine too closely, as you can imagine, so I'd stick it in there'

'Interesting, but if you fill it with packets or bags wouldn't the resonance check give the game away?'

'Yes it would, but you could have an inner tank with its own separate outlet!, there would be say, a completely sealed welded steel tank permanently fitted in the boat. Inside it is another smaller tank, which holds the smuggled goods. Say the goods were drugs in powered form, the powder could be fed in under pressure like grain into a grain hopper, then sucked out again by vacuum. Then the outer area would be filled with sewage in the normal way. Now if it's sounded, it will be normal in resonance. If a dip stick is lowered into the sewage it will be apparent won't it.... by testing it or by the smell!'

'Well done Sidney that's a very interesting solution. My friend should be well pleased with that. Tell you what, would you just run it up on the PC and I'll drop it over. I'll make certain you get a research fee out of this. Thanks a lot old chap, thanks a lot'

Fenton Gesler was sitting at the window of his Thameside Penthouse idly watching a string of barges moving slowly upstream when his mobile phone rang. Rummaging around the papers on his desk he found it buried amongst a nest of invoices.

'It's Jack... Jack Delaney... Hi Fenton, hope I haven't dragged you out of bed. How are you?'

'Better now I've had coffee, burnt the midnight a bit last night, amazing isn't it how all my clients leave their returns until the revenue get nasty. What can I do for you my son? Business or pleasure'

'Fenton do you remember last time we spoke you mentioned a distribution situation you thought I could possibly help out with'

'That's right I thought you had the ideal background to handle the products I'm in touch with. Why?'

'I've been thinking about it for sometime actually, but I had some sorting out before I came back to you'

'And have you come to a conclusion'

'Yes, transport was a stumbling block but I think I've got enough answers now'

'Not over the phone dear chap. Come around to my pad. We're less likely to get interrupted here. What about a spot of lunch? I'll get something tasty sent in'

'Yes that sounds fine about one o'clock then'

'See you shortly then.'

Kings Quay is the sort of place one brought Call Girls to thought Jack as he waited on the marble steps having pressed the big brass button for the third time. A voice from a polished grill invited him to come up. Inside the lofty marble hall the CCTV camera swung silently around to stare at him with its single eye as he called for the lift to take him to the top floor.

'I suppose your evil eye has got me on videotape now has it, those things make me jumpy'

Fenton laughed, 'stop twitching and drink your drink. You're as safe in here as in church'

'That's not saying much these days, nothing's sacred you

know'

'A quiet drink between friends is sacred enough I hope and we have been a little more than accountant and client'

'Sorry only joking, it's just the subject. Did I say too much over the phone?'

'Relax, we didn't really say a thing. It's your imagination. Listen Jack, cards on the table I act on behalf of the Bayswater Boys, have done for ages and through this I've built up contacts importing some 'Class A' stuff from Colombia. It's big money but all I get is my fee for handling the financial end paying the bills and laundering the money. The fees are generous of course but peanuts compared to the profit the boys make on distribution. Now it's never occurred to me to set up on my own until that is I did your first audit and saw you had the perfect distribution set up within your night clubs and amusement arcades. Together we could make a killing. I haven't brought the subject up again with you because I thought you needed time to sort things out in your own mind. I guess you have now or you wouldn't be here'

'I don't mind telling you Fenton I'm attracted but... I'm frightened of the consequences. Drug dealing is a high-risk occupation not to be undertaken lightly in spite of its rewards'.

'Don't worry I'm the same. I didn't plan my involvement, it just happened almost without my realizing, but there was no going back after that. I don't think of myself as a villain Jack it's just a service somebody else would provide if I didn't. There will always be junkies in our society, people who can't face the harsh realities of their life and we are in a position to offer them a little relief, the chance to get away from it all for a few hours. It's no big deal if they keep it under control!'

'It's not the moral aspect that bothers me Fenton it's how your other clients would react. I mean we would be treading on their toes. I don't want to be on someone's hit list. You don't go against these type of people'

'It wouldn't come to that I can assure you. They have their own territory and we'd be pushing the stuff only in your clubs, and arcades using people you've obviously checked out for loyalty. It shouldn't be a problem if your people keep their mouths tightly shut'

'Sure I know my business. Even my cleaners are paid off with eyes shut mouth closed money and protection is well taken care of and not by the Bayswater Boys I might add.'

'Vodka and tonic, ice and a slice?'

'Oh thanks, that's lovely. No I'm not really worried you know but there are a lot of questions to be answered before I go any further.'

'Of course there are, but I take it you're interested enough to talk further. yes?'

'Yes I am, I've got one foot in the game anyway so I might as well dip another toe in the water.'

'Good that's fine, let's eat and talk at the same time. Lobster mayonnaise, a glass of Chablis do you?'

'I must say you've got a lovely view from here. Houses of Parliament look most impressive in this light'

'Yes you'd never believe it was such a den of thieves would you. I bought this place from a backbencher. He even had a division bell fitted so he could get off his floozy when it rang and rush off to vote.' Fenton raised his glass. 'To a profitable new life'

'Yes' said Jack 'I'll drink to that, let's talk detail'

'Well firstly let's set a few parameters. Where does your sphere of operation finish and mine begin? We're talking cocaine here, from the leaves of the coca plant picked and brought from farmers in remote areas of Colombia sometimes by donkey-back to jungle factories. There it's processed into powdered cocaine hydrochloride'

'Which is how you buy it is it'

'Yes that's right we buy direct from the South American cocaine cartels, Peru, Bolivia, Colombia they're all in it. It's a

64

multi billion-dollar enterprise centred around the city of Medallin. It's big business Jack and I mean mega big. For instance one 44-kilo importation of good coke is worth something like 10 million pounds sterling on the streets, so you can see why someone said drug dealing was more addictive than drug taking can't you. Anyway I buy a shipment which by now is refined white powder bagged into easily handled kilo lots. These will be packed into boxes ready for shipping. Now to save going down through the Panama Canal to get from the Pacific to the North Atlantic ours will usually be flown over land across Colombia to the port of Caracas to join its ship.'

'Whose ship or aircraft are used'?

'Their own. The Barons of the drug cartels own factories, laboratories, aircraft, ships and even islands. They ship the stuff across to Amsterdam and that's where you come in'

'But if my input is distribution this doesn't start until it gets to London does it?'

'True but the leg between Amsterdam and London is like I've said a stumbling block. The Customs, and Drug Squad are getting a bit too good at sussing out our moves even before we make them. They're using undercover agents to infiltrate our lines of communication and making matters very difficult whatever means we try. Individual smugglers (or mules as they are called) stuff pods of it into every single orifice and as I said the other day even swallow condoms full, coming on scheduled air flights. But there is a limit to how much a single person can handle. And to get it here in bulk, aircraft, small yachts, lorries through the channel tunnel are all coming under too much scrutiny so a really foolproof system needs to be found.'

'Well' said Jack 'I think I may have a possible solution'

Fenton sat up 'Do tell me more. Do you mean using your boat?'

'Well let's say a boat like it, capable of making thc trip from

65

Amsterdam across the North Sea and into the Thames Estuary, at speeds up to forty knots, a boat with the general appearance of a Customs or Trinity House vessel and what could be a secret stowage space that sounds undetectable'

'Where did you dig that one up?'

'Down at the boat club at Milehaven. Over a heavy drinking session'. Jack described his conversation with Sidney in great detail.

'Hey this sounds promising. Do you think he'd be interested, He'd have to do all the work himself, to avoid security leaks, no cutting corners. Christ there would be plenty of cash for him. Do you realise if we only stashed twelve kilos into the storage space we'd have two million quid to share between us and from what you've said we'd do at least three times that amount. Would he be prepared to come in with us, and can he be trusted. That's the most important thing'

'I'm certain of it. He's been living beyond his means and he's well in debt at the moment and I'm sure he really needs the money right now. He runs a mistress and now this new boat. He's into it well over his head I should say. Oh yes, Sid will be keen. I'll sound him out if you like. But I'll be careful not to give the game away, till I'm sure. Very careful indeed.'

'How much does he know already?'

'Not much, no worries on that score. I told him a friend was writing a novel and I was doing the research'

'Well done that should keep things quiet for the moment. Anything else you'd like to know'

'Only about the cash involved. How's that to be organized because as I've said, Sid is short of a few bob and I'm not a lot better off. If it's a case of injecting big time capital up front, we will need some backup'.

'Leave that to me. I think I can organize a little working capital in advance using my offshore connections'

'Laundered money you mean. That would of course be your side of things Fenton'

Fenton smiled, 'A very important area. Well Jack it seems my gut reaction is going to pay off. I felt we'd be in business together one day. Now when you see Sid, don't say too much. Suss him out and arrange a meeting between the three of us. Here will do. Be sure you can trust him before giving away anything. No phone calls, e-mails or conversations in public places... OK. I'd offer you a brandy, but I know you're driving and we wouldn't want you to break the law now would we'

On Monday morning the pontoons were quiet, (in sharp contrast to Sunday afternoons when families had packed up and left their boats). Now only a few black headed gulls strutted and postured, picking up crumbs where a picnic basket had been emptied. Sidney made his way along to where Jackpot was moored. The message on his office answer machine was brief. 'Can you meet me on my boat at nine on Monday morning, if not give me a ring and we'll make another time' This was strange as Jack was always in London like most others weekdays unless there was something special like a Greyhound training sortie. If he were at Milehaven at all it would be at the clubhouse in the evening for a function, or a committee meeting. Monday was a dead day with only residents like John Crowther who lived aboard around. As Sid approached the grey shape it looked deserted, no lights in the wheelhouse or deck housing. No blue flag flying from the Jackstay (which in boatman's language meant the Skipper was aboard) 'Damn, don't say this is going to be a waste of time. I suppose I should have phoned him back to confirm' Sid muttered to himself as he climbed aboard and tried the wheelhouse door. It was unlocked, pushing it open he shouted 'Hello. Jack, you there, anyone aboard.'
Out of the gloom a voice said 'Sidney old son, there you are. I didn't hear you crossing the deck. I had my head stuck into a few papers. Thanks for coming. You obviously got my

message. I'm sorry it was such short notice, but I wanted a quiet chat'. Sidney looked surprised. 'Have you come down from London this morning?'

'No I slept on board last night. I must say it's very useful having a bolthole from the claustrophobia of town. I come down here from time to time to chill out. That's why the flag isn't flying. I don't tend to advertise the fact that I'm here.' There was a slightly awkward silence for a few seconds before he continued. 'Thanks for helping out my friend with his research the other day. He was very grateful. Funny thing to ask I suppose, it's just that I remembered you saying that was your area of expertise. Actually he's got a lot of knowledge himself on the drug trafficking scene. D'you know that just one trip across in a boat like this could bring in ten to twelve million pounds, staggering isn't it. Almost beyond belief. Not surprising he wants to write about it. It's the stuff dreams are made of.'

Sid formed his lips into a silent whistle. 'Beats fishing for mackerel or giving demonstrations of synchronized boat handling. I suppose if you were prepared to take a risk, but it would be a hell of a risk. I'd hate to end up doing 15 years wouldn't you? It's not worth it.'

'Oh sure I agree of course but the risk isn't as great as you would think these days. It's planned down to the last detail like a high tech military operation. Nothing left to chance, some of the best brains in the country are involved if only you knew'

Sid took the mug of coffee from Jack and sipped it very slowly. 'Like your friend you mean. There's no book is there. It's for real isn't it? All we've been talking about. It's going to happen. Don't tell me you're involved in the drugs scene...I don't believe it'

'Hold your horses Sidney, I'm not saying anything, but for the sake of argument, if I was, would you really blame me for a split of around a million'

Sid looked down at the dark blue carpet beneath him, then looked up sharply 'You might as well know Jack that the way things are at the moment money wise I would hi-jack the QE2 for less than half that figure if I could get away with it. This isn't a wind up. You're quite serious aren't you?'

'Never been more so Sidney, my friend is already involved. I thought you might be up for it, but didn't know how to ask you in case you went all moral on me and turned me into the Police. I should have denied this conversation of course. But just talking about it is a risky business for me'

'Well let's say I'd be interested as long as the planning is like you say and   the risk is cut to the minimum. There has to be some risk of course that's what makes it exciting isn't it. Do you know I can't believe we are having this sort of conversation'

'Don't worry, nor can I Sid .You realize this is the same sort of excitement Rodney Blake is looking for with the Greyhounds, but he's just playing games with big boys' toys. We've got the chance to get ourselves involved in something like the real thing'.

If Sidney had expected the first full meeting of the conspirators to prove to be a bare bulb suspended over a backroom table he was to find its formality exceeded even that of the MMYC Annual General Meeting. The venue was the function room of the Bank of Almenia whose Doric portals looked out across the plane trees of a shady London square. At precisely 09.30 hours a quiet voice from the end of the table spoke. 'I only know one face here so I think we should introduce ourselves. I'm Justin Rosenstein and I'm a Merchant Banker. The reason I'm speaking is because Fenton here suggested I chair this meeting because it's what I spend most of my time doing. He and I are more or less covering the same area, finance that is, only I get it together and he spreads it about. That's this side of the table, now you two over there.

69

That's Jack Delaney on the right, yes? OK Fenton tells me you've got a slice of the nightclub scene with aspirations towards a casino, fine. And Sidney Arthur on the left you're in the boat business fitting internal systems, I think that's correct yes? OK now state the objective. Why are we all sitting here together this morning in this charming room? The objective in brutal terms Gentlemen is to illegally import cocaine into this country and control its distribution and sale to our advantage. Now given the gravity of this statement in the light of current media pre-occupation with the control of Class A substances, if any of you have any misgivings, now is the time to mention them because this meeting is a commitment for all four of us. Let's not underestimate the task we are taking on. We must outwit not only the regional crime squad, customs blokes and of course the drug squad themselves. On the North Sea legs there's offshore fast customs and police boats and sometimes the Royal Navy themselves to contend with, and we mustn't overlook another factor. Fenton's Bayswater Boys, they control a large area of London, now they're not going to let just anyone muscle in I can tell you. Raise your head above the wall and they'll blast it off without a second thought...well that's the bad news. All depressed OK here's the good news. We can win if we do this thing properly. I would not have come here this morning if I didn't think it could be done. Is everybody with me? Well nobody has left the room yet so I'll take it as a yes. Right let's take it stage by stage. Buying, Transport, Distribution, Funding, Cover Security. Buying is Fenton's area. He's been dealing with Colombia cartels and knows how they work and can get the best possible deal including shipment as far as Europe. Transport...this is an area most people fall down on but from what Fenton has told me we have something quite unique. As I understand we have access to a couple of very fast boats which are not only similar in colour and profile to naval units but fly the blue ensign of the Royal Naval

Reserve. Whilst this in itself is impressive Jack and Sidney, you Sidney have I understand come up with what sounds like a foolproof method of concealing our precious cargo. Distribution this would be in Jacks hands. It's a big area and we might just have to recruit a fifth member to the team. Funding is down to me, we're going to need quite a bit of capital to get things done properly so as I've said to Fenton I will set up a Barents Sea oil exploration company. On paper only of course, and then arrange to fund it with venture capital. Cover, I've given this a lot of thought as it's an important factor. We need a respectable front we can work behind, something that sinks into the background without attracting too much notice. I suggest we form another bogus company and call it 'Sanitation Services' which can cover a multitude of sins. It should operate at least one lorry and then we need a safe house, where we can store stuff and do any work, which must be done. And talking of work brings me to operatives. Every time we employ anyone they are likely to find out what we are up to, which means we have either got to pay them a lot of money or frighten them to death to stop them giving the game away. So we shouldn't employ more bods than are absolutely necessary and be prepared to roll our sleeves up, and do things ourselves. Lastly security. This is something we must all be conscious of. The wartime slogan says it all. "Careless talk cost lives" one word in the wrong ear and we're done for. So it goes almost without saying that we talk to nobody about the project, that includes other halves, wives families, trust nobody. Keep contact to a minimum and although it may sound silly now, use these code names I'm going to give you when we talk. It could save being found floating down the Thames at Wapping or getting knee capped in Knightsbridge. Don't forget them. Fenton you're Diane. Jack Joyce and Sidney you'll be Katie and oh I'm Joan, no funny remarks please. Speak always in the third person, never in the first person singular, per essempio. If

Jack wants to check on the time of the next meeting he should ring me and say Joyce wants to check on the time of the next run. Could you let her know? That sound quite innocuous doesn't it. Now if I'm sounding a bit autocratic I don't mean to. There is no boss in this operation but somebody has to take the lead. I'm out of the country quite a bit so I suggest Fenton is point of contact between us in the weeks to come, you may need ready cash as we go along so he'll act as treasurer in any case. Just one more thing information is on a need too know basis. No point in getting mixed up in one another's areas We'll meet here again soon to review progress on all fronts, until then keep a tight ship and your mouths firmly shut. For the record you're all my clients here this morning, being advised of an investment opportunity. Oh, one thing we need a cover code for this operation we're about to set up. I suggest 'School Run'

Dave and Gloria had mixed feelings over Sid, when not in his company they dined out on his success. In the Milehaven Men's Club they dropped his name as of the upper crust 'See a lot of him? Oh yes we're often on his boat. Known him for yonks, officer of the yacht club and all. We'll probably be cruising round Monte Carlo with him and Jan next year if I can take the time of work that is...or I'll have to go sick eh!' It was as though as close friends their status had been raised a little above that of their cronies in the bar and at the meat raffle on a Friday or line dancing on a Wednesday. But in his company it was different. Dave would pick away at Sid's new polish in a jovial way of course, ready to parry offence with 'Only jokin'...you know me' For now they felt beneath him, that the bingo and Newcastle Brown showed through like rust bubbles on a ten year car. They would niggle on in the hope their little jibes might perhaps expose just a little of the grimy jobbing plumber they knew lurked beneath the doeskin blazer with the gold wire MMYC badge. Their weeks and holidays were working class as it should be, comfortable amongst their friends. Sid had no business to leap out of overalls and start talking la-de-dah 'Oh this is very posh Sid I must say, Champagne in an ice-bucket, eh what next'

'It's Asti Spumante' corrected his host 'Jan likes it better cause it's sweet, doesn't like it dry, do you luv. I said you don't like it dry, she can't hear me in the kitchen. It's the food blender. She's doing the avocado fillings. Damn I think that was supposed to be a surprise...More lager Dave, drain your glass and I'll top you up, there's plenty more outside...Gloria a tad more Asti. Oh excuse you, I know it makes Jan burp too. Don't worry you're among friends. Have that one on me.' Gloria giggled, hopelessly effervescent. She left the room, napkin complete with ring to her mouth mumbling 'Can I do anything to help Jan' Conversation lagged as the ladies filed in bearing the avocado pears in avocado shaped glass dishes.

'Oh very nice' piped up Dave again. 'Very yacht club eh. Shall we dig in'

Four spoons scooped into Jan's blended thousand island dressing and frozen prawns but none made any impression on the avocados which seemed to have the durability of smooth trainer soles. Faces contorted as pressure was applied in ever increasing measure until at last Gloria's spoon sent her avocado half spinning around the table dispensing pink dressing as it went. Dave primed now with a blend of Asti and lagers attacked his with a knife but succeeded only in liberating little wedges, which ended up mostly on the floor. 'Let's go on to the main course' suggested Janet 'Sorry I should have given them a squeeze at the Coop. There's more thousand island and prawns, I'll do a few little squares of toast to keep us all going'

Sid smiled a sickly smile and said 'What are you doing for holidays this year?' This was more in terms of a smoke screen to cover the exit of the failed avocados rather than interest in

Dave and Gloria's plans. But Dave read the question as a possible prelude to cruising in the Med and perked up visibly. 'Us? Oh nothing settled really, we'll probably take Gloria's Mums caravan at Selsea Bill for a week but that don't count cause she comes with her dog and us. It's unhealthy, farts all night and if you put it out it howls and wakes up all the others. Do you know there is over a thousand'

'What dogs?' asked Sid

'No caravans' cuts in Gloria. 'Lovely it is really with a shower block and bar and burger bar too. No need to walk anywhere'

'But nothing is settled as I said' cut in Dave to shut her up. 'So you could say we're at a loose end really as far as holidays are concerned. What are you two up to? Nice bit of cruising I shouldn't wonder'

'Not him, not my Sid' wheezed Janet lowering a big steaming serving dish between them. 'Buys a nice new boat then says he's taking it out of the water to do some work on it. Mind these plates are hot, gravy just coming'

'What broken down already. Nothing major I hope'

'Oh no Dave nothing's wrong just some changes I need to make' Sid turned away to serve Gloria with cauliflower but Dave seeing their cheap holiday sinking slowly by the bows hung on with terrier-like tenacity.

'So you won't be cruising with it then, it being out of the water and all. Something below the waterline is it?'

Sid thought mind your own business you nosy little pratt but said simply 'No I just want it in the boat shed where I've got all my specialised equipment. Actually I'm fitting a prototype air conditioning and water treatment system using my boat as a test rig. If it's successful then it could make SA Marine a lot of money. At the moment it's a bit hush hush until the thing's been protected by patent so it has to be worked on in private. There's no problem, other than I can't make any immediate plans for using the boat and may have to back out of the clubs

annual cruise across and through some of the French canals'
Dave speared a roast potato with a force, which expressed his horror facing two weeks at Selsea Bill with Gloria's Mother and the dog.

'Do you know I've never had a single night aboard that boat' whined Janet 'Let alone a weekend, but then I hate the sea, always have. So I suppose it's no bad thing, as long as my husband keeps bringing home the bacon that's all that matters eh! So we can entertain our friends. There's two more Yorkshire's outside. Go on Gloria, they'll only go to waste'

'Well what do you think, impressive isn't it?'
'Oh yes reminds me of the engine room in a supertanker, bit taller perhaps but same sort of thing'
Jenny laughed, tossing her hair back from her face. 'You're hopeless John Crowther. You're here to update your understanding of modern art not talk about engine rooms although of course this was the turbine room of a power station before it became the Tate Modern'
'Actually Jen I'll amend my first impression. It's a cross between a supertanker and Selfridges with escalators to floors packed with milling people. Here we are third floor garden furniture, sports and gym equipment'
'Behave yourself Captain Crowther or I'll never take you out again'
'Yes ma'am! but don't move too far away or I'll lose you in this crush. Is it always like this?'
'Not too sure, last time I was here I was working and there wasn't really time to take it all in. It's the coaches that do it of course. It's on most school and tour guides' itinerary and if you don't look where you're going you end up getting explanations in Thai or Japanese'
'Well it wouldn't make much difference in many cases would it. I don't know how anybody could describe that... It's just a

cardboard box with nothing in it. Good God there's loads of them. You sure this isn't the packing room?'

She took him by the arm and guided him into another room. 'I daren't leave you in there any longer people were beginning to gather round. Now this is a little less confusing. More contemplative perhaps'

Her pupil slowed down to a stop and took stock of the situation 'Well it's less crowded. One can see what is going on, only nothing is going on, except.... bloody hell what's a grand piano doing hanging upside down from the ceiling?'

'It's in spatial harmony with the total volume of this room'

'Is it? You are serious this time not taking the Mickey or anything. Only we had a Steinbeck in our garden room at home down by the river. That also was a major object in the room. It too was spatially satisfying even though it wasn't being played. It was in audio and visual harmony and it didn't have to be suspended from the ceiling upside down to achieve it. In fact there's only one advantage to the way they've got this one.... it won't collect dust on it's lid like ours did'

'Oh dear John, I'm beginning to think you might be a lost cause and there was I thinking I might have introduced you to a new aesthetic dimension'

'You have Jen. You really have. Only I'm not sure I'm happy with it. Let's go and grab a coffee shall we or at least join the queue'

They sat outside on a little balcony overlooking the Thames hands round huge beakers of frothy coffee. 'That's better, places like this always make my feet ache'

'Funny you should say that' agreed John. 'When I used to go round the National Gallery with the school it was deathly quiet and my shoes squeaked on the polished floors. There would only be a handful of people walking round and others sat on seats back to back in the middle of the room to gently take it in. But that was many years ago now of course. Things seem to have changed and I keep forgetting I'm nearly twenty years older than you. You're Tate Modern and I'm still National Gallery. That's an interesting analogy isn't it'

She caught his eyes and held their gaze. 'If we're talking fine art terms then think of me as your risorgimento John, your rebirth into a new dimension which will have changed things for both of us even when you, Tradewind and Bosun are on the other side of the ocean and I'm well wherever journalism chooses to take me in the years to come'

'That sounds depressingly final. Is there something I don't know?'

She nodded very slightly. 'The only reason I said we should meet up here in town for lunch is that I've been up here for an interview this morning at Syndicopy. I've been offered a job as reporter on their crime desk'

'That's great isn't it? You want to get where the action is don't you? I'm pleased for you Jen I really am.'

'Problem is, this opportunity has come up quicker than I thought and it means I've got to find a place in town. Which of course will be expensive and inconvenient. But that's the way it goes I suppose. If I've got a lot of travelling to do I shall be living out of a suitcase anyway. I'm told that comes with the territory. I shall just have to play it by ear. I start next month. Sorry I didn't tell you about it before, but it just sort of happened. Do you think you will be able to get up to town a few times before you actually leave these shores and sail off? We could meet in Soho for a spot of lunch or something...like today. I'm going to miss our discussions; I think we're good for one another Mr. Crowther'

'And you know it's the same as far as this old water rat is concerned, don't you?'

They stayed for sometime saying little but staring at the almost sullen flow of the Thames along the South Bank until he said 'If you're at Canary Wharf and the Thames was frozen down to Milehaven we'd be virtually living in the same street wouldn't we?'

She put her hand very gently over his and said' 'We've been living on the same street for sometime now haven't we at least that's how I see it'.

There was a gap among the grey boats on Pontoon five during the week that followed. No.3 had slipped her moorings and gone through the open sea lock on the last high tide, motoring up river the odd two miles to where a rusting hangar-like boathouse bore the sign, S.A. Marine. Within an hour the boat had gone from view, winched slowly up the rollers of its slipway into the dark cavern of a workshop, which housed several boats in varying stages of repair. Two sets of tall steel doors then rolled across on squeaking rusty wheels to close activity from the world outside. Within six hours the ebb tide would have drained the river leaving Sidney's little empire more part of an industrial site than the sea. Wedged securely within the dry dock pit which brought it's deck to ground level for ease of working, the forty feet of power sat almost insignificantly amongst the jungle of air hose cables, overhead gantries and dangling lifting chains. The air was heavy with the smell of engine oil, marine varnish and oxidising metals the usual raucous symphony of high decibel pop music clashed with the squeal of jigsaw, popping air rivet guns and the hiss of sanders. Sid's army was at work. He stood one hand cupped to Tina's ear for a moment then steered her towards the little office perched well above the workshop floor. He slammed the door behind them shaking the little portacabin with the impact.
'That's better, couldn't hear myself think down there, seems worse than ever today, even though there are not too many jobs on. Anyway thank goodness that's the last Sea Sprite fitted out today which leaves us clear on the water system side. There's only the two replacement tanks then, plus the anti fouling job in the corner. What I was trying to say to you

was it's a good job I've got that special project work on at the moment to keep us going. Mind you it's development stuff so it's not instant payment... more's the pity'

'Where did you pick that up from? I haven't had any luck yet from all my phone calls'

'Oh Jack Delaney. It's for a friend of his. Could mean a profit if it comes off.'

'It's kosher then. I mean we don't often do casual work. You know for a friend of a friend. Not until we have at least checked them out'

'Yes it's fine they're a big group, international in fact'

'Well then we had better open a job sheet for the boys'

'No need I'm doing all the work myself'

'You are! But why? You haven't done any hands on work for ages. You've always said why have a dog and bark yourself'

Sid thought quickly 'Well for one thing I'd like to keep my hand in. Anyway it's high security and I just can't take the risk of one of the boys blabbing details to the trade. You know what they're like. It's not that I don't trust them, but industrial espionage is a fact of life isn't it. Thought I told you about it the other day, don't you remember?'

'Yes you did mention something. Said you were starting with a prototype on your own boat first but I'd forgotten why it was so special'

'Well we won't go into details again but it's a new type of marine air conditioning, where air coming into the boat can be cooled down or warmed up. Whatever temperature you want really.'

'There's nothing new about air conditioning, is there? You can have it in your car these days. Surely a boat is the same sort of thing. What's so special?'

'Well sweetheart' explained Sid carefully. 'Take it from me that it is very special. Enough to make sure it is kept from the competition'

'And you want to make sure nobody around here sees

79

anything of what's going on whilst your boat is in here?'
Yes, tomorrow after this last Sea Sprite goes out I'll lay off
the boys for the rest of the week, we can have the whole place
to ourselves can't we.'
Tina raised one eyebrow quizzically. 'But darling aren't you
worried that I might be an industrial spy. Don't worry I'll
look the other way. Your secrets will be safe with me. I'll be
too busy making the coffee and keeping your strength up with
lunch'. She winked at him and gave a quick peck on the
cheek. 'Anyway joking aside you'll need someone to man the
phones. You never know what bread and butter work might be
around the corner'
Explaining his absence from his allotted berth in the marina
had been easy enough in the case of other boat owners but
with someone he worked, sailed with, and slept with, it was a
different matter entirely. In the first two days working on the
plan in the office it was bad enough as Tina had a habit of
looking over his shoulder. But when it came to the practical
side on the boat itself it began to get even worse. With all
work having been stopped on the other boats there was an
unnatural silence. Every sound he made echoed into the dark
vault of girders and corrugated iron. Even the tuneless whistle
of a plumber at work assumed the intensity of an excited
parrot. He changed over to a tuneless hum as he squeezed
himself into the space beside the starboard engine where the
40-gallon sewage holding tank was situated. It was now
pumped out and flushed clean in readiness for handling. In
thirty minutes it was disconnected from all pipe work and
electrical connections and the fixing brackets which held it in
place.
'Phew that'll do for starters, yes that's not too bad at all' Sid
sat back for a breather whistling softly to himself. He realised
with some surprise that he liked being back in overalls. Here I
am crouched awkwardly in a corner with a mole wrench in
my hand instead of a phone and a sewage tank for company.

Doesn't make any sense really. Sidney you're a plumber at heart he said to himself and that's your trouble mate. Now to get this bastard out. He eased forward and grasped the big polypropylene tank and pulled it towards him.

'Can I give yer a hand Guv' inquired a voice behind him causing him to sit up and bang his head.

'Christ Tina I didn't hear you coming'

'Just brought a flask of tea over. What you up to?'

'Er just trying to get this tank out. Like to give me a hand now you're here. Just squeeze along me and grab the other end will you'

'OK now we've got to get it over the engine, it won't go round'

'Pongs a bit doesn't it'

'It's been washed out but there's always a bit of a smell left'

'Why are you taking it out anyway? Is there a leak?'

'No nothing like that. I'm replacing it with a different one. It's part of the new system I was talking about'

'Can you stop now and have your tea'

Sid nodded. 'OK luv' He wiped his hands down his overalls like he used to and eased himself out of the engine room. They sat side by side on the bench seat in the wheelhouse with the red knobs of the throttle levers between them waiting for their tea to cool. Tina looked sideways at him for a moment and then said suddenly, 'What's a sewage tank got to do with air conditioning Sid I would have thought the two things were poles apart'

Her lover examined his mug of tea intently as though it was in some way connected to the problem. 'Well it's all part of the project luv in a way'

'You're very cagey on this job Sid. Preoccupied. Is everything OK? If there's a problem perhaps I can sort it out. I've done it before. I may not be technical but I can often think things through. You've said it yourself. Go on admit it'

'Sorry I can't talk about it. I promised. It's more than my

life's worth, really Tina I mean it, you'll have to take my word for it on this one' She laughed pushing him on the shoulder so his drink slopped and nearly split over.

'God Sid you're a funny one. You really are. I just don't believe you're making a drama out of 30 gallons of pooh and a new air system. I've heard of "when the shit hits the fan" but this is ridiculous. What are you going on about'

'It's no joke that's for sure' he explained. 'I just knew I'd never be able to keep it from you when it came to it. Not when we live in each other's pockets the way we do anyway. They did say don't tell your wife and family but you're my mistress, I suppose that lets me off the hook'

Tina gazed in exasperation at the deck head above them. 'Sidney will you please tell me what on earth you're talking about'

He explained his meeting with Jack in the Wardroom and the operation that was being planned. Tina's mouth gaped wide open 'Good God almighty Sid what have you done?. Have you any idea just what you're getting yourself into. This is highly dangerous stuff I can hardly believe what your saying' Sid covered his face with his hands. 'And I can hardly believe I'm sitting here telling you about this. God I must be barking mad' She pulled his hand away gently 'No you're not mad my love, just plain stupid keeping it all to yourself. Too much for one person to cope with. I knew something was afoot. I know your moods only too well. Look we have always shared everything. We've got to think it through together. Only don't shut me out that's all'

'It's sorted as far as my commitment is concerned. You can see I'm going ahead already, adapting my boat for the work it has to do'

'Importing drugs into the country you mean'

'Yep, that's it. Plain old fashioned smuggling across the North Sea from Amsterdam to Milehaven Marina, under cover of our cherished Blue Ensign. Brilliant or what?'

'But it's a hell of a risk. Do you think you'll get away with it'?

'Yes, two of us will make the run, Jack's boat and mine. Two official looking boats flying the flag of the Royal Naval Reserve on training exercise. What could be more above board. If that's not blue chip cover I don't know what is, and before you mention it I've been through all the moral recriminations a hundred times. I know it's hard drugs and not just fags or booze but as Jack says if we don't do it, someone else will, and anyway the users have free choice. Nobody forces them to buy the stuff. The great thing is we should clear a cut of around 2 million quid apiece. One trip that's all it needs. Just one quick there and back and we'll be set up for life. Now can you think of any better deal than that?'

'But think of the ones that get caught. There's always something in the papers every day. Thailand has its death sentences or a lifetime in one of those stinking prisons. That's if you don't get shot by one of the gangs you're trying to muscle in on. Have you really thought this through properly?'

'Yes love, I've thought about it till I'm blue in the face and we're not going anywhere near Thailand so don't worry. I know you're talking sense but even if I felt able to stand the shame of having to sell the boat to clear my debts, that would also mean having to leave the club. Anyway I can't back out now I know too much about the "school run" and all that's involved. Without this money I will have to close down the business and go back to jobbing plumbing and I really couldn't face that, not now after all this time. One trip Tina, just one trip that's all. I promise, just this one, then finish'

'I suppose this means you want me to come with you. Now I'm in the know as well'

'I don't know what made me tell you except I think you'd guessed already'

'Pretty well, we're too close for secrets me and you. Well as you say you're already working on the boat so that's the answer Sidney Arthur and as I certainly can't just stand by while you risk your neck you'd better count me in. If you think I'm qualified that is'

'Well I'm going to need a crew. It will certainly look less suspicious with a woman on board. I must say it's a relief to be able to talk things over with you. In fact with your help I'll be able to get on a lot faster. Nothing like an extra pair of hands so when you've drained your cup we'll ease the new tank into position'

To the casual observer the portly figure of Justin Rosenstein, dressed in slacks and casual shirt would have passed for any boat owner as he ambled along the pontoon. But the arch manipulator of underworld finance never ambled mentally; he took in everything in seconds and assessed it. Like the shape and character of the grey boats as he approached them. He paused at the one with the name 'Jackpot' inscribed on the bow, then stopped at the gangway before gingerly making his way aboard. The wheelhouse door was open and a voice within said 'Morning Justin, you've found us then'

'I hate boats' he replied by way of a greeting 'Always have, always will. Damn things won't stop wobbling about. Makes my guts heave even when they're tied up to something solid. Think I'd better take a tablet'

'The others are all here in the saloon' continued Jack. 'Down the ladder to the right. I'll organise us a drink'

With the three members of the school run round the little saloon table Justin had to squeeze his bulk onto the end 'God it's cramped in here isn't it' he wheezed, adding claustrophobia to his list of ills. 'I don't know how you stand it. I thought the QE2 was bad enough but this is like a broom cupboard without the brooms. Is this our North Sea boat?'

'No' answered Jack. 'That's Sid's but it's identical. It's in his boat shed at the moment having the compartments rearranged to cope with our needs'

'Good good I must say they look very official don't they these boats. You've chosen well and they'll make excellent cover. I thought it was a good idea to hold our next meeting of the school run in here so Fenton and I could get to see something of our marine hardware without drawing too much attention to ourselves of course'

'No problem on that score' reassured Jack 'We're all dressed casually and arrived separately. The cover is you're all friends of mine down here for a jolly. If anyone's really that interested that is!'

'Good that's it Gentlemen let's get on. Time is money as they say. As we're on the boat we'll deal with transport first. Sidney let's hear what stage you're at'

The addressed hesitated for some seconds remembering his conversation with Tina. 'I'm working on the boat as Jack has just said, in the boathouse near here. I've laid off my fitters for a couple of days and locked up the place so no questions will be asked as to what I'm doing. Except for my PA that is. She knows, she guessed and I had to let her in on it. She crews for me anyway. I'll need her when we do the job in any case'

'Can we trust her' said Fenton sharply 'You know what we agreed about security'

'She's OK. We always work together. She'd never grass on us I'll stake my life on it'

'You've just done that Sidney ' added Justin. 'But we'll take your word for it and as you say you'll need crew on the day. She's your problem Sidney. Make sure she keeps her lips buttoned and yours as well if you know what's good for you. Jack what about your crew on the day?'

'I don't have any problems. Sid's boat is where the action is going to take place. Mine is going for the ride so to speak just to give credibility to the idea of a training exercise but anyway Mario works for me. He's been checked out - Fenton can vouch for that'.

'OK that answers that one. Go on Sidney so you and your sidekick are working at the moment are you?'

'Yes we've unshipped the old plastic sewage holding tank and are in the process of replacing it with a larger steel one which has a secret inner chamber accessed from the upper deck. The inner one will contain the cocaine while all around the outside will be sewage solids floating in Elsan blue toilet fluid. Very nasty if you open the screw cap'

'So we're in the shit so to speak'

'Sort of. It should keep out the Customs and Excise interest. You see they'll always be looking for the usual one-kilo plastic packs of powder stacked behind lockers or under floorboards or in the bilges As suggested at the last meeting what they will probably do is give a knuckle tap test. If a water tank echoes it's empty and could be hiding something. If it sounds dull and heavy it's full of liquid and probably OK. If they open ours up the pong will drive them back, hopefully'

'But how do we get the coke packs in and out of the secret container without anyone seeing what we are doing?' asked Fenton.

'Jack and I have given this a lot of thought. Jack would you like to present our little concept as it comes under distribution'

'Yep fine Sid. Well you've outlined good cover is vital as we move the stuff around. We need to appear as ordinary as possible so nobody gives us a second look. The name Justin has come up with Sanitation Services is great. Vans with this name on could be seen anywhere around here without causing any attention. We'd need a bit of cash to set it up, but this is how it would work. Firstly as already mentioned we should get away from plastic bags of white powder in cardboard boxes. That sticks out a mile. So we have changed the packaging to start with and ask the Colombians to supply

86

wrapped like a sausage only thicker. Could be in lengths of say ten to twelve feet, tied off every six inches, the way sausages are'

'You're joking' laughed Justin.

'Never been more serious. Next a small tanker like Councils use for drain cleaning (sludge gobblers I think they're called) is driven from the docks to where our boat is moored. On its side will be the words "Sanitation Services, Sewage Removal". Ostensibly it will be there to pump out from the boats on-board holding tank via a three-inch thick connecting pipe. But actually it will be pumping in the other direction down the pipe a stream of liquid in which is floating a long chain of plastic cocaine pods. When our boat returns to the UK it goes alongside the loading quay at Milehaven where the reverse takes place and the same tanker sucks out the precious cargo'

'And where does it go from there' asks Justin who was now beginning to treat the idea as a serious proposition.

'That's stage two' replied Jack. 'It goes straight to our safe house, an old warehouse on the Grand Union Canal in West London. It was used for loading timber onto narrow boats years ago, but I've been using it as a storehouse for surplus furniture from my clubs'.

'What happens then?'

'That's all worked out. Once under cover the little tanker pumps out the cocaine chain which is then dried off ready for the stage three... the toilet rolls.'

It was Fenton's turn to laugh 'Toilet rolls what next'

'Well Sanitation Services as the name suggests supply paper towels and toilet rolls for lavatories in clubs pubs casinos, dog tracks, you name it. They buy in bulk and we just add a little packet of something to each consignment. You see our little coke pods will be exactly the right diameter and length to slip as a push fit into a cardboard tube, which forms the centre of the toilet roll. All we have to do is unwrap one end of the roll

87

cut off one cocaine pod and push it in carefully and then re close the wrapper. Now who is going to break the cover of a little white van from Sanitation Services delivering a box of toilet rolls to the back door of a London club? And finally a Pusher can sit on a toilet seat in the privacy of a cubicle and measure out individual doses for sale. So what do think of the plan gentlemen?'

'Pretty water tight from what you've just said' conceded Justin 'I can't fault it. All we've got to do is put it all together. It's going to cost a pretty penny but then we're talking millions not hundreds if we pull this off and we're going to do just that, I've no doubt on that score because I don't work with losers. Right let's throw what Jack has proposed for open discussion. I'll be devils advocate and start things off. Now we are going to use two boats which look like naval vessels and they'll be flying a Royal Navy flag so are we taking too many precautions with our secret compartment and our chain of coke pods. I mean do you think the Customs people will suspect a vessel like this?. Could we not save money by hiding the stuff in the bilge compartments like other boats have done?'

'Possibly' said Fenton. 'But if by taking a little extra trouble we can reduce the risk of getting caught still further I think we should do it. We know what happens if we fail. I like the suggested cover of Sanitation Services very much. Everything ties in so well from sewage disposal right down to toilet rolls. I think both Jack and Sidney have done us proud and I know Justin agrees. What I'd like to do is run through the critical path as I see it. My Cartel contact in Medellin can have our consignment flown from the jungle factory across to Caracas for shipping out as soon as we are ready. But if we want it packed in a special way it's going to take longer and cost us more of course. We can firm up on that one later. I think the four of us can formally agree on the company to be entered as Sanitation Services Plc. with a registered office as my city address and trading to be from Western House Warehouse 61 Canal Street. Cranbridge WC5. That correct Jack? Good! Now as soon as Justin has organised working capital we can purchase the vehicles and have them suitably painted. I'll leave the technicalities to Sidney here. Now if the Colombians can't pack the stuff in the special pod shapes we'll have to work round the standard kilo pack. How big a problem will that be Sid?'

'Well obviously we can't be seen handling kilo packs of white powder so what I'll have to do is instead of having a three inch cap on deck which marries up with the tankers hose pipe fitting is cut a little square hatch the same size as the kilo pack and then slide them down an enclosed chute from the top of the tanker straight into our chamber below decks'

'Fine Sidney - that sounds as though it could work as an alternative. Now Jack how does that affect your distribution?'

'Well what it will do is destroy our nice little toilet roll cover. It means we're still dealing with the very recognizable plastic packs of powder. It's much more dangerous. We could perhaps repack them into boxes of paper hand towels. At least it's similar in character'

'Good thinking Jack. If we have to change our ideas we'll keep that idea as a standby. This affects you Sidney, at the moment you don't know which deck fitting to close off your inner tank'

'Yes that's true. What I think I'll do is fit the small inlet and then widen if we have to later'

Fenton smiled 'Fine Sidney, that leaves the ball in my court to speak to my contact. I think we have covered a lot of ground this morning. I don't think we have any other business so I'll leave it to the chairman here to sum up'

'Thank you Fenton I think we have the makings of a good little import agency here between us. It's shaping up very nicely. As I've said I hate boats and water except in my malt whisky. These two boats are different, not the usual gin palaces so I think they will do a very nice job for us, but I'm glad I'm not going with you, at least not physically. Thanks Jack for providing the safe house that's one big problem solved. The fact is your work won't start until we're established inside there. But in this operation I must stress we are all in together. Although we've been talking of it in sections we must all look out for each other at all times because if one of us goes down we're all lost. Anyway we all know what we're doing I think, so I'll close this meeting of the school run. Next time we meet I hope it will be to fix the date of the run.'

Justin was glad to get off the boat not exactly ashore but at least on the terra almost firma of the pontoon which was only rocking very gently. He waited until Fenton came over the gangway and they stood looking out across the marina together. 'Nice little backwater this isn't it, but very handy for getting out to sea' he touched the accountants arm.
'Close to London as well, useful eh'
'Yes very useful, amazing to see all these boats and so few people around. It's like a deserted village, hundreds of thousands of pounds of floating luxury wherever you look and nobody enjoying it...I suppose they're in their city offices slaving away trying to pay for it all. Mad isn't it'
'Except for that guy along there in that scruffy old boat. He's got some work to do on that alright. Enough to keep him going for years I should think. Rather him than me swinging around at the top of that mast like that. Doesn't look safe to me'
They paused staring up at the bronzed figure in denim shorts and tee shirt suspended high above them in a flimsy Bosun's chair. Like him they didn't notice the woman in her thirties. She had long flowing hair and was dressed casually but somehow purposefully in black leather jacket and close fitting

jeans. Slung on her shoulder was a well-worn camera case to which was tied a scarf. She had also stopped short of the old wooden hull and looking up towards the dangling figure high above, aimed her camera and fired off a fast sequence of automatic wind on shots. Then shading her eyes against the sun shouted 'You coming down or shall I come up for coffee' The figure turned round with circus-like agility until the master mariner was smiling down between his knees at the fresh uplifted face below as his audience of two moved on. 'What's a nice girl like you doing in a place like this, we're not used to London media types down here. You could of course put the coffee on while I wind myself back to sea level if you like young Jenny Wren' The block and tackle squeaked as the chair jerked its way down the mast until John Crowther's frayed canvas boat shoes hit the cabin top. 'That was not much fun up there this morning fitting the new wind gauge I couldn't get the old one off. Good view though. Not that there's much going on round here except Jack's been having a coffee morning on his boat by the looks of it' She laughed and tossed her hair back. 'Yes they were all watching you at work you know'

He touched her shoulder gently 'This is an unexpected pleasure having a visit from you this morning. What brings you in this direction'

'Well ostensibly I'm over this way to do some interviews in connection with a rather nasty case of child abuse in a church run children's home not far from here. I was on the road and suddenly decided to divert here and get some fresh air first'

'You mean exchange the carbon dioxide of Fleet Street for the methane of Milehaven marshes'

'Don't be such an old cynic or I won't make the coffee. Anyway it's Bosun I've come to see really. I don't know why this dog stays with you. You never take him for walks or anything'

'He's a sea dog, doesn't like walking, actually he's a watch keeper. He'll come on deck at eight in the morning and sit there till eight bells chime at noon, then go below and sleep. That's the forenoon watch. Keeps it every day he does without fail. They probably named the dog-watches after him' 'What's a dog watch?'

'Television in the evening... No sorry a dogwatch is from 4 to 6 pm. That's the first one, then the second dog is from 6 to 8pm. They're the only two hour watches in the navy. All the rest are every four hours. How's that for useless information' She patted wiry hair on the dog's head. 'You make me laugh you two, do you know that. That's why I like coming over. It's sad to think you won't be here soon and that one day I'll walk across the pontoon and Tradewind will be gone for good. I can't believe this old creaking shadow of the sea will be a thousand miles away somewhere'

'Do you mean me or the boat young lady? Stop being sad, you're upsetting Bosun. Look his ears are going down. Let's go below and get this coffee you keep talking about. Tell you what; I bought a jam doughnut to have this morning. I'll cut it in half for us with my seaman's knife after I've wiped it clean that is'

The saloon table below was obscured by the components of a Stuart Turner bilge pump, Rice Crispies pack and a carton of semi skimmed milk. Jenny swept everything to one end of the raise edged wooden surface with one movement of her arm. 'God it's like Age Concerns white elephant stall down here. You'll need to clear up when you go to sea, that's for sure'.

'If I ever get there. At the moment everything that can wear out, fall off, rust or become incompatible with other new components is doing so. I guess we'll get there in the end but at the moment it seems a long way off'

'But you haven't changed your mind. The plan is still the same isn't it?'

He looked at her steadily. The fun had left his eyes. 'We'd always planned to do it she and I, for years it's been there if you know what I mean, always in the background but never forgotten. One day when I retire we'll do it, I would say. Find the boat that wants to go with us and take off. I knew someday the boat would show itself, ironic wasn't it that some six months after she died I came across the boat down here half buried in the creek mud. Well when I say I found her, it was Bosun really. He ran out chasing seagulls and I went to get him. The rest is history and we've been together off and on ever since. What I'm trying to say is although she never lived to see it, this boat would have been my apology for leaving her alone so much when time was running out for us. My way of saying this time we'll do it together for once, share this experience. It's not that I'm actually looking forward to sailing halfway round the world alone, sometimes it frightens me to death, after all I've always had something like 40.000 tons of steel at least beneath me not just six. And I know that however rough things got out there, at the end of my watch there would be a something hot and a chat with fellow officers down in the mess. No this lone trans global passage is an inevitability for the three of us now, Bosun, Tradewind and me. Something that has to be done. Oh no listen to me rambling on. I've never bent anyone's ear like this before. Sorry, what have you been up to with your work then?, sounds so much more exciting than mine. Come on tell me while I top up the coffee jug.'

She shrugged her shoulders rather sadly 'Me? Oh this and that. I've settled into my new flat. Getting used to sharing with the three other girls. Fortunately we are all in the same business so we more or less talk the same language. Actually I feel a bit of a hypocrite going on about the state of your living space on here. You should see the state of our place at times. We all work quite unsociable hours so it's a bit like a transit camp at times. I never know when I'm going to be called out. It's like being in the police really I work so closely with them around the scene of the crime, sometimes all night then I have to attend court during the daytime. I must confess I have actually dozed off when a boring bench of magistrates goes droning on. It's a life of great contrasts mine is, strong light and shade. One day I'll be stuck in archives sifting through a sea of statements till me head aches and the next I'll be standing on a dockside wharf at say four in the morning as a police boat pulls a body from the river. Sometimes the images resurface in my waking thoughts.'

'But you wouldn't change things would you, I mean it's what you want to do isn't it.?'

'Oh yes. Yes it is, warts and all. It's the work I want to be doing, it seems a along way from the weddings and parish reporting I used to do'

He looked up and caught her eye. 'We're driven, you and I aren't we? In different ways, but just as positively. Almost as if it's beyond our control'

'Yes we are I agree with that, but perhaps not beyond the point of our control, not quite but that remains to be seen. You've left your half of the doughnut. Shall I give it to Bosun before it's time for him to go on watch!'

The Blue Orchid by day belied its name, for there was nothing exotic in closed shutters or unlit neon tubes. It was passed by with hardly a sidelong glance by the citizens of Soho, until the business of the working day was done. Then as twilight drained all greys leaving just stark contrast of black and white a metamorphosis took place. Neon lights flickered and then shone like dancing fireflies and amongst them the Blue Orchid flowered with intensity such as to almost hurt the eye. Beneath the flower itself the words trailed off into a bright blue line which traced the outline of the entrance then went on to enlighten the area of shutters and into the basement below. Concealed blue fluorescent lights shone upwards in a mist, which transformed dusty shutters into the magic of a

94

tropical night. This illusion was instantly dispelled by Big Erickson and Twister the Bouncers, their bulk and stance spelt menace more than magic, but that was what doormen were paid for, to vet and then perhaps eject. But their presence was usually enough. Erickson was six foot three inches, and only moved to nod slightly at each entrant or mumble a few words into his 'portie', and Twister was only visible by the flash of gold in his mouth when he accidentally smiled.

This nocturnal reawakening was also taking place on the top floor where gambling would soon be active again, in the ground floor bars, and deep in the dive where intimate bays and corners concealed a multitude of sins and expense accounts were squandered on exorbitant cocktails and cheap champagne. In general the patrons were portly and the air in latter hours heavy with a blend of tobacco and cheap perfume. The rooms were rarely empty but filled to capacity when the floorshows began. There were several at intervals throughout the evening, each one in turn a little more erotic, until the final performance of practically pure pornography. This was carefully designed to wind the patrons up into a state of sexual excitement at which point the hostesses would circulate amongst the tables. Some to be seen later leaving on the arms of slightly unsteady guests to continue the floor show elsewhere. Jack's main office on the top floor looked a little like the control room of a submarine with one normal TV monitor, three CCTV screens and a computer station. To one side was a glass screen behind which an operator sat at a control panel for lights and audio presentation. On Jacks' desk was a mike for a p.a. system, which he now spoke closely into. 'Gloria to main office please, Gloria to main office'

Four minutes later the door half opened and a head poked round it. A mountain of blonde hair rose up like a volcanic eruption. Above it a diamond encrusted band securing three tall Ostrich feathers that dipped as if in salute to her employer. 'Come in Gloria, how's it going tonight?' The feathers dipped in response. 'Yes fine Mr. Jack the new routine's working a treat now on the first show. Pity about the strobe lighting flash effect. Was that guy OK?'

'Oh yes he came round after passing out in his Plat de Jour. Gave us all a bit of a turn though, nearly drowning in Chicken Korma. What a way to go. Mind you he'd drunk enough for a platoon of squaddies. Served him right'

'There's another thing Mr. Jack. It's George the Python in the third show, he's a bit off colour. Brenda wants to give him the night off'

'He seemed alright last night. How do you know when a Pythons off colour anyway Gloria? I wouldn't like to have to take its temperature'

'Well it's the bit where he rises out of the basket and up under her dress. It really gets them going. They stand up in their seats and clap some nights'

'Well what's wrong, won't he do it or something?'

'Well sort of, he comes out of his basket and then flops back limp over the side'

Jack smiled 'Perhaps he's gone off Brenda. No I'm being flippant, sorry Gloria, OK give him the night off and call in the vet if he won't rise to the occasion tomorrow. This may sound stupid but do we have a spare snake?'

'No I don't think so'

'Tell you what, give Patsy the third spot. She does that trick with a ducks egg. Hold on sweetie don't go yet there's something I wanted to say, just pop into the side office for a moment will you.'

The rest of Gloria emerged from behind the door. She went in and out in the right places, and out meant spilling over with the basic joy of a well-pulled pint. What didn't glitter undulated beneath a silky body stocking that would make a snake look baggy.

'Cigarette?' asked Jack 'Take a pew and shut the door' He smelt her perfume and heard the rustle of inner thighs in tights being crossed together as she settled on the swivel stool. She looked tense. Drawing deeply on a filter tip as he said 'Don't worry there's no problem, it's just that you're one of the people I can really trust, so I thought I'd have a word with you first. The thing is, fairly soon if all goes well, we'll be getting a new supply of coke and some crack for sale in here. It'll just be those two in addition to all the usual stuff we have. Now the last thing I want is to upset all our existing suppliers so take everything they offer as usual, yes? Nothing changes. So nothing need be mentioned about any new stuff, Ecstasy, Speed, all as usual, but the new crack and coke will be available and slightly cheaper. I'd like you to be my contact with this lot. They'll get the stuff at a rate that gives them a good margin and on top of that I'll give you a bonus, which we can agree on later. How's that sound?'

'Fine Mr. Jack, you've always been straight with me and you know I'll play fair with you.'

'I do Gloria. That's why I'm talking to you now. We work in a dangerous scene, you know as well as I do that the dealers who supply don't take kindly to the club taking stuff from anyone new. That's why this has got to be handled with kid gloves. You've always dealt with all our girls so well. The stuff won't be ready yet for a while but I thought I had better forewarn you. Whilst you're here there's just one other thing. If the capital becomes available I'm thinking of opening up a casino in a major coastal resort, Blackpool maybe, where the lights are bright, you know something in the Vegas direction. I think it would go over big I really do. No porno stuff, that'll stay here in Soho. I'm thinking more up-market, you know gambling on the grander side, glittering girls and great musical cabarets. It would have to be opulent of course and cost an absolute fortune. But it's on the cards and I want you to be part of it, help me set it up. We work well together and your stage spectacular experience will be invaluable. Keep it in mind eh'

The showgirl's eyes lit up under her outsize eyelashes. 'Sounds great, what a fabulous idea. I'll cross my fingers on that one'

'OK Gloria I'll let you go, it's nearly time for your first spot. Keep what we've discussed to yourself mind'

'No problem, my lips are sealed' She rose to go and sitting at buttock level he watched the fluffy pom-pom on her cat skin wobble as she minced towards the door. 'Let me know if George goes limp again and we'll let Brenda pick another python' called Jack laughingly. She turned her head and let her sealed lips smile the famous lip-gloss smile.

Tina puckered up her lips to take the champagne pink she always wore then talking to the reflection of Sid clad only in socks which filled her make up mirror said 'Funny that e-mail just come through, what do you make of it?'

Sid picked up the printed copy, which said, *From School Run Group. Karen says sausages OK for event. Arrange container to suit. Confirm when set up'*

'It's from Fenton' he explained 'The bloke I was telling you about to say the Colombians have agreed to pack the powdered coke to suit our preferred system of concealment and means I can now use a three inch connecting hose between the tanker and our deck intake point. Jack has tracked down a second hand agricultural tanker that at present is being resprayed, lettered with the logo Sanitation Services, and the words Sewage Disposal, and fitted with a three inch coupling system. That work is being done in a friend's garage in Wembley. Then it will be driven to a lock-up in our safe house on the canal ready to go over to Holland. It's all happening isn't it'

'Amazing I didn't think everything was so far advanced. I have to admit that I'm impressed at the detailed planning that goes into this sort of thing. It's certainly not just a case of jump into the boat and go is it.'

'Too much at stake for that. Look I don't know how I've got into this operation Tina but I have, and the fact is if the school run fails I probably won't be here at all. I'll be doing time! So I'm going to make damned sure that as far as my part is concerned nothing goes wrong...for both our sakes. You do realize this will be the making of us don't you sweetheart. With that sort of dosh we can do anything. Go anywhere we want. This is big league we're about to play in. When Jack first talked about it I was scared to death, didn't think I had the bottle to go through with it. But now I've told you and you'll be with me I must admit I'm beginning to feel excited'

Tina turned round to face the real Sid. 'Do you know I think I am too. The drugs bit worried me a little when you first explained what we would be carrying but if I put that out of my mind and think of it as a sort of treasure hunt that's going to be fun, with a huge prize to be won as long as we get it right then it's a different thing entirely'

Sid slapped his bare thigh hard 'Now I can understand old Rodney, at least where he's coming from. He had an exciting war rushing about in MTB's in '45 shooting up German E boats. Can't face retirement so he's trying to recreate that action with these grey boats. A sad old man playing war games. We're going one better aren't we? We're actually going to sea on active service against HM Customs only we're not aiming to sink them, just to see them off, outwit them. Right!'

'Covert Operations is what they'll call it' suggested Tina

'I read it in some book. And speaking of secrets you haven't said anything to Janet about this have you, now you've told me everything?'

'Good God no. I daren't do that. She couldn't keep her mouth shut for five minutes. It would be all round the men's club meat raffle crowd on the first Friday. No that's not fair but there is no point involving her at this stage'

'But you'll have to tell her something when you get your share won't you. How will you explain all that money being around'

'It wont be around, that's the whole point of Fenton's laundering service. It'll be safely tucked away in some obscure numbered offshore account, say the Caymans. All I would do is draw out the interest plus a lump sum when I needed it. Then that could be paid into the SA Marine account, great thing is to keep it moving. No Janet would never know anything. As long as there's enough money in the joint account to pay off all the credit cards and enough cash around the house she'll be as happy as a hippo in river ooze. The one thing you have to remember as far as I'm concerned is that as long as there's plenty of cash coming in my wife will never question my absences, you see her mind tells her I have to work all hours to keep the family in luxury. But the second things get a bit tight like they are getting now, she'll say if I haven't got enough work around I can come home and do some of the jobs that need doing around the house.'

'Is she asking questions now about the nights we spend on the boat?'

'Yeah once or twice lately but I say I'm doing lots of cold calls trying to get new business'

'What all night? She doesn't fall for that one surely to God'

'No course not, I tell her I've been ratted after a session in the club with Jack and had to sleep it off on the boat rather than risk driving home after midnight. Only problem is she thinks I'm becoming a bit of a piss artist says I should cut down a bit. She'd have a shock if she could see what I've been doing these last few days to the boat. Still the work is nearly over now and we can get Plumb Crazy back in the water. I'm sure to get a few questions from old Rodney I just hope he bought the rubbish I've been telling him about fitting a new air conditioning system. Let's hope he doesn't want to come on board and see it working'.

'What will you do if he does, you can't very well say no. Can you?'

'No I'll just have to spin him a yarn and say it's not working properly yet even though I've been putting in extra trunking behind the panelling. I'll blind him with science hopefully I'm quite good at that. I've had lots of practice conning old ladies remember, telling them that their plumbing was knackered and needed replacing. You know something on the lines of Bad news Mrs. your header is back feeding into your thermal rise and needs a new non-return self acting block valve and that could be a bit difficult cos' it's a non standard unit now. Just your luck though I think I may have a spare on the van, bit pricey they are, but it'll do the job proper. Bit of luck I came along today otherwise that dripping tap of yours could have got very nasty, oh yes very nasty'

'And what really would be wrong then?'

'New tap washer, two-minute job. So you see I'd fix it then go for a smoke up in the loft or get my head down for half an hour banging my spanner on the pipe for effect every now and again of course. Then I'd come down and charge 'em on the emergency call out rate say twenty five quid and she'd be ever so grateful. Never fails that one'

'But didn't you worry about conning people who trusted you to help them'

Sid raised his shoulders 'If I didn't do it someone else would. They were asking for it most of them. Anyway I did do genuine repairs as well. I'm a good plumber you know deep down it's the job I've been trained for. Look don't think I'm going to let this new money go to my head because I'm not. SA Marine will still be here as though nothing has happened only there'll be no pressure, that's the great thing. We can have a nice little flat darling together on a waterfront with a mooring, somewhere nobody knows us. We can start from scratch. That suit you'

Her eyes brightened 'You mean really live together like you

said we would one day. You'll tell Janet, get it over and done with. No more lies having to remember where you're supposed to be when she phones. Oh Sid, that'll be wonderful'

'Yep' he replied uncertainly 'Wonderful, I'm definitely going to tell her soon as we get the money sorted. Promise'

Giggling Tina blotted the champagne pink lips on a tissue. 'Hey, don't just sit there Sidney in your socks you never know who's going to call'

Rodney was well pleased with the way things were going for the MMYC. His little exclusive greyhound group had received good press coverage not only in the local rag but also nationally in yachting magazines. His book of cuttings was getting more and more impressive by the day with shots of the boats performing at regattas and sea festivals around south coast resorts. Rodney was particularly pleased with the shots of himself at functions giving after dinner talks on boating in the British Isles, traditions and responsibilities. Headlines such as *'Ex Royal Naval hero shows the need for discipline at sea'* and *'Old sea dog sets example for better safety at sea'* were stirring stuff, there was no denying that. This was going to put Milehaven on the map, maybe even become the Cowes of the motor yachting world. 'Hmm' he said out loud, 'Now there's a thought for the future why should the wind sailors have it all their own way' He could see the Milehaven marina enlarged, yes there was bags of space on the marshes after all, just waiting to be dredged and dug out to take the bigger sea going boats. Town houses with moorings. The private sector would be falling over themselves to fund that sort of prestige development. Why not, that type of land could not be reclaimed for much else. There may not be as much sun as the French Riviera but now the London docks had been allowed to die there was a need for some new contact with the sea. He smiled, the confident smile borne of thoughts of becoming an entrepreneur, adding whisky in good measure to the waiting rocks. This was the way history was made having the courage to take a broad view of the way ahead. Churchillian that was it. Why had he not thought of this before? Rodney raised his glass to a new concept and went in search of Liz his lady wife. He found her potting Azaleas in the conservatory and briefed her on his vision of the reclamation of the Milehaven marshes. Rodney always ran his thoughts past her. In her capacity of devils advocate she was calm and objective as he was impulsive and headstrong. She listened quietly as he laid bare the bones of a six-year plan standing behind her and looking towards the apex of glass panes where flies grilled to a husk in the heart of noon now hung suspended by unseen threads. There was a silence when he had finished, broken only by the tap of trowel upon pot before she said 'It's an awful lot of mud!'

'Mud' he repeated

'About ten square miles of it nothing but cockles and tiny little crabs' she explained packing down the compost with practiced fingers. 'Good place for twitchers to catch glimpses of Egrets, lovely little birds. I'd rather watch them on TV though. This is as close to nature as I want to get. Marsh should be left to seabirds. I should think it would be too unstable for building on a grand scale. Never know what was underneath, developers nightmare. You're talking foundations of rafts on piles with the tides tugging away. Huge costs before you've even laid a breezeblock. Can't see investors falling over themselves to get on board that one I must say my dear'

Rodney rattled the rocks in irritation at this reception. 'Come on old girl, you have to look beyond the obvious. Take a broader view of something like this otherwise nothing would ever be accomplished. The London Boat Show could move out there and how about this...it could provide the very first

London Marina park and ride'

'You are joking Rodney I hope'

'No I'm not. Look other than St Catherine's at Tower Bridge there are no small boat moorings for cruisers coming up the Thames and it's a daunting prospect anyway for many people. What better than to be able to moor up safely this end and get on a train straight into London.

'But they can do that already by coming into Milehaven'

'Not really we only keep a few berths clear for visitors. I'm talking of around fifty pontoons at least. We could push further back on to the marshes from the marina. We could still use our sea-lock, and perhaps even change the name to London Marina. How about that for an idea then?'

'And what would that make you if you head it up, Commodore, Harbourmaster, Captain in charge?'

'It would certainly be a high profile appointment. Now can you see why I would like to see this idea go further to the planning stage for presentation at the highest level? Who knows it could attract Lottery capital. It damn well should with all the benefits it would bring in terms of extra tourism. I'm getting excited over this I really am'

'I suppose you'll end up Sir Rodney then' chuckled Liz.

Her husband looked up towards the apex flies as though the idea had not crossed his mind. 'Oh I don't know about that' but nodded in approval as he drained his glass, which had now become just tepid water.

Fenton Gestler's glass was taller well-charged and chilled with ice, which still tinkled well when swilled around as he was doing. '*Si Juan. por favor OK si, estupendamente, continua. Yes of course, no problem, yes I'll do that, no hay deque, adios, speak with you soon*' He snapped his mobile shut, threw it on the sofa beside him and punched the air. 'Yes! Yes! By Christ we're on our way. It's down to you now Justin to come along with the cash. Here's to the School Run!' The glass was raised and replenished with Vodka before the next call was made. *'Mr. Rosenstein please, It's personal...hello Justin sorry to intrude with domesticity. It's a message from Karen about the school run, seems it's starting up and they need some cash to get it sorted.... isn't it... fine... .Yes if you would...thanks I'll be in touch about the next meeting...Wednesday? . Yes OK we'll try for Wednesday morning here if you like...OK then I'll contact the others...Bye for now'*

Fenton walked across to the computer screen and immediately emailed Sidney and Jack. Yes that sounds about right he said to himself then read out loud again before sending *'Message from Karen. Meeting to finalize school run rota fixed for Wednesday 10.30 at my place. Advise if inconvenient. Love K.* Fenton recharged his glass again. Well this is it, Juan had never let him down when he was wearing his Bayswater hat and made no comment now when he had placed the order from "Atrium Associates". So it had to be assumed that all was in order. He tapped his finger on the glass. Yes there shouldn't be any problem...as long as nobody at the jungle dispatch centre mentioned anything to any of the Bayswater mob. Not that they had any cause to make contact direct when he had handled all transactions so far. Anyway if they tried to trace Atrium they'd find only an accommodation address. It certainly paid to cover ones tracks at every stage of the game....mm…and this game was just beginning to get interesting.

The sense of purpose in Fenton's flat on Wednesday morning belied apparent card school casualness as the four conspirators sat looking out to where the brown swirl of the Thames moved almost imperceptibly towards the sea. Justin put down his coffee cup 'Gentlemen thanks for coming at such short notice but as you've probably gathered things are moving ahead on the school run. Our shipment is being processed at the Cartels jungle factory and will shortly be moved by air across to Caracas to be loaded onto MV Aquila Nera for the sea passage over to either Rotterdam or Amsterdam. The Cartel keeps its options open just in case intelligence reports a possible customs reception committee in attendance. Nothing is left to chance by our Colombian friends'

'They own the ship then' inquired Jack.

'That ship and at least another four, all specially adapted for carrying cargo like ours. Then they have their own aircraft, and landing strips all over South America, not to mention islands with refuelling facilities. You don't know the half of it boys. Fenton here can tell you about the organization, in some respects it makes the Mafia look small fry. Never under estimate the Cartels; cross them and you're dead meat, very dead meat. However both Fenton and I have a good relationship with their key figures going back some years now. So long as we pay up and keep our mouths shut we should be OK and on the subject of payment, the usual arrangement is one third on ordering a consignment and the other two thirds on delivery. I can confirm funds are now in position under our trading name of Atrium Associates, so Fenton has issued the first transfer to Bogotá on our joint behalf. Atrium has also purchased and paid for the tanker lorry now signwritten under the name Sanitation Services our cover company. Now as soon as we know whether it's going to be Rotterdam or Amsterdam it will be driven to the docks to await the arrival of Aquila Nera. Then the stuff will be transferred to our boat. Fenton reminds me that we need to recruit two or three bods to act as back up, one to drive the tanker around and then another to work processing the stuff at our canal side warehouse once everything's safely there. Yes Jack'

'They'll need to be checked out as trustworthy won't they. If it's any help we can use one of my club van drivers and two of our cleaners. They'll be keen to make a bit on the side cos they're up to their necks in debt and doing the drugs bit, so they can be trusted to keep a tight lip. They're not going to grass us up cos they know what will happen if they did'

'Thanks Jack. I'll leave the arrangements with you then. Next the technical stuff, Sidney how are things with adapting the boat'

'Yeah all ready to go. Boats back in the water and nobody is any the wiser. To outsiders I'm testing out a trial rig for a new air conditioning system.'

'Good well-done Sid, sounds as though we're in good professional hands. I'm sorry you had to go ahead without seeing what the cargo looked like. Now I know it's a bit late but Fenton received a parcel yesterday which he's brought with him'

The accountant opened his briefcase and displayed a parcel which he unwrapped to reveal what appeared to be a length of rather white looking liver sausage divided into four sections by metal clips. He held it up 'There you are my friends, this is what it's all about, only this is a dummy. If customs had opened it up, all they would have found would have been common white flour. But it shows Sid and us in particular what to expect when our shipment arrives. We are taking a 50 kilo batch on this run and each of these, let's call them pods, is a quarter of a kilo, therefore we will be looking at a chain made up of two hundred. Each will be 110mm long with a diameter of 41mm (for those of you like me, who still work in inches, that's just over four and a quarter inches by a little over one and a half inches) This system has been devised to ensure that at no time in its transit will our coke come into view to give the game away because every time it's transferred from ship to shore or vice versa it will be inside the three inch suction hose of our sewage transfer tanker. That's the transport stage. Now once inside our sanitation safe house we switch to the distribution stage'. He picked up the four-pod chain. 'It's no coincidence that each one of these little chappies fits snugly into the centre cardboard tube of an average toilet roll. So our chain of two hundred is then broken up and becomes part of a bulk consignment of toilet rolls. Our little membrane parcels however are safely and hygienically contained in a very light solution of sterile oil during transit, just enough to help them slip along easily during the process of pumping in and out. OK that's enough. on the technicalities. As for timing we're in the hands of the shippers, but I think both Sid and Jack should be on standby from the latter part of next week when the Aquila docks. The Master won't want to spend longer than absolutely necessary alongside where the Dutch Customs can come nosing around. So the second I get the final point of arrival I'll contact you Jack and we'll flash the green light for our two boats to move into position. Now I'm pretty certain that Rotterdam is a red herring and the actual destination will be Amsterdam. Have you anything to add Jack'

'Yea, well as previously discussed Sidney and I feel it would be best if both our boats are used. We've got excellent cover anyway. But if there's two of us it's even better, the story being we're on a training exercise. We'll contact the Coastguard in the Netherlands and let them know we are coming. Aquila will probably go to the modern docks, northwest up river. If we find a berth alongside the Central Station somewhere, that should be far enough away from any unfortunate connections to be made. It'll work quite well. The whole thing is that a yacht carrying drugs would normally sneak in and out everywhere. The fact that we have such a high bold as brass profile puts us above suspicion. All we've got to do is look the part and we'll carry it off, and that includes Mario, he may look a bit swarthy but he's okay. Tough as they come, been out with me on my old boat. Useful bod to have around I've used him on the doors before, nobody takes liberties with him. What I'll do is get him down to the boat for a few days to adjust to everything and he'll be on standby for when the call comes through'

'Fine Jack, that's sorted that out. Sid you okay on the crew side?'

'Yes I've no problems. We can be ready with about three hours notice'

'This all sounds very exciting' interrupted Justin, but I'm glad I've only got the finance to sort out. But I'll be on tenterhooks as zero hour approaches. Until then all I can do is raise my cup and in coffee dregs give you a toast.... The School Run.... go bring home the bacon boys!'

Big though Rodney's home was with only he and Liz, the gardener, and a daily woman to run around seven bedrooms (and a hall you could hold a village fete in), he still went out when he had things on his mind. It was to his pride and joy, Grey Lady his flagship. With due and reverent ceremony his first task was always to go up to the flag locker, take out the neatly folded flag, attach it to the flagstay halyards and slowly hoist the blue ensign closely followed by the MMYC club pendant. Only then did he enter the wheelhouse having walked the deck to ensure that everything was shipshape. It was as if the phantom crew of MTB B406 Coastal Forces had piped him over the side then lined up for Captains rounds. His Steward would be in the Galley preparing breakfast. All gunners closed up for inspection at the bofors and pompoms. He would whistle quietly to himself and say softly 'Carry on number one, stand down from inspection and secure for sea' But all that was gone now, no bustle or barked orders, not a sound except the lapping of water along the side between the pontoons. Everything was squared away on the navigation table. All papers filed. He filled and put on the kettle. He walked into the shower room, brushed back his hair and smiled at his reflection in the mirror. Rodney liked what he saw. He was ageing well. A creditable mop of steel grey hair still graced his head. Best side was his left he thought, must remember that when interviewed. He smiled again, not too many wrinkles either, strong chin line. A face of a leader. The kettle forced an end to further contemplation and he put a spoonful of instant coffee into a mug catching the aroma in the jar as he did so. Now to business for there was much to be done. He took the mug over to the navigation area and put it down beside the plot. Must set down the best way to handle the promotion of the reclamation project. This Rodney old fellow is a concept of immense national proportions, which could secure a place in history. He saw a blue circular plate set into the wall outside his house.

'Here lived Sir Rodney Blake Founder of the London Marina
Right he said to himself, plan of action, firstly contact Herewood Chase. He was fortunate to count among his friends an architect with civil engineering connections. He would describe the idea to him and get him to prepare a feasibility study. Next...Get in touch with Royston Hayter MP and arrange meeting to present Herewood's study and ascertain the political and legal implications. Then with an accredited engineering and architectural plan backed in principal by Government it should be possible to put out feelers in the private sector with regard to possible funding. After all the commercial possibilities were endless. Then...yes that would be the time to bring in advertising to raise the profile, to stimulate not only market forces but national pride in having such a wonderful symbol of London's historic links with the river and the sea. Rodney sat back, checking his agenda, shaking his head in amazement at his own breadth of vision. It was incredible that this hadn't been thought about before after London Airport and Eurostar there had been nothing dramatic. There was the Thames Barrier of course, that was a brilliant defensive measure but in effect just a gate

110

across the river, this was something different like Milton Keynes, only better, much better, because it would attract the outside world. He stood up, poured black coffee into his dark blue "Captain" mug walked back into the shower room and addressed the mirror with reserved smile and loud voice. *'Gentlemen I have the honour to place before you a concept which could revitalize London and our River Thames'*
His last words were drowned by the sounds of a big diesel starting up, closely followed by a second until the two produced the unmistakable throb of twin engines warming up at low revs. 'Must be Jack turning over, but he's normally in London this time of the week. Strange unless he's going out, but then surely he would have said something thought Rodney to himself. The sound intensified as the process was repeated by a second pair of diesels, the coffee in his cup rippling in response to the low frequency vibrations. Curiosity got the better of him and Rodney went out to the wheelhouse door and peered out. He found himself staring into the beefy face of what looked like a Cuban Revolutionary hanging over the stern; black hair of a Southern Latin, softened by a blue cloud of diesel fumes. It nodded mutely in Rodney's direction. The Commodore sniffed, who was this foreigner on Jack's boat destroyer of peace and solitude of his Tuesday morning. He nodded curtly in response and murmured 'Morning' stepping out on deck as if to help. Seeing Jack now on the Bridge he cupped his hands to shout 'You going for a run out?'
'No' came the reply 'Just going round to the pumps to refuel'
He stood watching first Jackpot then Plumb Crazy with Tina out on the deck swing slowly out from the pontoon with engines ticking over leaving a static haze behind. The growl of their four huge engines lessening gradually as they picked their way through the forest of masts and white hulls to the fuelling dock. 'What are those two doing' he mused. Both refuelling midweek. Jack said they weren't going out and there were no Greyhound outings scheduled for another ten

111

days or so at least. With two 138-gallon tanks the Sea Beavers didn't often need refuelling so there was something in the offing that he hadn't been advised of. Anyway it was none of his business what the five boats in his Greyhound team did individually, he was just being possessive, couldn't help it, they were his team.'

In an hour or so both boats were back alongside in their normal berths and all was quiet again. Only a slight tang of diesel hung in the air as Rodney sat down to a working lunch. Had he been aware of it however another fact might have given him cause for concern, which was that his two grey boats weren't just refuelling but topping up the extra long range fuel tanks they were fitted with, extending their cruising range by at least 25%. Enjoyment of his lunch might also have been somewhat impaired had he known that only a boat length away another working lunch was taking place, down in Sid's boat which had in fact more the character of a council of war. Whereas on Grey Lady it was smoke salmon salad with half a bottle of white wine. On Plumb Crazy a plate of sandwiches sufficed as those who would take the key role in operation School Run compared notes around the dim glow of the navigation chart plotter screens. Jaws alternated between chomping corned beef and discussing what their functions would be when the final call to action came. 'So then that's decided' said Sid. 'Jack and I will navigate once we are underway while Tina and Mario take the helm, when entering and leaving harbour it's the other way around, with Jack and I on the wheel while Tina and Mario work the deck...agreed?' Heads nodded. 'OK now I think we all know that there will be no time for cooking or chart work at sea, now all preparations must be done beforehand. On the galley side of things Tina I suggest we make up some rolls and plenty of coffee flasks and get a few chocolate bars for us all, that should do. As to navigation it's going to be a case of way points, buoy hopping nearly all the way across. We've both got the same Raytheon systems, which makes things simpler, and we've checked the area CD ROMs so that's OK. Also I've worked the harbour pilotage out on Amsterdam unless we hear to the contrary and we'll use VHF channel six for contact, plus leaving channel sixteen open of course. Are we agreed?'

'Yep that sounds fine Sidney no problems at all' said Jack 'Now as I imagine we'll be cruising line ahead you'd better lead as you've done the run before at least as far as Rotterdam. And as we are travelling as greyhounds we'd better stick to our usual codes of Red Two and Red Three as if all the others are with us. That'll keep things normal. When we arrive if you go alongside and I tie on your outside it'll tuck you nicely from other river traffic won't it...that's if of course our berth situation permits. Now there's just one other thing Sidney. Rodney is very interested in our movements. So to keep him quiet I think we should tell him that you and I are taking our boats to carry out sea trials on the new heating and air conditioning system designed for the Sea Sprite. I think that sounds plausible don't you?'

'Nice one Jack I hadn't thought of that. We'll email him a transit report as we go off, that should shut him up. Now time is getting short, if we can it might be an idea to stay close to the boats. Tina can stay aboard and I'll stay at the office so we've covered the phones. What about you two you'll be in London I suppose'

Jack looked at Mario 'I should be but I'll only be on tenterhooks the whole time so I think I'll stay aboard. We can always play cards and chill out can't we Mario'

'I think we're all going to be twitching a bit from now on' agreed Sid. 'The sooner we get this show on the road the better as far as I'm concerned. It would be nice if we could do it in day light, I'm never at my best at night'

Night and day made little difference in the newsroom at Syndicopy. Strip lights overhead and desk lamps below evened out what little sunlight survived dirty windows and smoke pollution, to create a visual plasma until darkness drew its blinds again. The screeching of a hundred phones like monkeys in a rain forest canopy, went largely unheard by the natives below, each one concerned only with their own incoming update on the doings of humanity at large. At 02.30 the scene would be little different from noon or 2pm just a few new faces maybe. It was rumoured however that Jake Drage never slept for it was his gruff tone, which received most of the calls which mattered. His many friends in fire, police and ambulance never let him down and he in turn would always find the right reporter to cover.

'Hi Jake, that you?'

'Whose asking!'

'It's me you nut head DC Glazer, Dock End CID. Did I wake you or something?'

'Unlike you I don't sleep. What's moving your end?'

'Shootout in club land. Looks like gang war stuff. Just after midnight, doorman dead, armed response unit in attendance. Do you want to cover?'

'Thanks chum I owe you one, See yaw'

He wrote the details on a message pad, tore it off and slapped it on the keyboard of the shirt-sleeved operator.

'There you are Frankie boy, take a pool car and drag your evil trainers over to that address. Raise Jenny on her mobile and take her along as well. Don't take too long otherwise there'll be sod all left to see. Those armed response lads don't hang around. Go on take your coffee with you.'

The pool car smelt of beef burgers and old butt ends enough to turn the stomach of someone who was only half awake with eyes screwed up painfully against flashing lights ahead. A hand slapped the roof above and a face with a flashlight of the uniform branch thrust itself through a half wound down window. 'Oh Press, you can't stop here, better park up on the pavement over there, well clear of the tape mind'.

'Thanks mate will do' Frank looked at Jenny and grinned. 'You did well Jen. D'you sleep in that bloody jump suit or something? I would never have done it so quickly. Look you get out here, I think I've parked a bit close to the wall. Grab your camera and we'll get as close as they'll let us. Run a few shots off while I find out what's going on' She nodded and ducked under the blue and white tape that was sealing off the road. Her black jump suit and black baseball cap mingled well with the dark combat suits of police units standing huddled talking in the darkness and she wasn't challenged or ordered off. Forensics were already at work to one side of the nightclubs entrance where the body of a man in evening dress lay sprawled amongst some potted plants. Electronic flashes lit a little group in silhouette for blinding milliseconds as their photographers recorded every angle. Jenny didn't hesitate, with the calculating arrogance of the press she approached the group, dropped down on one knee and pushing her compact SLR camera between their legs added her flashes to those authorized by law. A group of nightclub staff stood talking in shocked whispers as some guests emerged, now keen to leave the scene. She quickly changed the lens to telephoto and backed off a little, securing a sequence of reportage close ups, her further flashes going unnoticed in the general explosive character of light. Camera back in case she now approached the group of what appeared to be employees. Selecting a young mini skirted hostess and adopting an authoritative concerned tone said 'Nasty business, you OK?' The girl nodded mutely, then in a shaky voice said 'It's terrible he was only doing his job. Such a nice chap he was, had two little kids and all' The girl's shoulders shook and she was racked with sobbing. Jenny put her arm around the bare white back and held her tightly. 'I know, I know it's not fair is it, not fair at all. How did the fight start? Did you see anything?'

'No, I've told the police already I was in the restaurant working and I didn't even hear the gun shot, first thing I knew was when Julie on the front desk came down and screamed out that Gerry had been shot and Tony too'.

'So both doormen were shot at the front door then?'

'Yes Gerry shot twice in the head and Tony in the shoulder. Julie saw it all, there wasn't a fight. Two men on a motorbike roared up and shot them, then roared off again, quick as that. It's murder, that's what it is'

'Professional hit men I think' explained another girl with feathers on her head. 'All over in seconds just like she said' She looked at the plain dark jumpsuit warily. 'You're with the police are you?' 'Yes' answered Jenny firmly. 'Intelligence Service. Now this is the Red Apple right?, and the owner is!'

'Gino Modica,' replied the feathered head. 'He was here just now. He owns the Green Goddess strip club in Bayswater too. Poor guy he had a letter bomb there last month, burnt the cloakroom nearly down and all the naughty boys like Bishops and MP's who shouldn't have been there had to tell their wives how their overcoats caught fire'

A heavy hand fell on the newshounds shoulder and a voice said 'Allo allo what have we here'

Jenny jumped guiltily round. 'Oh God Bob you made me jump'

'DC Glazer to you Jenny I presume Mr. Drage pointed you in this direction. I see you've got your ear to the ground already. Nasty one this but quick and clean, contract job by the look of it. It's got all the hallmarks, close range, small calibre straight between the eyes no messing. How are things with you, getting plenty of work? It's people like me who keep you lot in business. Come on over to the car, I've got some tea and bagels on board' He opened the car door 'I'll just check in first...Control this is Romeo Alpha, Romeo Alpha attending incident at Red Apple Club, scene of crime sealed off, uniform now in charge, forensics and ambulances now clear. Armed response stood down, negative resistance. DC Glazer out. Good that's me clocked off for the time being. Have you got all you need? I see your oppo is still ferreting around inside. Now obviously we've got a lot more statements to take before we go to the CPS but it seems on the surface that it's a case of someone not coughing up insurance, or protection money if you like, and that's the way my DI wants it treated by the press. But entree nous, I'm pretty sure it's drug related. I've got a nose for this sort of situation. If I'm right I don't want the big boys to know what's going on at our end, so if you play ball with me and keep this on the cool side perhaps we can work together to our mutual advantage. Do you catch my drift?' He leant back in the car seat and lit a cigarette offering her one. She refused. 'Our problem at regional crime squad is we're a bit too close to things sometimes, I mean although I'm dressed in plain clothes a villain will come up to me and say 'Hello Bob how's it going' They know who most of us are and exactly what we're up to most of the time. It's a bit disconcerting, that's why it pays to have as many outside contacts as possible. We liaise with the drug squad, narcotics and the customs boys of course but people like you often have your nose closer to the ground than we do'

'Because we're constantly sniffing around for a story'

'Yes but the problem as far as we're concerned is the second you dig up something, you splash it over the front page'

'Of course we do, that's our job isn't it'.

'I know that, but what I'm saying is if someone like you would be prepared to work more closely with my outfit, under cover if necessary and then pass anything you come up with through us for clearance before publication it would speed up our investigation lines no end in certain cases and won't do your career any harm either'

'That sounds fine, but time is money for a freelance you know, if I spend say three weeks on a line of enquiry and end up with enough material for a feature I need to sell it quickly to get paid.'

'OK, maybe I can convince my Guv'nor to sanction

reasonable expenses in some cases, after all we pay our informants on the other side of the fence don't we. Look tell you what, if you come up with anything remotely interesting give us a ring first, keep in touch, as I've said before, it could do us both some good.'

There was a tap on the window. 'There you are partner. I've been looking for you everywhere. Didn't dream you'd been arrested'

'Sorry I took her in for questioning over a bagel and a teabag. You can have her back now. I'd better get back to the cop shop anyway. I've got a report to write before the morning.'

Jenny got out of the car and shivered as the first grey light of a watery dawn appeared over the horizon. She looked around; two uniformed officers inside the police tape were the only remaining signs of the human tragedy which had been acted out in the last few hours. 'Bye then Bob' Jenny half waved her hand as the police car sped away.

'This car smells like a rugby club changing room' moaned Jenny as Frank swung the pool car into Euston Road 'There must be about six months fast food wrappers stuffed under the seats. Come in for a bacon sandwich when you drop me off if you like. It's hardly worth going back to bed now'

They sat in the tiny kitchen munching on the buttery bacon sandwiches 'God knows how much coffee I've drunk in the last few hours. It's a wonder I haven't got the shakes. Look surprisingly my hand is quite steady isn't it'

'Only because chain smoking has calmed you down. You're an unhealthy specimen Frank do you know that, but then I've never really known a wholesome journalist. It's the lifestyle I suppose, which reminds me I had an interesting chat with DC Glazer while you were in the club. He was virtually saying the crime squad would be interested in some sort of cooperation with us reporters where we exchange inside information to our mutual advantage. What did you pick up on tonight?'

The unshaven face yawned expansively 'Well they all said the doorman was a lovely bloke but had probably upset the wrong person somewhere along the line. I mean doormen do, it's part of the job' There was a pause while Jenny disposed of a doorstep section of bacon sandwich. 'I'm not sure my waistline is going to exist soon with all this snacking... I actually picked up a different slant. It seems the door security contract...and a very lucrative one, had always been with a group known as.... wait for it.... the Bayswater Boys, but the club dropped them in favour of employing their own Bouncers, that's Gerry and Tony. The owner did the same thing at the Green Goddess in Bayswater and got fire bombed for his trouble. I think it's mob rule stuff. Who ever controls the door has their fingers on the pulse of the place, never mind who actually owns it. They can direct punters to other strip joints and porn houses and of course push all sorts of drugs. So to lose control is not taken lightly. I'm not saying it was that group that did it but somebody had to be mighty upset to want to take out the opposition in that way. Let's say I don't think an individual would have gone to such lengths. The club scene interests me in terms of crime, it's something I'd like to delve into a bit more, but let's get this item written up and I'll whack these rolls of film in the lab for process'.

Newspapers the following day carried the headline CLUBLAND KILLING, dominant on the page.

The copy read - *Two doorman at Soho's leading nightclub were shot at point blank range yesterday by a motorcycle gunman. Gerry Perks was pronounced dead at the scene and Tony Mancely suffered serious injury. The motive is believed to be a gangland dispute. Metropolitan Police are investigating. Mr. Perks leaves a wife and two young daughters. Colleagues at the club said he had only recently taken over the job having retired from service in the army. He was well liked and his welcoming smile would be sorely missed at the front door of the Red Apple* With. dramatic shots of the figure in evening dress lying sprawled amongst the foliage of a fallen Bay tree seen through the legs of onlookers. The by-line read *Jenny Sutcliffe and Frank Daven Syndicopy*

Another heading this time as email on a computer screen read simply SCHOOL RUN GROUP and continued BLACKBIRD SCHOOL PARTY -ETA AT HOTEL (NOW CHOICE 'A' HEMHAVEN) 14OO HOURS LOCAL TIME 10 JULY ARRANGE MEET AND TRANSPORT AS ARRANGED LUV KAREN

'That's it. Green light Mario. Looks as though we are off' Jack stood back from the screen and pressed the printout button as his crewmate emerged from the galley bearing mugs of tea. 'I'd better explain this to you Mario' said Jack clutching the A4 sheet. 'Blackbird is Aquila Nera, Black Eagle, the Colombian freighter with our cargo (the school party) due to arrive in 'A' that's Amsterdam estimated time 1400 hours into the Hemhaven's basin on the 10th July. Karen, ...that's Fenton of course.... will now contact our road tanker and arrange for it to be alongside on the quay at Hemhaven. So we need to be alongside somewhere close to Westerdocsdyk just west of Central Station pier, that's the old harbour area at around 1400 hours local time. Now they're on central european time, which in July is two hours ahead of us so our target has got to be noon on the 10th. That's this Friday. We've got about 250 miles to cover which should take us approximately 10 hours depending on wind and tide. So we had better leave here at 0200hours on Thursday morning. Bit of an early start but can't be helped. As soon as we are alongside in Amsterdam we must contact the driver of the road tanker on his mobile and take it from there. Let's hope the weather is kind to us that's all I ask. Ten hours at 20 knots in a boat like this can be rough going if the swells are over a metre. Still it's going to be worth it, no doubt about that

120

Mario. Right I'd better give Tina a buzz so she can contact Sid at the office. We'll have to get together for final arrangements. There's a lot to get through before Thursday'

It was ironic that the atmosphere of adrenalin charged excitement missing in Rodney's ex service life was to be found in full measure not a boat lengths away. It was created not by painting pleasure craft like warships and putting them on parade but by instincts of a predators lust for combat, fear, and a greed for gold. Two of his little elite group were about to put their wits against the sea and the force of law and order. 'No violence Mario, whatever happens, that's why I said don't bring the shooter. We're going to get away with it by stealth, not fire power. D'you agree Sid?'

'Yes of course but not even stealth, I'd say by behaving absolutely normal all the way, and for that reason let's not operate undercover of darkness more than we have to. Now if we left here at a more civilized hour say 0600 in daylight that would get us over there about 1500 hours our time which I think would be better, that's 1700 hours local time which gives them more time for unloading in any case. Is that OK?

'Yeah that's fine by me. We'll have to get the lock keeper up early because the tide will be half out at that time, but that's no problem. Oh and we need some Gilders for petty cash.

'Yes we do need some currency. Good thing I sorted that out wasn't it I've got enough to see us through I think'

'Well done Sidney, that ties most things up then, I think we should get an early night we've got a long day ahead'

Like most ex watch keepers John Crowther could always respond quickly to any sounds on deck even when asleep as he did at 0500 hours that morning. Rope passing over the decks, the movement of fenders, voices and the rattle of block and tackle as a tender was hoisted inboard. He was wide-

121

awake when the first engine fired up followed closely by another. Pretty soon four V8's were all grumbling and bubbling away and the smell of diesel was strong in the air. He stretched, swung his legs over the edge of his bunk and opened the hatch just in time to see the dark shape of Jack's boat swinging slowly away from the pontoon followed by Sidney's until they were clear, leaving their moorings strangely bare. The growling of engines muffled now by lines of silent hulls lessened gradually until only masthead lights moving slowly above the mass of boats showed their position as they approached the sea lock. Once inside, hydraulic rams closed the gates and the sound of rushing water echoed as the level dropped to meet the sea and their lights went with it. The burly master mariner squeezed with difficulty into the upright coffin that was his 'heads' and aiming carefully into his porta loo looked out of its tiny porthole at the dawn sky reflected in clear water where the boats had been. 'Funny I thought they always went out as a group, never seen just two go off before' he said to himself.

An email to Janet just said Sid would be away two days to drum up business, back Sunday, which was true even if it was funny business. Another one to their Commodore informed him that Sid and Jack were out on a proving run to test a new system being developed by SA Marine.

By the time John had walked Bosun off the pontoon for a pee, Greyhounds two and three were just two slim shadows heading out to sea.

'Keep her on 045 shouted Sid from the plot table, that should take us to the next way point'

'I can't see much at all ahead' answered Tina in a slightly apprehensive tone. 'There's a bank of mist to port'

'Don't worry luv' it's all locked into our chart plot, everything. Tides, wind speeds; we did it all before we left if

122

you remember. Just hold her on 045 . We could even switch to auto helm if you felt like five minutes on the bed. Not that it would be very comfortable down in the bow at the moment. I can see Barrow Beacon on the radar so we're just off Maplin Sands now. Jack's keeping station astern OK. I think I'll just give him a call before we increase speed' He unhooked the mike from the bulkhead.. 'Greyhound Two do you read me come in please'

'I have you loud and clear and visual too, if a little hazy. Bit of a cross-sea running, we ought to increase speed to 20 knots. What do you think? Over'

'That's why I raised you, yes. I think we need to increase to maintain schedule. Let's give it a try. At 12 knots it's going to take too long. If the slamming gets too bad we can ease back a little. Over'

He turned to Tina 'Right luv ease the throttles forward. Let's take her up to 20 knots and see how she likes it' The drumming vibration beneath their feet increased as the two big diesels responded, raising their revs until both turbo's cut in, driving twin propellers even harder into green water astern. Churning it into a raging chaos of tortured spume and froth. It left behind a wake like a creamy motorway, which overcame all shapes of individual waves until the bow of Greyhound Three following behind divided it to renew the process all over again. Tina felt the change in power flow into the sinews of her arms, as the pulsing growl of the engines became more of a turbine whine.

'Hold on' yelled Sid's voice above the noise as the Vee shaped hull lifted high out of the water 'on the plane' only the squat stern biting deeper with the effort of the drive. The boat leapt from wave crest to wave crest like a skimming stone slamming down with bone shaking force after each short flight. Crockery crashed and cutlery in the drawers rattled as the crew of two grasped every handhold firmly before contemplating any move.

123

'Can you hold her at this speed? I'd like to maintain it if we could'

'Yes I can, visibility is getting better out here. Only don't suggest we pour out the coffee will you'

'Or do anything except hang on. You can see now why everything had to be done before we left our mooring. Don't forget what I told you about every seventh wave'

'That's balls isn't it'?

'Course it isn't, it's a physical fact. Look out ahead and you'll see. Now count the wave crests, there you are that ones the seventh. Feel how it shook us. Just count seven and you'll be ready'

'You'll be telling me to look out for a lone Albatross next. If your wife could see you now I wonder what she'd say'

'Not a lot, she'd be too busy being seasick or getting hysterical over the way this boat is behaving. Being here would be her worst nightmare. Not like Rodney now he'd love it. I must say I'm only here for the money. For what we hope to come back with, I'm almost happy to be tossed around like a cork in a tumble drier, but I don't think I'll tackle that bacon roll just yet though.'

At that moment amplified atmospherics blared out above the turbo whine and pounding of the sea. 'Greyhound Three, come in please. Over'

'Read you. Still with us then Jack. You're disappearing some of the time when you nose in it. You both OK?.. Over'

'Yeah we're OK, uncomfortable but fine. Wouldn't fancy going any faster though that's for sure. Sea time comes as a bit of a culture shock after sitting for weeks in a calm marina doesn't it. Our visual track along the electronic plotter makes it look so easy then you look out the wheelhouse window and see the real world. Things should get a lot easier when the tide turns and we lose a bit of this wind against tide. I feel easier now we've cleared the estuary sandbanks even though our track between way points takes us well away. Check with you later Sid. Greyhound Two out'

'They seem OK Jack and Mario considering they look more like a submarine half the time'

Tina grasped the small car like steering wheel tightly as a large wave hit the bow pointing it skywards where it hovered for some seconds before dropping into the shadow of the following trough. 'Ouch my stomach. That must have been the seventh wave. I think you may have been right on that one Sid. God this wind seems a damn sight stronger than the force 4 to 5 forecasted. I'd have said it was more like 6 to 7. Bleak place the North Sea. Pity we are not going to the Med to pick this stuff up, calm blue seas and all that'

'We'd still have the Bay of Biscay to worry about' reassured her skipper. 'Anyway look there's clear sky ahead, things could cheer up soon.'

'I hope so I'm dying to go to the loo, I mean the heads'

'But Tina you went before we left didn't you. Do you feel seasick or something?'

She laughed. 'No it's just all this water splashing around. It has this effect on me'

'Well cross your legs for a bit. The less walking about we do at the moment the better. We can't afford any injuries at this stage of the game'.

'What's the value Sid, what's it really worth, this cargo of ours?'

'Well if you're talking street value about ten million, sounds a lot but there are an awful lot of overheads to be deducted before we get to the profit part'.

'But we still stand to make a packet out of it, for the risk we are taking, all of us, don't we?'

'I should say so, otherwise we wouldn't be in the middle of the North Sea bobbing up and down like corks. You do realize we've got to come all this way back again don't you sweetheart'

'Now that's really cheered me up Sidney. Hold on. Here

comes another big one'

Bosun was ill at ease; it showed in the way his ears dropped. He did not approve of the smell of furniture polish, which now assailed his nostrils in the cabin. Or by the way that his cushion had been washed and ironed. He was going to have to do a lot of scuffing and rolling on his back to put his scent back where it should be, in the space he shared with his master. Brass had been polished, bookshelves dusted and upholstery sprayed with air freshener. He sneezed and had to go on deck. John smiled to himself, yes that looked a lot better. Should pass for inspection. God the dogs hairs, toe nail clippings and coins of the realm down between the leather squabs of the seat lockers. He was quite ashamed, but it was cleaner now, a good job done. However this still left the problem of where to re-house the spare propeller, wind speed indicator and toilet seat, all still awaiting attention. The forepeak chain locker, yes that would do. There should be room in there along with a dozen or so half used tins of paint and varnish. He poured himself a scotch sat down and leant back in his chair. Worse than stripping down an engine block all this tiding up. Up to now it hadn't mattered if his living space looked like the spares department of a boatyard and that he drank soup out of some old cracked mug, but now there was a chance that she might drop in on the off chance and have to lift a bilge pump off the seat to sit down. 'We've got to make an effort Bosun' he said half apologetically. 'We have to show we care what people think of us. Your basket is sometimes very smelly. Tonight is her birthday and don't ask me why but she wants to spend it here on Tradewind with us. Now you've had your charcoal biscuits for lunch so let's hope there won't be any bouts of silent wind from you Bosun like the last time she was here. We had to eat with the hatch open. You know I'm talking about you don't you. I can see your tail twitch. He put a candle on the table laid for two then took it off again. Can't have that it looks over the top. Too much in here. We'll just have a bottle of wine in the middle, yes that's enough. 'What are you looking at me like that for then? Oh I see, want some cheese and biscuits do you. Well only one. Here you are boy' He looked up at the ships clock on the bulkhead She's late he thought. I hope she turns up after all my efforts. Like a refill John? Well just a little one. Don't mind if I do. He poured a small measure into his glass and went over to the wheelhouse window to look casually along the pontoon. Yes there she was, walking with her usual casual swing between the lines of white rakish bows towards him. He downed the whisky in one and sat himself quickly back in his chair casually holding the paper as she crossed the gangway. 'Hello Jen. You made it then. Happy Birthday' He stood up, kissed her lightly upon both cheeks, then stood her back at arms length 'You're looking well for a journalist that is, and one that lives in London come to that. Sit down and I'll fix you a drink' But she stood for a moment looking all around her. 'Wow look at this, what have you been up to? Where are all the bits waiting to be put together? It looks so bare and Bosun's in his basket, that's a first for sure. But he looks a bit uncomfortable like you in a collar and tie. It's lovely but there is something unreal as if you'll pull a string in a minute and it all will be back to normal. Did you do all this for me because it's my birthday? I'd be embarrassed if I thought you wouldn't find all your bits and pieces of engine again and this poor dog' she bent down to Bosun basket level 'He smells of lavender air freshener. He'll take days to live it down'

'Oh he'll be alright' mumbled John rather guiltily. 'One quick roll in the horse manure at the riding stables will fix him. Now what will you have to drink. Still on vodka and tonic these days?'

'Yes that'll do nicely. Although I'm dispensing more of that than I drink these days'

'How's that then?'

'I'm doing part time bar work in a club'

'Good grief Jen. How do you fit it all in with your career?'

'Quite easily really it's shift work ten to two in the morning, only two nights a week. I only miss the odd assignment from Syndic'

'But why on earth bother, you don't need the money, I mean you're OK financially aren't you?'

'Well it's not that exactly, it's more a case of my needing to be there if you see what I mean'

'I don't think I actually do see unless you mean you're working under cover'

'Well let's say I keep my eyes open and my mouth shut. There's no substitute for actually being part of the scene. There's no telling what I'm going to pick up just ear wigging. You'd be surprised how much people open up in clubs whereas they get very careful talking to the press or anywhere the police are. The hostesses hear it all of course because they're around the tables serving drinks, sometimes sitting with the punters (and often in bed with them). They come up to the bar and I load the drink onto the trays. They're at the bar most of the time, because the punters aren't allowed to buy drinks themselves, A lot of the customers, in fact most of them, are company executives taking clients out for the traditional night on the town. They may be clever businessmen but really they're just a bunch of idiots on expense accounts and their clients are usually pompous boring old farts who moralize at home but want to be taken to private clubs where they can leer at showgirls and grope hostesses. But amongst this unsavoury flotsam of the so-called normal business world (who seem to need to create a stag night every night of the year) are the real targets. The Flash Harry's of the criminal world you can spot them a mile off. This is what I'm really after, organized crime, not the petty stuff, but the big boys. I knew I'd never stand a chance of getting anywhere near myself but some time ago I was called out to a shooting at a club, a doorman was murdered and whilst I was there I realized the hostesses were the real ones on the inside, the informed people I should be talking to. It occurred to me these girls spend most of the time standing at the bar collecting drinks for the sleaseballs then slagging them off to the bar staff. So I knew I had to get a bit of part time work in a club, which wasn't as difficult as I thought, because the hours are so dreadful people don't fall over themselves to work them.'

'So you're working under cover then?. It sounds a bit dangerous to me'

'It's not that bad. You see I'm one stage removed from the danger of being one of them, or pretending to be. I let my hostess friends eavesdrop on their conversations, then relate it all to me'

'But surely they wouldn't chat to you unless they thought you were one of them would they. You know a bit tarty'

Jenny raised her eyebrows 'I might tell you Mr. Crowther I can drop my aitches and use the double negative with the best of them, and I ain't a push over either so keep yer cork in, cocky socks'

'Very good, I'm impressed as long as you can keep it up'

'Joking aside John, it's not difficult one just listens to them and tries to think like them without overdoing it. That would be stupid. I try not to do the talking just let them prattle on and make the occasional comment, that's the way most of them like it anyway. I'm becoming a very good listener'

'I'm sure you are. Has your new role proved fruitful yet?'

'Yes it has, it's amazing just what a little hot bed of vice and crime Pandora's is proving to be. It all seems to be there for the taking. The place seems to be full of pimps and pushers working quite openly at all hours. Enforcers make sure the club pays its insurance against violence, if you know what I mean, whilst the dealers dine in style surrounded by their

hoods and hard men. It's a dangerous world just beneath the surface and yet it's all opulence and suave manners on the outside. There aren't many fights or drunks. They are usually surgically removed with the minimum of fuss'
'How long will you stay there do you think?'
'As long as it takes to collect enough information to put my series together. Could be some time I suppose'
'What's the series about then. This all seems very interesting'
'It examines the drug scene and how it affects juvenile crime. It's a long-term project, which might turn into a book. What's happening is I cover the courts for Syndic during the day and attend incidents and scenes of crime when my friends on the regional crime squad tip us off. I'm building up notes all the time that way and now of course getting bits and pieces of the inside story overnight at the Pandora's and getting paid for it. So it's not a bad scene overall. I've almost forgotten what it's like to write up a local dog show. Enough about me anyway except to say thank you for inviting me to spend my birthday on board here. So what's been happening to you since I saw you last. Have you fixed a sailing day for your great adventure yet?'
'Not exactly, every time I get one problem sorted out something else pops up. The engine is working fine and I've had it running for quite some hours now, no problem when it's in neutral but when I shove it in gear there's a vibration in the prop shaft, not much but I wouldn't like to trust it going across the Bay of Biscay. I know what's causing it, wear and tear in the external gland, unfortunately it means taking the boat out of the water to have it replaced. Then there's the caulking in the deck planks that needs redoing. I'll get there in the end but it's time consuming and frustrating'
'When you get to your target area, the Windward Islands. Is that it the end of the rainbow or will you just keep wandering the oceans'
'Like I've always done you mean, I suppose it's just become a

habit over the years, a sort of human Albatross. But you never know Tradewind might have other plans. This boat has been around for a long time. She may decide to fall apart in Bridgetown or Martinique in which case I'd probably stay there. But I've got to get there first. I'd like to end up somewhere not too far removed from the equator though, some place it's 'dolce far niente', nice to just become a beach bum. I'm beginning to sound like a crazy mixed up kid. Perhaps it's time I grew up and acted my age. Anyway let's not get maudlin, not on your birthday. Knock back the vodka and I'll open some bubbly'

'Oh you're spoiling me'

'Shall we take our drinks out onto the quarter deck madam' He ushered her out into the open cockpit area. They sat on either side of the working area looking out across the marina. She stood up and looked along the pontoon. 'It looks very empty today, what's gone'

'Oh it's two of the grey boats they went out early this morning on some sort of training exercise I expect, only Grey Lady and the others haven't gone this time. Strange because they usually go off together'

'Last time I was down here (you were up the mast remember, fixing your new windy thing with the cups on) I took some photographs. I've got them here in my bag. Here we are you look very impressive high up there. Incidentally who are those blokes standing looking up at you? Do you know them?'

'No never seen them before. Tell you what though, I think it might be the same people who were on Jacks boat. There had been some sort of meeting that morning; there were four of them on there as I remember. Why do you ask anyway?'

'It's just that the tall one, rather elegantly dressed, he looked vaguely familiar. I am sure I've seen his face somewhere, before but it's not important'

They sat for some time as shadows lengthened on the pontoon and the bollard lights came on, their reflections dancing obediently on the dark waters below.

'Another drop? Might as well finish this bottle off. It won't keep'

She placed her hand delicately over the tall tulip glass. 'Better not I'm driving don't forget'

'Don't drive then...there's some very fine red wine to come with our dinner and I've got some Baileys to go with our coffee afterwards'

'It would be a birthday treat to doss down here tonight I must admit. Not to have to worry about the traffic, that would be a real indulgence, do you know that Captain John'

'It's your birthday after all go on indulge yourself'

'Happy berfday me then. I can't say berfday properly'

'Nor can I, but it's not mine so I don't have to'

'Greyhound Two, Greyhound Two, come in please. Over'

'Sidney how nice of you to call, got you loud and clear...go ahead.... over'

'Now things have settled down it's a bit smoother ride, we'd like to reduce speed down to 12 knots for ten minutes or so, we can get a hot drink then without throwing it all over ourselves. Is that OK with you? over'

'Suits us fine, we'll do the same'

Sidney turned and cupping his hands shouted 'Tina, throttle back, reduce speed to 12 knots and pull both throttle levers back together'. Instantly the bow dropped as the turbo drive came off and the boat levelled off to plough through the swells now instead of bouncing over them.

'That's better lass, much more civilized. Now we can move about a bit. I'll take a turn and you can have a stretch of your legs. Then we can have a quick bacon roll yes!' The view ahead was now clear and the sea no longer menacing but sparkling under an almost clear sky. 'That's better' he said to himself. For in spite of radar, sonar and electronic chart display it was still an act of faith to be hurling 15 tons of boat blind into thick mist at a speed of some 35 knots with no effective means of stopping quickly. 'Blessed relief' repeated Tina. I had to go for a pee I couldn't hold on much longer. I wish I had a bladder like yours. Don't you need to go'. Sid shook his head 'No I'm OK I'll stay on helm while you pour us a drink. Everything OK down below. Nothing broken?'

'Not that I can see, I haven't looked in the lockers though'

'We'll check everything when we get alongside. Funny how this boat doesn't like going slow, off the plane, does it. You feel it wallowing can't you. I mean this wheel is slack, slow to respond. We'll get back up to speed as soon as we've had our snack. 'Get on with the job in hand eh'

The twin diesels growled and grumbled to themselves as if anxious to get the bit between their teeth again. The revs increasing occasionally as the props lifted clear of the surface momentarily.

'I'll tell you what' said Tina sipping carefully as her drink sloshed around the mug 'This gentle motion is more sick-making than running at speed' Sid laughed 'Ironic isn't it. You're right though. I had a Citroen car with a special fluid suspension system once. It was so comfortable almost like flying, but everyone in the back got car sick, even on short journeys, same syndrome here really. Anyway now we've rested our backs a bit we had better resume cruising speed. I'll just let Jack know what we are doing now. OK luv?'

He unhooked the VHF mike. Let's try to get up to 30 knots now Jack, the conditions have improved greatly...over'.

'OK Roger to that, take it away cowboy...over'

Sid reached across to Tina's shoulder. 'OK wind her up sweetheart, full ahead on both'.

The dozing diesels roared back to life thrusting the slim pointed bow like a jousting lance at oncoming swells, Stern dropping as twin screws bit deep into the green water and the boat reared skywards causing the crew to grab once again for the secure hand holds. 'Yee haa!' yelled Sidney in exhilaration as they became airborne before crashing down upon the next wave crest fifteen feet ahead. 'Now we're going places, Christ we are really motoring ain't we sweetie pie. This is what the boat was made for. You can feel it now can't you?. Thirty knots, spot on, and we're not slamming quite so much. Bit more comfortable now. I'll take over again for a while luv, give your arms a rest. They must be pulled out of their sockets. Check our position on the GPS track. See if it's still 045 degrees magnetic. We should be level with Cromer and the Wash yes?' We'll be starting to swing in towards the Dutch Coast soon and Texel Island. Call up the harbour authority on their working channel and give them our name and destination soon. Better do things by the book. Say we're aiming to berth in the old harbour by the Central Station oh, and give them our eta. I gave our transit report to Thames Radio when we left so nobody can say we are being furtive anyway'. Within minutes of transmission a reply was received on the open channel. 'Milehaven Greyboats your position and eta noted. Have you on radar now. Proceed to Amsterdam Old Harbour where you will be met'... So far so good Tina crossed her fingers.

'Listen' shouted Sid. 'Before we get there let me just say this. If anything goes wrong and we're caught I shall swear you know nothing about this Tina. You know nothing about what's on board. You just came for the ride. There's no point in us both going down, but hopefully nothing is going to go wrong, we are too well prepared. So uncross your fingers. I'll just have a quick word with Jack'. He called up the grey shape ploughing through their wake and passed on the official news of their arrival. 'Nice to be recognized and so well received isn't it Jack, as flag bearers of the blue ensign. We've made good time so far. We'll reduce speed now we are approaching the coast. Our Dutch friends will meet us at the old harbour entrance according to the radio message. Keep close astern as we follow the buoyed channel round to the sea lock at DenOever and through into IJsselmeer...over'

As sea became channel, narrowing gradually between flat areas of land and sand banks, the wind decreased. Once through the sea lock free of tide and with the speed now down to seven knots the diesels idled at tick over and the boats were once again stable platforms 'OK Tina luv I'll stay on the wheel. You observe and keep visual contact with Jack as we make our final approach' After the drama and excitement of their North Sea passage the slow procession into the heart of Amsterdam seemed an anti climax except for the reality of what they were about to undertake. Fortunately the massive shape of the Central Station when it came into view was an unmistakable landmark dominating a mass of piers providing moorings for mostly tourist trip boats and river police.

'Here we are. We'll go in further up the river where that sign says Westerdoksdisk, see it?' Tina nodded passing on VHF directions to Jack now close behind. Greyhound three swung across the tideless river in a wide arc, coming up to where a concrete jetty protruded its tyre cushioned flank into the murky water. Sid brought the bow round and then tucked the stern in neatly, using both engines before taking off all way with a quick burst of hard astern. Tina was ready with the fenders and her heaving line coiled ready to throw. A river police crewman caught it neatly and made for the bollards. Within three minutes the two boats were tied up side by side with the gangplank in position. Two uniformed police officers climbed aboard causing butterflies to flutter madly in both crews' stomachs. But hands were extended for shaking and with flashing smiles and perfect English the spokesman said 'Welcome to the Netherlands. We are honoured to have a visit from two Royal Navy Auxiliaries'.

'Thank you' replied Sidney acting as spokesman 'But this is not an official visit we've been out on sea trials and just decided to call in'

'No matter the Netherlands Navy will be pleased to see you and look over your boats if there's time. See you later perhaps.' They saluted and roared off in their jeep with siren and blue flashing light.

'Gods teeth' exclaimed Jack 'Breathe again'

'Amen to that' laughed Sid nervously. 'Talk about guilty conscience. They were both standing virtually on top of where we are going to stash all the stuff. I thought I was going to shit a brick and that someone had tipped them off'

'Relax we've done nothing yet. Nothing to worry about until the evidence is on board. I think we're all a bit jumpy. Look according to that clock tower it's only 18.00 Let's get together in G3 saloon for a quick drink, then contact our tanker'. Johnny Walker did much to relax both crews and in some thirty minutes they were primed and ready for the most important phase of the run. Jack dialled the drivers mobile number 'Hello Charlie. Yes it's Jack, yes fine, no problems. We've just arrived. We're just west of the station at the old harbour. We're ready for a sewage pump out when you're ready. I take it Aquila Nera arrived OK...Really that late. So you're still at Hemhaven's Basin then collecting...OK...Yes we'll expect you within the hour. Look out for you.' Jack put the phone down. 'You heard all that I take it. Ship was late arriving. He'll be here within an hour he hopes. I suggest we take it in turns to keep a look out. I'll take the first watch, rest of you can go below and get some rest' He lit a cigarette and sat himself down on the edge of the jetty. Odd groups of people were strolling along the harbours edge but few gave the two boats more than a passing glance. An evening tour party of noisy Germans boarded at one of the piers by the station and cruised past singing lustily on their way upstream. Then after a while the tanker appeared in the distance. Bright yellow, it stood out easily from embankment buildings. Moving slowly along as its driver scanned the assortment of moored vessels, it hesitated several times before Jack stepped into the road waving his arms. 'Hi Charlie, over here. It's good to see you'

The driver got down and assessed the scene, then rubbed his chin reflectively 'I can't get very close to the boats.'

'Have you got enough hose to reach across?'

'Yes, there should be enough'

Charlie explained while securing the coupling hose 'I'll start pumping then as the units flow in, each time one of the little metal clips passes your electronic counter it'll show up on your screen and mine and I'll know when to stop. At the end of the chain there's a rubber plug, which closes the aperture'. Within five minutes the process was completed and Charlie unhooked the hose. '160 agreed'

'Yep' said Sidney.

'It's all yours now' said Charlie wiping his hands 'Good luck for the return journey I'll see you in the UK' They shook hands and the little yellow tanker drove off to catch the Hook of Holland ferry. Sid slapped his thigh as they sat rocking gently on G2. 'Did you see those people stepping over our hose across the pavement. All chatting away while a fortune was running underneath their feet'

It was tempting to cast off right away now the cargo was aboard, but in the interest of normality the two boats stayed in Amsterdam. After a nights rest, early the next morning they headed towards the Deoever sea lock and out to the open sea again. The weather forecast had been good and the return trip much smoother allowing a cruising speed of 30 knots. An uneventful trip until off Southend on Sea a big Sikorski Coastguard helicopter flew high above them, descended and circled back.'Oh shit! It's tracking us' reported Tina. 'Do you think something's gone wrong?' Her question was answered in the next few seconds when a metallic voice cut through atmospherics on VHF channel 16. 'This is Coastguard Rescue Bravo Tango Echo to Milehaven Greyhounds below. Do you read, please come in... Over'

Sid raised his eyes 'Oh dear what now... Hello Coastguard I hear you loud and clear. Any problems. Go ahead... Over'

'No problem. Just to say you're looking good from up here. Nice straight line ahead. Only two of you today. Where's the family. So used to seeing you boys out together.'

'We've been over to the Netherlands, socially with some of their naval boys. Rest of the hounds are confined to kennels making money. Some of us have to work you know'

'Invite us the next time. We can get there quicker, safe trip back. Over and out.'

'Phew' Sid looked at Tina. 'They had me worried for a bit'

'You and me both, still it's nice to be recognized as a friend I suppose. My God if only they knew what we were carrying it would be a bit different. I can hardly believe it myself. Ten million quid. Some school run chalk that on the blackboard!'

'Yeah, some run indeed but it's only worth that when it's been distributed to the pushers and sold on the streets. In other words when it's been turned into cash and even that's got to be laundered before it can safely be spent. Sorry to be such a `Jobs comforter Tina my love but we can't count our chickens until the jobs complete. The first leg is nearly over, now we get ready for the next'

'You're right Sidney I was getting carried away, there's no cause to be complacent yet. What's the next move?'

'Well we all return and tie up back on the pontoon again. Let the dust settle and wait a call from Charlie on the road tanker. As soon as he's back he'll arrange to get alongside and take off our school children (or pump out our sewage holding tank as far as the rest of the world are concerned.) But I don't think he'll be able to get near the pontoon so we shall have to moor up alongside the quay to make the transfer. I hope it will be sometime tomorrow'

'And that's the end of that as far as we're concerned?'

'Well that's how it was going to originally be, with Jack and I simply bringing the stuff back into the UK and being paid off.

138

We would have got about five grand each. But then as I explained, we formed a syndicate with Fenton and Justin to take care of the whole thing so you could say it's only the beginning as far as we're concerned the way things are now. This way we get a cut of the whole ten million. So far the planning has been faultless. We're in the big time now luv' No more fitting pipes and water tanks to an endless production line in that draughty old boathouse day after day. We're going to make a pile, then sit and spend it some where the sun never stops shining. Miles away from grey skies, cold seas, my bingo loving wife and Milehaven men's club. All you need in life Tina is an exciting concept planned down to the last detail and the will to see it through, and I've got all that .Just stick with me and you'll see'

The planning committee meeting was impressed by item forty three on their agenda entitled London Marina: a concept for reclamation of extensive marshland in the Thames Estuary. It detailed the development of this bleak area into something that was described as being what London docks had used to be and Heathrow Airport had now become. Its creator a retired Royal Naval Officer by the name of Rodney Blake had spared no expense it seemed in setting forth its virtues using precise plans, an artists impression, and a virtual reality computer presentation. His CV included the development of Milehaven marina itself already established on the estuary and his scheme was summarized as being Britain's biggest tourist park and ride and international boat show stage for London. What had at first been just a doodle on a blotter now consumed Rodney's waking hours; he talked nothing else at breakfast, dinner parties, to his wife, friends, and colleagues on the parish council. 'Once he gets a bee in his bonnet there's no stopping him' confined Liz on the phone to a friend. 'First it was those greyhound boats, morning noon and

139

night, till I thought I would go mad, now it's this London marina business. It's the Julius Caesar syndrome sweetie. He keeps trying to build Rome all over the place. It's getting so expensive I mean the roof of this place needs replacing and English Heritage just don't want to know. Truth be told he wants to be remembered for something, that's what it's all about. God preserve us from the male ego. Only good thing about all this is, it keeps him in the office a lot of the day on the phone or busy with papers so he's not under my feet in the greenhouse'

If Rodney's pre occupation with planning matters meant he was not around to get in her way socially it also meant he was not around to see Greyhound Three transfer its costly cargo via the suction hose of the yellow sewage disposal tanker. An operation carried out on the clubhouse quay in full view of the members drinking in the bar. This caused no real interest other than a chance remark to the effect that 'There must have been quite a run on Sid's heads for him to need a pump out'

There was a tense moment however when the owner of a large motor yacht asked Charlie the tanker driver to come and pump his boat out as well. 'Sorry Guv' replied the driver quickly, 'I've got all I can take this time around'

'Gee Charlie that was a close one' said Sid later on. The burly driver laughed 'I only told him the truth mate, I'd got a full load.... only not just of crap'

His load went straight to the premises of Sanitation Services, an old furniture storage warehouse down on the Grand Union Canal. The building, a relic of the hey days of transportation by barge. A rusting narrow boat lying still and silent beside the loading dock locked in by a carpet of green weed that looked solid enough to walk on.

Four days later Ted Jollyman gate keeper, caretaker and trusty handyman opened up the creaking gates again to admit this time a trickle of visiting cars containing the school run principals. One by one he ushered them through rooms piled high with the dusty surplus to requirement junk of countless bars and clubs. Rusting slot machines, plastic bar stools, gaming tables, sofa's and sets of matching chairs. On the second floor a door marked 'staff' opened onto a space where room to move still remained and chairs were placed round two restaurant tables pushed together. Justin Rosenstein and Fenton Gesler were already there when Jack and Sidney arrived. 'Ah there you are gentlemen' welcomed Justin 'Nice to see you both again, and congratulations on your North Sea run. It seems to have gone off like clockwork, great stuff, and Jack thanks for allowing us to use your store rooms, this is a first class safe house, a backwater in every sense of the word and will suit our purposes very well indeed'.

'Very few people come down here' said Jack. 'You probably saw when you came in here it's surrounded by eight foot razor wired walls, with plenty of parking space, three floors of storage rooms in this building and a separate empty building over on the other side'.

'Let's make good use of it' said Fenton.

'Precisely' Jack nodded 'Here's what I think we should do, first consider distribution. Our cover, Sanitation Services now operating in and out of this building and ostensibly supplying toilet rolls and tissue to clubs, bars and hotels. The way it works as we've already discussed is we buy toilet rolls in packs of six, carefully open selected rolls and insert our little coke pods into the cardboard centres, marking the loaded ones with a 'double strength' sticker over each resealed end. We deliver directly to our customers. They will sell on in the usually way for further breaking down. We can also break some stuff down with baking soda for sale as crack if required. The outhouse I mentioned which used to be a crockery store is already stocked with packs of toilet rolls ready for processing. So I think we are now ready for stage two of the school run. Any questions'

'Where's our precious cargo then?' inquired Fenton 'Just in

case anyone should come nosing around'

'Still inside the tanker in the garage here until we need it'

'Who's going to do the packing' asked Justin.

Jack touched Sidney on the shoulder lightly. 'We'll cope with that, us two, and Mario of course. I gather Tina will lend a hand also. So we should see it off in a day or two'.

'Good' said Fenton rubbing his hands 'Charlie will make the deliveries and collect payments in cash. We'll pay ourselves say ten grand each as capital builds up, then when the whole lot's in I'll change it into Gilders in large denomination notes and send it out of the country for legitimising. At that stage we can settle all our debts with Justin's capital investors in the Barents Sea exploration company. So next time we meet we should be on the way to becoming offshore millionaires'

Female staff at Pandora's were both ostentatious and exotic as the job demanded, but in general terms discreet. Hostesses minced expertly between tables dispensing hugely expensive drinks in an aura of body perfume and casual innuendo. Their demure attitude was found to be more titillating to customers than overtly sexual mannerisms and dress. Proprietor Ronnie Terrano was very positive on that point. A student of Freudian sexual psychology he was forever expounding on how he had applied its classic principles to the business of making money out of the needs of maladjusted men.

'Sex today is far too open, too obvious' he would exclaim 'Now I'm no moralist far from it, you know me or I wouldn't be in this game. Sex is great for business always will be it sells books and films, live shows, and catalogues of kinky clothes and objects. It's probably the biggest profit making entertainment, short of drugs that is, and gambling of course and yet most club owners get it wrong. They over cook it, just like most of the present generation they casualize it; strip it of its mystery. The Victorians now, they knew how to treat it...with respect. Not in a moral way but with understanding. The impressionists knew it too; they didn't draw in every detail like the Dutch school, that was boring. They just hinted at it and let the imagination do the rest. Now that's exciting, just like the 'lost and found' line in the pencil sketch. I employ this thinking here for our nightly audience and they lap it up, love every minute of it. No naked parts flashed everywhere, shaven or unshaven, while people are eating. No prancing girls with rings through everything and glittering G-strings round their middles. Simply suggestion, which still leaves a lot of latitude. We have theme nights, tonight may be St. Trinians with our hostesses dressed in school uniforms, straw hats, shirts and ties, short pleated black skirts, suspenders and black stockings, and high heeled shoes. I've known some of our old boys nearly have a stroke when a hostess bends over them serving at table. We've had nurse night, air hostesses, little French maids, teachers, even housewife nights, all good fetish stuff, they love it'

Tonight was Teachers Night and Georgina wore her hair in a severe black bun, her glasses were black heavy Michael Caine style and only the nipples of her ample breasts protested her femininity against the tight stretched nylon of a schoolmarm blouse.

'Christ these damned stockings aren't long enough they're pulling me suspender belt down as I walk and me knickers are riding up, fit to cut me in 'arf. I'll be glad when I'm finished tonight I can tell you Jen' Now let's see it's two G & T's, one Tom Collins and two Rum and Coke and two Carlsberg's right'

Jenny pulled a face 'You poor old thing Georgie, still at least you've not got a class full of teenagers to keep in line'

'You're jokin' luv', this lot are ten times worse. I've had two punters hands up me skirt in the last 'arf hour. Still I did rap their knuckles with this.' She waved a plastic ruler 'Trouble is the bastards enjoy it. One actually asked if I'd give him a good caning on his bare bum. Hold on a minute I think I got it wrong, add a vodka and orange will you, that's it. Tell you what Jen, do me a black coffee and I'll pick it up on my next round. Got to keep myself going. Didn't get much sleep today, what with the kid next door learning the bloody drums. I'll shove his head up his bongo's if he does it again in a hurry'. Georgina melted away in a haze of smoke and spotlights to be replaced by another bun and black glasses.

'Hi Angela, what can I do for you' A tray of glasses rattled and clinked its way across the bar. 'Two gins, one whisky, a rum and coke, snake bite and a bottle of mineral water. God I hate guys that blow cigar smoke in my eyes when I'm serving them. That Tony character thinks he can buy anything, trouble is he can most times, always tips a tenner at least. Wouldn't like to get on the wrong side of him though, not with the bunch he hangs around with. Keep away from Bayswater that's my advice darling'

'Why's that' asked Jenny casually.

'Bayswater Boys, that's why, they're big on the drug scene, doesn't interest me, not the hard stuff anyway. I might use the odd joint or two, that's nothing is it, we all do that from time to time don't we'

'Sure thing' said Jenny. 'We all do that. Got to get a lift somehow. Do you want a coffee I'm doing one for Georgina in a minute'

'Thanks babe' said Angela wearily pushing her heavy black glasses up on her head. 'These damn things make my nose sore and this hairpiece is so hot with the lights and all' As Angela steered her recharged tray off into the gloom of lights now dimmed for the next live stage show, the undercover newshound smiled to herself polishing the endless stream of glasses. Well at least the girls were talking to her on equal terms in spite of the fact they knew little about her. She must be careful when the questions come. Remember you're at catering college, studying hotel management. Things are

144

tough and you need bar work to pay your way. Now where do I live, student bedsit, she muttered to herself. Fulham Road. Let's hope they don't delve too deeply that's all. The floor show slowed things down a little whilst a sea of mid-life faces leered unwaveringly as two tall black females fully dressed in gowns of figure hugging jersey silk caressed each others curves with probing fingers to the tune of Moonlight in Vermont'

'Knocks 'em cold every time that one' explained another passing hostess as she slid her tray across. 'You can almost here them drooling into their drinks. Trouble is the drinking rate goes down and we're all on commission. Still gives us a break I suppose. How are you coping in this madhouse then babes, not too easy giving change in this gloom? Not that a lot of them would notice the wrong change. I do it all the time, short change them. Trick is to look them in the eye, sexy like; usually they're pretty stoned, high on coke or something like that from snorting in the gents, which means they don't notice what change is on the tray. Serves them right, fringe benefits you might say'

'So they can pick up stuff from here then' whispered Jenny.

'Course they can silly, lavatory attendants a pusher. It's probably why his place is called a convenience. He sells them a single dose and they go and shove it up their nose. Sometimes there's more people shooting up in there than having a crap, mind you they do pay 20p for the privilege of using it so at least the club gets something out of the deal'

Jenny polished the tray and passed it back over the bar. 'And can they pick anything up down there?'

'Drugs yep, you name it, for a price, coke is top seller of course even at £18 a snort'

'Why's coke so popular if it's so expensive'

'It's a good hit, good value, it's what those in the know go for but the real reason is the Colombian connection to the Bayswater Boys, they buy in such quantities that they get discounts...so it's coke that gets pushed the hardest, around this joint anyway'

'But I guess Ronnie Terrano makes that decision doesn't he, being the boss man. I mean the Bayswater Boys as you call them don't have shares in this place, do they?'

The hostess looked puzzled 'Say where you been brought up kid, that don't make any difference at all. Sure Ronnie owns this place but those boys run the door which means they call the shots around here that's what I mean. Nobody gets inside unless the bouncers say so and by the time they get down here they know what's on the menu and what it costs, get my drift' She lowered her voice and leaned closer. 'It's protection you understand, and those two door goons are enforcers.' The music changed and the house lights went up. Hostesses, white teeth gleaming, descended again on the tables and Jenny wilted beneath the subsequent clatter of trays and barrage of shouted orders. Not until 3am when hordes of red eyed revellers had shuffled noisily upstairs and cleaners began clearing up the litter of their lifestyles was conversation again possible and then only in a series of one liners between girls who saw the same thing every night and slept most of the day, sometimes alone or sometimes with those who had wads of ready cash that could buy them what their charisma couldn't. Some went straight to their shared dressing rooms to change from their show clothes into jeans and tee shirts. They melted off into the grey of the coming dawn with prickling eyes and hair in which the odour of spent cigars still clung. Others felt the need to wind down at the bar, with now only stacked chairs and empty tables for company. Like an air lock between two compartments in their life.

'Give us a black coffee Jen if there's any left, three sugars. I'm shagged'

'You would be if King Tony had got his way. Couldn't take his eyes off you tonight, or his hands come to that'

'Tell me about it, the thing is he never looks at you when he does it, almost as if his hands don't belong to him'

'Yeah well at least he's a reasonable looker eh. Not like that one that looks like a toad, Jesus, one of these nights he's going to pop his clogs. I'm sure he works himself off during the show, filthy old pervert'

'Now now Jen, the gentlemen pays his way'

'So he damn well should I'd charge him double'

'I usually make a point of it.. Jen you look absolutely bushed yourself. You ain't got a day job as well 'av you?'

Jenny felt her face flush and hoped it didn't notice. 'Me? No being a student takes enough out of me as it is. So, er, we can get all our drugs here from the boys, if we want, can we?' she went on, changing the subject

The hostess eased off the black hairpiece and shook out her hair. 'It's simpler to do so if you want to be a user, but if you're pushing it must be with their stuff sweetie. They'd take you out as soon as look at you if they caught you muscling in on their territory. Most people know better than to cross those boys. Mind you there's a few pushers in here on an average night and when it's jam packed with punters it's difficult to tell who's selling what to who. A little sachet slipped into the palm of someone's hand and if the user is on a regular basis with the supplier, no money need change hands, so there's very little to see if it's done carefully' She placed her manicured hand over Jenny's 'If you're thinking of pushing a little something to boost your income luvvie, listen to me, have a word with Susie in the downstairs Ladies next to the cloakroom, she deals around here a bit and knows all the sources, but be careful it's a very dodgy scene' She downed her coffee in one gulp 'God that's strong, that and a fag or two will keep me mobile till I hit the sack. Well that's Teachers over for a week or two, it's Bavarian night tomorrow or should I say later on today, pigtails and Lederhosen shorts, funny way to run your life isn't it'.

147

A traffic warden stopped to fill in the date on the ticket she was writing out, then walked on slowly to where a white Thames van was double parked in a congested side street. Its driver bending over into the open rear doors straightened to face her holding a pack of toilet rolls in his arms. 'Five minutes luv', that's all, promise'

'That's what they all say sir, you're double parked'

'Medical supplies, special delivery, see'

She glanced at the package 'Mm border line case I'd say. I'm not sure that toilet rolls can be classed as urgent medical supplies or that this Casino looks like a clinic, so I shall stand here and if you're not back in four minutes I shall enter your name on this fixed penalty notice'

A dedicated observer might have found the Sanitation Services van infringing parking regulations in many similar situations in the following days, including a dog track, gentlemen's clubs, an army barracks, a public school and even a travelling fair ground. Fenton's connections continued to prove invaluable in supplying new outlets for the school run product in and around London and the painstaking and meticulous trouble taken over advance planning was now seen to be paying off. Some two weeks earlier than expected Charlie was able to report all packs delivered. All rolls having given up their expensive centres, were now assumed to be performing a far less exciting function in life.

The toilet of Sid and Janet Arthur's house was looking good with a make over which had transformed it from vinyl wallpaper to ceramic tiles, which reached right up to the ceiling. Gone was the chain and cast iron cistern, which clanked before each delivery of water, and in its place a rose pink low flushing suite with gold plated handle quiet as a mouse in operation. The matching pink pedestal hand basin also had gold taps and a smart liquid soap dispenser just like the men's club. Janet could not believe just how their luck had changed these last few weeks, she knew of course Sid was a survivor, always had in the past, ready to put in all the hours that God sends to make things work. She certainly hadn't seen much of Sid at home over the past few months but things appeared to be looking up for SA Marine so she couldn't complain. She couldn't wait to tell them down at the club about all the new things that were being done to the house now their ship had come home so to speak, especially to those who had said how sorry they were to hear Sid's business was in trouble when you could tell they were really pleased, jealous of all he'd achieved since being just a jobbing plumber. Gloria for one and Dave, supposed to be best friends, all they wanted was free holidays most times, well they could whistle now. Anyway Sid would be too busy for things like that with this new marine air conditioning system the company was importing. What a difference it was making already. It was lovely to be flush after being told they couldn't afford this and that. Obviously all those business trips had paid off at last. Easier to have the cash around rather than write cheques or use a credit card, she always got flustered doing that and he knew it, so considerate, she must remember to thank him. Come to think of it he'd mentioned possibly getting a safe put in, now that sounded a really grand idea, something not many of their friends would have. Her bingo that was another thing, when things were tight she never seemed to win, now with a wad of notes in her bag she was often calling 'house' But then of course she would never have considered she was buying a lot more cards these days. Janet in fact was buying a lot more of everything, it was so easy to flick out a fiver from her purse and know the purchase would never come back to haunt her as an item on some future credit card statement. Ready cash was what she had always wanted not just for its buying power but also as something to flaunt in front of others, a measure of status within her social group.

149

Life was no longer just a matter of keeping up with the Jones's suddenly was it, but in getting one or two points ahead. If things kept going on so well they could be changing their car quite soon maybe even the house, although she liked living there, even better since they were smartening the place up. She tried hard not to bring it up in Sid's absence but the temptation was too much when at the club's meat raffle on Friday night Gloria kept going on about their windfall when Dave's aunt died and left him £15.000 (plus two Yorkshire terriers and a Vauxhall Viva which had never left the garage in the last two years). You'd think they'd just been elevated to the peerage, she just had to be put straight, and after all they were milking it for all they were worth. 'How lovely for you' Jan cooed 'Now you'll be able to go on a proper cruise like P&O instead of just coming across to Guernsey with us won't you, well one at least, once you've found a kennel for the dogs. Don't forget they were always kennelled at Pets Paradise at £200 per week. Had a wonderful time, the little darlings, TV radio, gourmet meals, and shampooed twice a week. You'll be getting your guest room ready I expect they'll like that, she never split them up you know. Pity about the one with the bladder trouble, couldn't help it the poor little mite, just used to spray out when it got excited.... every morning when the postman came and if it saw a cat. Oh my there's your cat isn't there, still that could have the utility room I suppose, best thing to keep them all apart, What with all this going on it won't leave you too much time for gadding about. Pity Gloria 'cos with the income from Sid's business I'm going to have so much more leisure time, Won't know what to do with myself will I. Said I didn't need a cleaning lady but Sid insisted, so thoughtful you know that man of mine. I mean this place of ours isn't big enough to give me any grief, but if we did move we might have to have a gardener as well .Did I not say, thought I'd told you Sid's new business has taken off. He said not to breathe a word yet but you two are almost family so that's OK, only keep it to yourselves won't you. What's it all about? I'm not sure, you know me, if the business is going well, I don't rock the boat. I only ask questions when our overdraft can't pay off the credit cards. No that's a lie I did ask him once and he said this American air conditioning system needed selling over here so he'd built the prototype into our boat to demonstrate it to boat building companies, you know like a show house on a new housing estate, that's how he put it anyway. Now apparently it's selling well. Busy at Milehaven boathouse? Well yes of course I expect so, it's always on answer phone these days whenever I ring. Sid says even Tina is working on the boats. They'll be roping me in next, perhaps even you Gloria if you want to earn a bit on the side'

But the huge boathouse doors on the slipway were closed and padlocked as they had been for sometime. Should entry have been accessed by the side office door every footfall would have echoed across an emptiness as total as though a plague had struck the work force but left no bodies, just a scattering of tools on work surfaces and some unused copper piping on the racks. A few old burger cartons and Pepsi tins lay under the racks on which the boats had once rested and a scruffy pigeon scavenged for crumbs until frightened off by the phone which had now rung four times then stopped. The answer phone clicked in with a recorded message of Tina's voice "I'm afraid Sidney Arthur cannot take your call at present" This much was true as he was in fact still working in a building close to water, but of the stagnant variety on the Grand Union Canal where he and the others were packing up the last of the domestic packages for distribution.

Domestic packages were stacked in a neat row inside a long white painted locker beside dried food, and basic essentials for survival during long periods at sea. 'Let's see now' said John to himself. 'Beans, mixed fruit and cereal, salt beef, melba toast, and for you Bosun my lad, you have a choice of rabbit, chicken or meaty chunks in tins which must be horse if I'm any judge, still it's got so many added vitamins you'll never suffer from scurvy or dandruff for that matter, if push came to shove we could possibly eat each others rations the way things are today. Anyway we've got plenty to tuck into. Keep us going for weeks eh!' Bosun sniffed dutifully along the line of tightly wedged packs but detecting nothing of immediate edible interest turned away and went outside on deck to check his bone from last night was still tucked up in some old sacking. John started up the big Perkins diesel which gave a shudder as though shaking off its sleep, coughed and then settled to a throbbing if slightly erratic tick over which rattled his glasses on the shelf. He did this every day to give it a run but in fact it was because he liked to feel its heartbeat running though his feet. She was almost ready now, this boat of his, to push off out of this smart little backwater and meet the elements head on as she was designed to do. To dig her deep displacement hull into rolling swells, becoming part of them instead of just skimming and slapping noisily across their surface. Was that what most of us did perhaps? Just skimmed and slapped our way through life without ever really dipping into it. Not him, after all most of his days at sea had been spent at cargo vessel speed with ample time on watch to stand and stare at far horizons and maybe wonder at the meaning of it all. Lonely? Yes at times, but then she was always there on his return, waiting at their window overlooking the Solent when his ship passed through Spit Head to tie up at Fawley. The window would probably still be there but with a strange face now watching other ships. Her face was still with him though; he'd seen it many times quite clearly. In the shadows, in the clouds, in dappled light reflections sunlight on water made along the side of boats.

Bosun had such visions too, he was convinced of it for he would see the dog go rigid at times, staring at a spot on the water for what seemed like hours. John knew he wouldn't change anything by running away, for that was what he was doing. There would be shadows on clouds on other skies and shapes could form on spume as it slid down the backs of breaking rollers on any ocean in the world. All he could hope for was to be so busy working the boat and so tired when he wasn't that all else would fade. 'That's the plan anyway' he muttered to himself 'Unless anyone comes up with a better one and right now I'd better get cleaned up if I'm going ashore' He never wore a suit these days and getting cleaned up meant putting clean jeans on with socks and shoes, maybe a shirt and jacket, but certainly no tie.

The five thirty going into London was quite comfortable with most of the rush hour coming out of town at this time of the day and it pleased him to be sitting quietly reading his yachting magazine while passing trains were stacked full of standing, swaying figures. The surge of London's human tide on subway and street level seemed to be louder and more oppressive with every visit and he was glad to let the black cab insulate its passenger as it ducked and dived its way to Jenny's flat. He paid off the cab and went up the short flight of well-worn steps to the front door. One of many in this long line of Victorian terraced houses. The bell echoed inside and feet clip clomped on the stairs, then she was in front of him. There was a pause, then both spoke at once. 'Sorry I was going to say it's nice and quiet here after all the hustle and bustle of town. I'm just not used to all this excitement. Anyway you look well and you've had your hair cut short, it suits you'

She motioned him in, giving him a peck on the cheek as he passed her in the doorway 'Yes it is quite quiet here in this street, anyway with cars parked on both sides there's not much room left for joy riding' The slight embarrassment he felt in calling on her at her home address faded as they chatted on their way up the lino cladded stairs. Arriving at the top a little breathless their ease of conversation had returned. 'One more flight and I'll be needing oxygen. It must be something carrying shopping up all these stairs'. She laughed and he found himself noticing how she screwed up her eyes like a cat. 'Oh it works out OK I only do a little at a time usually at the corner shop'

'Mr. Patel?'

'How did you guess, but then we do eat quite a bit of curry'

'It's working out then is it. I mean with the girls?'

'Yes fine. It gets a little fraught from time to time especially with the hours I keep'

'So the job's keeping you going all hours then?'

She shook her head and the short hair cut stayed in place 'Not exactly but I've got two on the go at present'

'Two jobs, still working on that nightclub undercover thing are you?'

She explained her undercover night work at the club was paying off and was providing all the background information she needed.

'But if they did check up on you and found out you're lying they could kill you, do you realize that. I mean they're not playing around you know Jen, their professionals. Look at that doorman murder you covered, taken out because he was on the take from the wrong people. Can't you go about this in a safer way? What is it you're trying to achieve anyway? I mean you've established yourself as a credible crime writer in general terms, you're getting good by-lines aren't you?'

'Yes John, in all humility I can say I'm being used to cover all major crime scenes. I've made good contacts with the drug squad and the customs people and the regional crime squad but it's big out there, they're calling me in when all the action is over just to tell Jo public how clever they've been. It's really just for a press release, a fixed statement. I'm after something more exciting, something to titillate the palette of the tabloid   readership, sell more papers. I want to make some sort of contribution. I see myself as uncovering facts, the truth and then reporting it for the public to react, not sitting around waiting for other organized bodies to use me like an intelligent form of word processor'.

'OK Jen I understand that...you need to make a more active contribution but how can you go out and write about a crime that hasn't happened yet. Don't you have to wait until it's been committed so there's something to get hold of?'

'But that's the whole point, it has happened, it's happening all the time just beneath the surface. What I've got to do is put on diving gear and get to the bottom amongst all the slime, then pop up and expose it!'

'And you think you can do that better than our professional police force'

'Yes I do, well on the drug scene anyway. This situation may turn out to be more than I can handle, I don't know, but, it's something I'm really concerned about. Drugs are a dirty business John, make no mistake, especially with what they are doing to young people, turning them from intelligent useful members of society into crazed creatures simply living for a fix, ready to rob, kill just to fuel the ghastly habit. Fags and booze are bad enough but drugs especially hard drugs are the end of the road, a black pit from which it's almost impossible to climb out of. I've been to drug rehab centres to see for myself and believe me when you've seen a frail sunken eyed young girl, somebody's daughter, going cold turkey you wouldn't need to stick your fingers down your throat to be physically sick. Some will never make it, their guts destroyed forever. Others have to exist with their nasal membranes burnt to a cinder from endless snorting. I've got masses of photographs and statements in my files already on the subject. Now I'm after the real villains, the suppliers and to do it I've got to go amongst them. Get to the horse's mouth you might say, only I prefer to think of it as the face of the dragon. What I intend to do is to write the whole story from beginning to the end so everyone can understand it. The types of drugs and where they come from, who produces and imports them and how they're distributed. That's one side of the coin, then as I've said I'll go into case histories of those whose lives have been destroyed as a result'

'Do you intend to name all the places and people involved in the information you collect'?

'I'll have to if I'm to get any sort of credibility. I mean this isn't some sort of evil fairy story John, it's documentary'

'But they'll come after you for God's sake as soon as the facts are published. You'll never be safe'

'You're right of course that's why everything will be written under a non-de-plume to keep my identity secret'

'I see but it still sounds a dangerous area to be raking over however morally justifiable. How deep are you in already?'

'Just probing the crust at the moment really. I think the girls at the club (that's the hostesses) accept me more or less. My cover is I'm a hard up catering management student, trying to make a few bob on the side in bar work. It's the perfect situation with them waiting on tables and picking up on conversations as the customers in their drunken state mouth off about what they've done that day. Then it's all us girls together as they come up to the bar for me to sort out the orders, and you know how things get passed on. I'm a good listener, always have been. It's as easy as that really. I make notes of the names they drop, then once back home here I begin to piece the jigsaw together. I'm very careful over how many questions I ask lest they think me too interested. So you see hopefully I'm not taking too many chances'

He looked at her and she saw the concern in his eyes. 'You're a single minded person Jen and a brave one when I think of the difference between your life and mine I didn't realize until just now what your work entailed'

'We are both professionals you and I, both our jobs entail taking risks. At sea you fought all your life against the elements and now you're even planning to take it on single-handed. That takes courage I would say so don't put me on a pedestal Mr. Crowther.'

He rubbed his stubbly chin thoughtfully. 'Is there anyway I can help, with background work I mean, say research of any kind. Even moral support or when you need a second opinion. I've got the time you see. It's just a thought. I'm probably being silly though, just forget it I'm talking out loud'

'Of course you're not being silly, it's very nice of you to offer...in fact...that's not a bad idea at all. You've got your PC haven't you? Look if I were to pass over some names of company's and individuals you could check them on the web for me. Would that be a problem'

'No problem at all I often browse the net aimlessly for something to do in the evenings. It would make it more enjoyable, give me a sense of purpose'

'Right then if you're sure that's OK I'll give you a list of all the bones I'd like some flesh put on before you go'

They sat in the little living room with the panoramic view of chimney pots and television aerials receding into the haze of central London united now by what seemed a common involvement. Late afternoon transcended easily into a noisy gathering in the public bar of the Three Nuns at the end of the road until a vision of Bosun of passing water or worse on the upper deck of Tradewind brought John to his feet.

'Look at the time I should have been on the train hours ago. I'd better grab a taxi molto quick, poor dog will be desperate by now'

'I'll drive you to the station silly; I've only had Pepsi's tonight. Grab your coat'

He was on the train rattling across the Thames before he realized that he had kissed her an extended goodbye.

Like most financiers Justin Rosenstein seemed to be a cold fish because he played his cards always very closely to his chest. Dealing, he once said to Fenton, is very much the same in money as in cards, a game of bluff. If you want what your opponent has, never let him see it! Laid back is the attitude at all times, affect the lazy eye, a stifled yawn to hide the flow of adrenaline. A low bid when the stakes are high will often change the scene. Now Fenton waited, having presented the School Run profit and loss figures in what could only possibly be described as a half term audit. Justin sat back lips pursed, eyebrows knitted computing tabulated figures, then tantalizingly twirled his glass and drained it until the slice of soggy lemon touched his nose before looking round him with beaming smile to say. 'Capital.... in every sense of the word. Well done everyone. Well done indeed.' That seemed to add up to pretty well perfection. 'Sanitation Services seems to have been an excellent choice of cover, so far at least. Nice and non-descript like cleaning windows, something one expects to see everywhere without warranting a second look. Now at the point of sale Jack are you having any problems?'
'Not on my patch, everyone seems happy with our quality and price. Crack is going quicker than the pure stuff but then that's been the case for sometime especially with the young. Bit like the way they take to fast food more than meat and two veg I suppose'
'Interesting analogy Jack, now what about the competition. Any reaction yet? I do hope not, especially as we're undercutting by 10%.'
'They will only find out if a dealer or pusher grasses us up and at our prices they'd be cutting off their noses in terms of profit if they were to spill the beans'
'Anyway Jack we could always arrange a little nasal disfigurement if we chose eh!'

'I imagine we could Justin, but as yet we have no problems'
'Good so life in the domain is going well. I'm glad to hear it; one can never be complacent in our world. But of course we are supplying areas not overseen by your good self Jack which is just a teeny bit more worrying. We ought to put a few feelers out to see how sweet things are out there'
'Justin's right we can't afford to get to take any risks' butted in Fenton. As you know I work closely with the Bayswater Boys and my heads on the block if they get the slightest whiff that I'm buying from their sources and undercutting them. So believe me I'll be keeping my ear to the ground, so close that weeds will grow in it. Jack, you've got contacts amongst doormen in other areas in town, can you cross their palms with silver so they'll drop the word if there's the slightest hint of trouble'
'Yep OK I'll get on to it'
Justin held up his hand. 'Well that's the bad news (the dark side of the coin) the good news is most of our cash is now in hand, and it's the turn of Fenton and I to put the hose on it, clean it up a little, so it's ready for us to spend. Now I know you've all been waiting for it and we're almost there. We can wind up Sanitation Services and Barents Sea Exploration no problem, dispose of the tanker and the van, move out of Jack's warehouse and stand down the north sea school run boats.... if that's what you want. Fenton has already opened numbered accounts in various places across the world in which bonds are registered in our names. We can draw the interest as it accrues, or cash in as required and that will be the end of it. It's Graduation Day for us unlikely students at 'O' level in Class A drugs. Unless we four go on to 'A' levels in more than one sense of the word. Why give up now? We have spent an enormous amount of energy and organization into putting the school run together and I think you will agree it's been well worthwhile despite the risks. You Sidney and Jack together with our trusted supporters are the task force

159

and you may well feel the task has been successfully completed and want to stand back and reap the rewards, that's understandable. But our machinery is in place and working well. We could do worse than have another go...make another school run.' He held up his left hand, palm outward. 'Don't chip in with comments yet; hear me out, and then you can chew over the fat. First we use both boats as carriers on this run, this doubles the payload. Think of it twenty million. If Fenton can abstract a discount from the boys in Bogotá based on our double sized order. I can fund the purchase as before from Barents capital. Everything else is in place, as we know. All it needs is for us to agree and set a new date' he looked from side to side slowly. 'Well Gents what's the feeling. Have we got the guts to carry this off again? Think of all that lovely money'

For a moment there was a depressing silence whilst everybody waited for someone else to commit themselves. Then Fenton said 'Makes sound accountancy sense to maximize existing assets before their disposal, thereby reducing depreciation against hardware'

Justin laughed 'Or if the cars in the garage don't take the bus'

'Sounds great to me' chirped in Jack 'In for a penny and all that. I'm game if Sid can produce another hidden chamber in my boat that is.'

'You're a bit quiet Sidney' prompted Justin 'Does the idea worry you'

'A little I must admit, it's just that I'd got used to the idea that we could relax now there would be no more risks to take. Perhaps I'm a bit superstitious about well returning to the scene of the crime. Is it tempting fate. I mean we've done so well already. What happens if we get caught? It's a lot to lose. It's not just the money it's the freedom to enjoy it that's at stake. I can't stand the thought of years locked up in jail. It would kill me honest'

Justin nodded sagely with all the decorum of a High Court

Judge. 'I quite understand your misgivings, Sidney, possibly we all feel a bit like that, it's the agony of the double or quits decision. But as we've just said. We've done it once. The hard work was in setting up remember and that's all in place now. It seems stupid to waste all that. Look we all knew what the risks were and the moral considerations right from the beginning but decided the rewards were worth it didn't we, you included, agreed!'

'Well yes but!'

'And nothing's changed Sidney except that we now have the opportunity to more than double our gains. If you chicken out you compromise the rest of us. And don't forget one thing. You're already in this thing up to your neck and if we five go down on this second run without you, you'll still go down with us. In for a penny, in for a pound Sid and we're going to succeed, don't you worry on that score, just relax! One last run then Gentlemen eh! Perhaps Fenton would be kind enough to set up a new deal on our behalf with our colleagues in Colombia. That's fine then, all decisions made. Let's drink to our continued association, in the second school run'.

The Thames dissipated much of its estuary flow to form dislocated mud flats. Yet within this labyrinth of creeks and bogs there was a sort of unity personified in village action groups, councils and societies, Milehaven marina, that microcosm of civilized society was of course the obvious venue for meetings such as the Urban District forum on crime being held on Tuesday evening in the club room of the yacht club. This suited everybody given the pre and après' meeting possibilities for a tipple in the bar. It also suited Rodney Blake as chairman putting him in the added role of host, a position he always enjoyed as he did the company of the Chief Constable of Police, someone he felt could be useful in his

161

great plan for the new London marina. A subject he would contrive to introduce at every given opportunity.

'Crime' intoned the Chief Constable in a tone of quiet satisfaction 'has shown a marked decrease across this area'

'That's no great surprise' remarked one of the old parishioners 'seeing as it's tidal mud'

'In spite of restrictions in available manpower' continued the officer 'our force can both cover large areas and respond to any incident using land based helicopters and units of the river police' he went on to explain how bigger and better offshore patrol boats could pursue villains far out to sea and in close cooperation with customs, coastguard and the navy itself cope with smugglers on an international scale. To Rodney waiting patiently for his chance to speak it seemed an age 'Homewatch' droned on the Constable 'should never be underestimated as the police force could not even with the best will in the world have eyes everywhere. We all must be on our guard at all times. Not just to report major crimes but report anything out of the ordinary'. At this stage road wardens with the homewatch badge began twitching waiting for the call to recount their experiences in the line of duty...their tales of daring-do. But the top lawman in the county held them back like a sheriff with his vigilantes knowing that an open forum would immediately ensue. That was 'any other business' stuff and the main course was still on the table as far as he was concerned.

'But restraint must be exercised' he warned 'At all times in approaching any suspect however obvious the interest for in these times of gratuitous violence grave personal injury can easily result'

Hands holding scraps of paper with notes on what to say were now held up high and chair legs scraped restlessly along the wood block floor. But it was to be half an hour before the chairman's gavel hit the table hard enough to spill the speakers water, and four more questions fought for answers before order was restored enough for him to get a word in edge ways.

'Before I thank our speaker I'd like to say just a few words myself on the subject of homewatch in this area. As the Chief Constable says it has to steer a very careful course between going too far and not going far enough in its attitude to wrongdoing. Obviously its members are advised not to have a go, just inform or a call for assistance. This problem of course is common to all villages, housing estates, and urban areas, but our venue for this evening Milehaven marina is a prime example of something different. A complete community designed as such from the beginning, to cater for those who either own a boat or just love living where there is water and boats to watch. It is modern in every aspect and yet in some ways resembles a Roman settlement in terms of its security'

(The homewatch volunteers were getting restless again on their chairs, sensing their foregathering on crime and the vital part they had to play was being steered into a lecture on sociology by Rodney Blake. But the chairman had the reins and wouldn't let go... 'A marina such as this with millions of pounds tied up on its pontoons is a prime target for thieves and villains yet there is very little evidence of crime of any sort. This has been achieved by a blend of harbour watch volunteers and paid security staff.... to very good effect.'

To the dismay of the captive audience the distinguished guest speaker and the bar steward (who had hardly sold a drink in the past two hours.) Rodney Blake went on to describe in boring detail the success he'd had in running both the marina and the yacht club single-handed. And just when they all prayed he would thank the speaker and let them stampede for the bar he went on to say how he would use this experience to good effect if given the mandate to advance his plans for reclaiming marshland for miles around to create a vast new London marina, his contribution to the good of Greater London. Many chins had dropped forward on to chests and

163

tongues dried in the absence of real ale before the monologue drew slowly to a close with the stirring line. 'So I can confidently state that our chief constable will find no major crime in Milehaven today.'

But in the SA Marine workshop less than a mile away that very evening another boat was being fitted out for use in the second school run.

Hostesses at Pandora's could suss out the scene almost at a glance in terms of the tipability of tables on any given night, and tonight indicated rich pickings. It was all to do with the size and disposition of incoming groups. Large parties of clients being entertained by executives on company expenses were well known good news. When the company picked up the bill nobody worried how much it cost as long as the business was done in the end. Stag parties once in their cups of course splashed out in all directions. Sugar Daddies always felt the need to look big and usually dug deep with a flourish while flabby foreign businessmen were known to get confused over currency, and mistakes once made were rarely rectified. Of all purveyors of perks however it was the villains who were most generous, and experienced hostesses fought tooth and nail to serve them. Most prized of all was a 'Godfather group' usually a table for as much as twelve to fifteen where two or three girls would work together and run a three way split to keep things fair. A party of this size would obviously book in advance, but if a 'family' well known in terms of notoriety should suddenly appear they would be accommodated immediately even if it meant uprooting others from their tables. No one complained if they knew what was good for them. When the Bayswater Boys came in there was no flash dress, it was smart casual Armani or even business type suits. But you knew who they were without a second glance, even if the face was unfamiliar. Something about their perfect manner and reserve showed menace. For them dinner in the nightclub was a once a week affair with or without wives or girlfriends depending on the business at hand for where business men would have the working lunch, with hoods and villains it was the working dinner, where matters of mob policy would often be discussed in an atmosphere they felt at home in. As one of the girls put it, because they extract protection money from the place they probably feel they've got a stake in it'.

'Good night tonight' smiled Georgina as she slammed her tray down on the bar and read out the first order from her note pad. I've got the mob all to myself, now ain't that grand'

'Which tables that?' asked Jenny peering through the gloom.

'The round one for eight, far right in the corner. Don't stare Jen'

Jenny quickly put the drinks together on the tray. 'Oh is the cognac small or large?'

'Bottle luv. Did I not say? This lot's just for starters, you wait till they get going. E're I think I'm going to need two trays for this lot pet'

'No probs' Jenny reached below the bar 'Here we are look I'll carry this one over, it'll save you a second trip'

'Thanks Jen, you're a luv.' They eased their way between the hazards of lit cigars and elbows to the table in the corner. Jenny stood back holding the second tray while Georgina bent forward and expertly unloaded the first. Through lowered eyelashes it was possible to get a close-up glimpse of some of the country's most notorious drug barons at play. Making use of every second, Jenny scanned the circle of faces talking in animated fashion. A face two places to her right tilted momentarily to the light and she froze. It was familiar! She caught the eye for a split second, and then it was gone, sunk again into the circle of nodding and laughing heads. Georgina tapped her shoulder 'Oi! Let's have it then' Jenny came to.

'Oh sorry' and passed over the second full tray to her

165

colleague.

'Where were you then, on another planet' came the comment as they got back to the bar.

'No just taking in the experience of your Mayfair Boys'

'Bayswater silly, smooth bunch of bastards aren't they. Quite famous faces some of them by all accounts (in police records anyway) 'Gawd they're shouting for more drinks already. Where the hell they put it I never know. It's all go.'

She dived back into the human tide of self-indulgence as other trays were slammed across the bar. Jenny tried hard to place the face she had seen for only a moment, but to no avail and the table was so tucked away she couldn't get a second look from the bar area. Was it worth the risk of a question or two, after all Georgie didn't seem to be all that perceptive? Her chance came in the second show when the lights went down and the hostesses could snatch a quick fag and coffee at the bar while lust replaced thirst as punters glued their eyes to the antics of semi clad females.

'Do you know all that lot then' she asked Georgina 'I mean the boys at the round table'

'Personally? Not really, just by name that's all...why do you want an introduction. One there that you fancy?'

'No nothing like that, it's just I thought one of them looked a bit like Harrison Ford the film star'

'Which one?'

'The guy sitting right by the pillar'

'Oh him that's Fenton Gestler, I think he's their accountant. He's with them occasionally when I guess they're talking money. I think he looks more like Robert Dinero myself'

'Not to worry, how are the tips going?'

'If they have another round I'm on the make big time'

Back in the flat that night lying in bed wide-awake Jenny could still see the after image of the face at the table. At least Georgina had put a name to the face, Fenton, Fenton Gestler that was it. But why should this face seem so familiar, where had she seen him before. At a scene of a crime maybe, yes that could be it. After all she spent a lot of time hanging around these places. She'd also seen a lot of crooked faces in the dock during the many court proceedings she had attended. Out of the window she could see the silhouette of a television aerial was gradually resolving itself in a lightening urban sky as her eyelids fluttered and she succumbed to sleep.

Jenny could work well into the small hours, keep sharp when others staggered with the need for sleep, but mornings were a problem, she did not do mornings. When she finally broke through that next day the smell of her flatmate's breakfast toast had long subsided. A shaft of sunlight drenched a section of patchwork quilt. She pulled herself up onto her elbow and with the other hand reached up to draw back the curtain. The resulting flash of sunlight blinded her for a moment but the flash reached deep into the recesses of her mind. In that instant Jenny put the face in context, she was sure it belonged to a figure in the background of a shot she took of John working on the mast of Tradewind. One of the group of men who she had seen coming off the boat next door. She'd given John the shot to keep, damn it! She would have to blow it up to prove her point. She'd have to ring him to locate it and then get down to Milehaven as soon as possible. A rush of excitement took over and Jenny got out of bed and showered in record time. Was it the fact of sorting out the face or the thought of seeing John again.

Greyhound Two sat quietly within the cavern of Sid Arthur's boathouse surrounded by pipes and power cables as its large holding tank was adapted for the next school run. All was peaceful, the work force sat around on boxes drinking coffee and eating fish and chips out of plastic containers brought in by Tina from the Happy Haddock fish bar on the corner. 'Should have this done by Friday' mumbled Sid through a mouthful of chips. It's always easier when you've done the

167

job once before, cos most of the problems have been already solved. Let's hope the second run goes as well. And the weather doesn't fail us. We were lucky the first time. Who knows? The Dutch police could be waiting for us, on this visit'

Jack paused, a forkful of haddock raised 'You're a right old Job's comforter Sid, cheer up for God's sake. It's all for one and one for all now. We've got to believe we can pull it off again. No reason to suspect otherwise. We know the drill and this holding tank compartment will fool them every time. If there was a search they'd never look in a tank of sewage' He looked across at Tina. 'You convince him luv will you, that we're all going to earn ourselves a bloody great fortune for just one more trip, then we'll never get our hands dirty again.... ever!'

'She's already said that' snorted Sid, 'but we've come out of the first trip with nearly a million each. I can live on the interest from that without ever touching the capital. Now we're going to do another run, a double run, that's 90 kilo's of the stuff between our two boats. Do we really need the money, that's another two million on top of what we've already got. What am I going to do with it? Can't buy a bigger yacht, cos that'll need a crew to handle it and will invite questions from everywhere. I can already see that Janet is well looked after and I can buy a nice little villa for Tina and me. Paid me debts off. You see Jack I don't really need the money that's what I'm trying to say'.

'Sid, as Justin said, were in too deep now, we've got to go through with it. Trouble with you is, you've no great ambitions, You've got to look further ahead than next week you know'

'Why, what have you got in mind then?

The Casino Sidney old lad, my big super play house in Blackpool, no holds barred, a palace of glamorous gambling and girls, Las Vegas style. Floor shows, extravaganza's theme

168

restaurants, you name it, I'll promote it. But it's going to need funding. That's where my three million comes in. That and the proceeds from my other two nightclubs and arcades and I'll be functional, fully operational. Running it would be a huge occupation. Now there's a thought you could invest your pot in my casino. You not wanting all of it, that is!'

'Jack, how are you going to buy anything that big without someone wondering where all the cash is coming from?'

'Fenton's worked it all out for me. He's going to set up a company in the Caymans. We've even got a name going, 'Global Glamour Inc' Like it!. Now all my cash gets paid into that and GGI does the business. I am then employed by the company to run things over here. It'll be legit, have a board of directors, all paid a nominal fee, but with no real power. Good wheeze eh. He's a good chap Fenton. He might even put some cash in himself. Seriously Sidney you could do a lot worse than throw your lot in with me. Both you and Tina. It would be good to have the two of you alongside. New life and all that'

'You really mean it don't you Jack. You're convinced it's going to happen'

'Of course I am, it's a dream I can realize. I'm halfway there. I'm always looking for the main chance'

'I envy you. I won't say I haven't looked for making a few bob on the side. That's why I was able to put away enough while being an emergency plumber to start up SA Marine. They were good days, Just an advert in the Yellow Pages 'Send for Sid' day or night, when pipes are your problem. Most times it was something easy but I'd hang around a bit, like I've said before, have a fag, then do the job in five minutes. Then an hour later have me tea and charge 'em a nice little emergency call out rate. They never questioned it. In fact a few called me back again… Know what I mean… But I didn't feel I was conning them, cos they got something out of it. But what we are doing now is evil if we're honest with ourselves. I mean nobody gets anything out of it in the long run, do they?'

'Course they do Sid, the users love the stuff, can't get enough of it. It turns them on. It's their life style, takes them out of themselves for a while. We're doing them a service. If we didn't someone else would. So it might just as well be us. Stop getting cold feet Sidney my boy. Come on now shake a leg. There's a good side and a bad side to everything. You tell him Tina'

'Jacks right, we're just the parcel service, if we're evil then so is the tobacco and drinks industry, and nobody seems to think too badly of them do they!''

'Do you know I quite like taking the punters money in my arcades, it's only a simple matter of adjustment to the machines which alters the balance in my favour, they're as happy as Larry loosing handfuls of coins all day long'

'Jack you're evil' sighed Sid. with resignation 'Perhaps I am being a bit over cautious. I can't pull out now anyway, not after I've done all this bloody work on your boat. As you say we've come this far together. Tomorrow this will be finished and we'll be ready to bring our second batch of children home. Perhaps you'd better cut us in on your casino, then we'll see what Tina looks like in nothing else but feathers!'

'Let go for'ard Jenny OK'

The bulbous bow of Tradewind swung slowly out away from the pontoon.

'Let go aft'

The gap of swirling water widened as John applied starboard helm and the big single screw slowly built up steerageway.

'Fenders in, standby boat hook till we're through the lock'

Jenny neatly coiled each line and tucked the white plastic fenders down alongside the guardrails 'Shall I take them off?'

'No we won't be out long and it doesn't look too rough'

The Perkins diesel eased them slowly down between the lines of moored boats with Bosun on the bow like a figurehead

'Look at that' said the skipper pointing to the bow 'If that dog dies on me I'm going to have him stuffed and made into a figure head, see if I don't'

Jenny stood half inside the wheelhouse door 'Poor Bosun, he takes his job very seriously that's all'

'One of these days he'll get washed over the side. I had a cat on Ocean Rover my first tanker that went over the side, wind caught it. We were all very upset at the time'

'You must have been distraught'

'That we had forty tins of cat food to get rid of yes' John laughed and gave a small blast on the Klaxon horn as they approached the sea lock. They glided quietly in. The keeper closed the gates after them and stood outside as the water level drained down. 'How's it been going John. Haven't seen much of you lately. Bosun's looking well. S'pose you'll be heading off sometime soon now?'

'That's the plan Jock if all goes well. But it never does. Fast as I tick one job off another crops up and something else packs up. It's the prop shaft stern gland at the moment. Can't seem to get it right. Leaks as soon as we're running at cruising revs. That's why we're out today. Give it a bit of a test. Perhaps you'd give it the once over, you're good at heavy stuff'

'Sure no problem John. Give us a shout next week. See you've got a crew today'

'Jenny yes, it's much easier with a mate I must say. Could do with her more often, but she's a busy girl our Jen. Keeps her head down nosing out the news in London most of the time'

The boat had now descended to the point where even shouting became difficult. Jock waved as he opened the gates 'Have a good run, see you on the way back'

John advanced the throttle and they powered out of the lock, Tradewind rolling and pitching out of the protected Milehaven water. Jenny came in and shut the sliding

171

wheelhouse door. 'That's better, much quieter with this door closed. 'What we doing?'

'Well I think we'll cut across the stream, and then turn up river for a bit. Thought we'd have a nose at Sid's boathouse first then turn and run out to sea OK with you?'

She smiled 'Fine Skipper, you're the boss I'm at your disposal. Sid's place is not too far up river is it?'

'No distance, you'll see it in a minute, it's got a big slipway, I think it was the old lifeboat station years ago when Milehaven was just an old creek. My dog should remember that I used to walk him along the river, that's when I first saw this old boat sitting in the mud and decided I would try and buy it. God little did I know what I was taking on. A lot has happened since then. A lot of water under the bridge (or through the lock should say)! Here look Jen this is it, see the name over the doors 'SA Marine' and look the doors are open. I think we'll hang around here for a bit while I check things before we venture out to sea. I'll bring us up to that yellow buoy. You go out and hold it with the boat hook, then take a turn with the head rope' With the engine cut, the only sound was the river swishing past. Let's get Bosun in, then I'll get the binoculars out and have a nose at Sid's place. It's always intrigued me...Hey Jen I can just about see inside the boathouse. Looks like they're wheeling out one of the grey boats on to the slipway. Yes it's Jacks, I can see the name clearly. Wonder what work they've been doing'.

Jenny laughed 'You're as bad as me. Don't be such a nosey parker.'

They watched the slim grey powerboat winched slowly down the slipway. John adjusted the focus on the area inside the boathouse. 'Well Sid hasn't got much work on it's completely empty inside'

John went back to check the engine and within ten minutes they were running downstream with the ebb tide, straight past the lock gates of Milehaven and on towards the sea. John beckoned to his crewmate 'Here Jen take the helm. I'm just going to increase the speed to fifteen knots and see what happens' He eased the big brass throttle lever forward 'There we are that's good, this is a more respectable cruising speed for this boat anyway, hold her steady on this course I'm going below to check what's happening to the stern gland. I won't be long.' Bosun having had a drenching, at last deserted his bow station and having been admitted to the wheelhouse did what all dogs do and shook himself over everything in sight. 'It's leaking again' shouted John through clenched teeth 'I've started the bilge pump, that'll take care of it for now. I'll have to get Jock to have a look at it. Least we've proved a point. There's only one way to test a boat and that's out to sea. We'll turn about soon and make our way back' He shook his head in some despair wiping his hands on an oily rag. 'Sometimes I wonder if I'll ever get across the Bay of Biscay. Oh! by the way, how's your investigation coming along?. It was strange recognizing the face in that photograph you took of me. It's definitely the bloke you came across in Pandora's then. Are you sure it's the same person?'

'Oh yes quite sure. I served him a drink, I was as close to him as I am to you'

'The shot was a bit grainy you know. You might have been mistaken'

'Possibly I suppose, anyway the man in the club was Fenton Gesler whom I am told is an accountant known for juggling with funny money and his table companions that night are collectively known as the Bayswater Boys 'a family' of hoods and enforcers with fingers in many unsavoury pies, and mostly known for their direct connections with drugs'

So this Gesler character if his face matches our photograph was one of the two men you saw on the pontoon having come from Jacks boat ...yes?'

'That's it. What's Jack like?. I mean what line's he in. Do you know much about him?'

'Not really but I think he's something to do with amusement arcades, or clubs, that sort of thing'

'Do you think there could be some sort of connection'?

'I don't know perhaps we're stretching things a bit, but I'll tell you one thing lots of business meetings take place on boats on these pontoons. It's private you see, no prying eyes or secretarial ears'

'Well anyway my nightclub job in Pandora's has paid off so far. I seem to have been accepted behind the bar and I'm getting some tittle-tattle via the girls. One girl Georgina is particularly mouthy I think you would say, she seems to be the key figure. What's Jack's surname by the way'

'Delaney. Do you think they might know him as well? I'd go very carefully my girl on this one'

'I will, if I mention his name I'll drop it in very casually just to see what reaction I get, if any at all. Will you keep an eye on any further unusual visitors on the pontoon from now on, and if you get the chance have a casual chat to Jack sometime. See if you can find out the name of his club and where it is. I don't want to write about the drug scene in general, others do that, I want statistics, real facts and real people. Show both sides of the coin, the supplier to the user. How it effects lives'

'You mean a actual expose' Name names. That sounds dangerous to me'

'It's the only way John. Anything else would be pussy footing about. It's time someone came out and shamed those who make millions out of human misery. Sorry John I'm not a do gooder. All I want to achieve is a sound piece of journalism, make an impact and open up a few eyes to this problem'

'I know Jen, you're a genuine newshound and I mean that in the nicest way. Here, take the helm will you while I dive down and check that blasted stern gland again'

She took hold of the old spoked wheel, it felt good to hold, strong and solid like a ships wheel should, and upright like John himself. Standing there legs braced against the slight roll she felt part of the sea itself, she sensed the flexing of the wooden hull as it ploughed deep into the oncoming swells. Timbers creaking in response to every turn. She felt very calm and relaxed as she played with the waves, turning the wheel, responding to its never-ending games. She felt a hand on her shoulder. 'Oh there you are. I was miles away then. Still on course skipper, and revolutions for fifteen knots'

'Well done mate. We're still taking in water at the stern; pumps got it well in hand though. So we should be alright. Want to stay on the helm for a bit?'

'Fine with me, I'm enjoying it. I know it sounds daft to say this but everything seems very boat like. I mean it's all part of the sea, in sympathy with it. The way the deck moves the solid feel of the brass and wood'

John laughed 'What you mean is it's not a GRP gin palace. Yes there's a world of difference. The chief one for me is that a boat like this is in the sea, a power cruiser just sits on it. Poodling along just suits me fine. Gives me time to think. I can't be doing with all the rushing about. There's cars for that sort of thing'

'The grey boats, Rodney Blake's greyhounds, they're like racing cars really aren't they. Built for speed I mean'

'That's true they're all engine and not a lot of living space'

'They would make useful smuggling boats I should think'

'What makes you say that?'

'Just that they could out run the customs, just like warships, German E-boats or something.'

'You not thinking Jack might be into drug running are you?'

'No I wasn't but actually it would provide a very good reason for someone connected with drug importation being on board his boat wouldn't it?'

John ran his fingers through his thinning hair 'I can't believe we are having this conversation, it's ludicrous; he's the flag officer of the MMYC. Smuggling drugs while flying a blue ensign. It seems a bit of a far fetched idea'

'Would make a very interesting story though'

'Interesting...it would blow Milehaven marina out of the water. Don't even think about it!'

The oncoming swells were steeper now and spray lashed the wheelhouse window as Tradewind's bow bit into foaming crests.

'I think it's time we went about Jen. We'll be losing the lee of North Foreland soon and it's beginning to blow. Let her head pay off to starboard now, that's it go on. Now hold on as we come beam on to the swells. There she goes'

The masthead whipped from side to side and Bosun slid across the wheelhouse as it rolled until the bow came round into the wind and they completed their one hundred and eighty degree turn.

'That's better OK steady onto two seven five degrees, fine. Let's head for home. You'll find the steering a bit more difficult now'

'Why's that?'

'Well a following sea tends to slew us sideways, not good news for the helmsman I'm afraid and we've got the tide coming in with us as well'

'Oh yes, I see what you mean, I'm not too keen on this corkscrew motion. It's making me feel a bit seasick. Hope it won't go on for long John, I've really enjoyed today'

'So have I. It's good for you to be able to get away and join me on my test run. It's just great having company'

'Hey John Crowther that doesn't sound like the voice of a single-handed sailor. Anyway you've always got Bosun'

'Yep I suppose I have, but he doesn't say much. Doesn't even bark when we're at sea. So I never know if he's a bit seasick. too late if he honks....Now listen to me I'm very worried that you're pushing you're luck with this undercover thing. I've said it before but please be careful. I know you say the girls at the club have accepted you, but don't forget they are part of it all and if they suspect you're a snoop, that could put your life at risk. I'm not saying lay off cos you're a professional, but don't stick your neck out too much that's all, and remember if you're in any trouble give me a call... OK?'

'Yes thanks, I promise I won't do anything rash. It's really a case of softly softly, but gut reaction tells me I'm going in the right direction. Anyway I've got you on the case this end, all you've got to do is let me know if you see a skull and crossbones flying from over Milehaven'

Fenton Gesler was well pleased; the school run had worked better than he had thought in spite of using two amateurs. It just showed what attention to detail could produce. Now the stuff was well into circulation and the money well hidden offshore. Quite a bright spark that Jack, got some good ideas. That casino of his could actually be a winner, even in Blackpool of all places. It might just be worth getting a bit of the action. After all Las Vegas grew out of the desert and look at it now. Right he said to himself, down to business. There's the balance due for the last Bayswater shipment to settle. Better get a payment note sorted for the Nagles 65 kilos, then two more to cover the 45 kilo's each for the Atrium and school run. Nice bit of profit coming up for just sending an email order. He pressed the 'send' button on his computer, printed a copy, and sat back with satisfaction. Gone he thought, off into cyberspace, all that commission for just so little effort. It made audit work look like slave labour. Still he liked juggling with figures. It was like playing Bridge. Anyway he had to have some respectable cover and being chartered did keep him in touch with the more legitimate client, (assuming of course that it was an advantage these days). Fenton jumped out of his thoughts as the door buzzed. He walked over to the entry phone. 'Oh hi Justin, come on up' 'Glad you could come over' Firmly gripping Justin's hand at the door and shaking it he went on. 'I thought it was about time we had a little chat on our own. I think sometimes we talk over the heads of Sid and Jack, without wishing to put them down in any way of course. Let me fix you a drink, Scotch or perhaps a slug of Grappa? Aids the digestion you know'

'Oh I think I'd prefer a gin and tonic please, got any ice?'

'Coming right up. I've just sent this off by the way' he waved the copy of the email at Justin. I was in two minds as to whether I should let it go or not'

'Why? Every things alright isn't it?'

'Well yes really'

'You don't sound too convincing Fenton. We don't want a problem now'

'Oh I think it's me being a little paranoid. Only Sidney seemed a bit short on commitment when we last spoke'

' I thought you were going to mention that at some stage. You don't think he's cracking under the strain do you? Because if he is we're going to have to put the frighteners on him, you know that don't you Fenton. Can't have him squealing'

'Oh I don't think it's that bad, he'll go ahead alright'

'The fuck he will if he knows what's good for him. Should we get him in and have a little chat. Set him straight on a few things eh'

'No not at the moment, he's got no ambition that's all, a small time chiseller out of his depth. He was in heavy debt; living way beyond his means and Jack showed him a way out with us. Now of course it's paid off and he's off the hook and of course delayed shock is setting in, unless his girlfriend has convinced him to stick his neck out a bit more'

'He'll get it chopped off if he puts the rest of us in the shit. He can be sure of that. OK I really feel we should have a word in his shell like. Do it for me will you? Now what about Jack. He's OK on everything isn't he!'

'Jacks no problem he's motivated 100%, He wants that new casino of his more than anything, sticks out a mile. He's an empire builder, our Jack'

'That's a relief anyway so we can count on the two boats then'.

'Yes Jacks just reported his boat is ready to go and everybody else is on standby as before'

'OK so you're happy about everything. No cloud on your horizon.'

'No unless you can think of anything Justin'

'Only that you're double dealing at the moment, playing with fire I would say. Doesn't that worry you? The Bayswater Boys won't be very happy. And that email you've just shown me has both orders on it, one for the Boys and one for the school run. Which means they will probably be dispatched at the same time. What happens to their stuff.'

'Oh it's stuffed into frozen turkeys and comes over via the Channel Ferry'

'Who supervises that or shouldn't I ask?'

'I do, it works well, customs and police are more interested in Asylum seekers at the moment'

'Fine Fenton, as long as there's no risk of the Bayswater lot finding out. I wouldn't give much for your chances if they did'

'Well thanks, I've covered my tracks pretty well I think. Anyway I'll be watching it, don't you worry'

'Not just for your sake Fenton, but for all of us, stir up a hornets nest and we could all get stung'

I know but I'm in almost daily contact with Charlie and Vic Nagle, (you know they're the King Pins of Bayswater mob) over at Pandora's and if there was any problem they'd let me know sooner rather than later. Then I would have to talk my way out of it pretty smartish'

' I hope so Fenton, cos I'm not going down with you'

'This casino of Jack's' cut in the accountant, eager to change the subject. 'I think he's under estimating the start up costs. He might have a bit of a shortfall, even taking into account the

money that will be coming his way, How do you feel about taking a piece of the action. We can let him play the big entrepreneur out front but pull the strings from the wings'
'I can see the possibilities' said the man of money.
'Blackpool is ripe for this type of development. It's brash enough with its lights but does need a major makeover from the cheap family holiday area to the glitzy big spenders paradise. Out go the donkeys, fish and chips and in will come the new British Vegas. I'm only surprised the Mob haven't got their foot in the door already. It's such an obvious opportunity. I think the sooner we can get Jack to produce plans the better. We want to be helpful don't we eh! The project should have a name...Northern Lights Casino, that says it all doesn't it. We could register the name offshore with our pot of working capital. Just think what a lovely umbrella this would be for many things, nice little place to push our stuff as well'
'All this is going to be too big for Jack to handle on his own. But hey let's wait until after the boys return home with the bacon. Then we'll move in.'

Whilst the Northern Lights Casino was still just a gleam in Fenton Gesler's eye. The London Marina had at least achieved the status of a set of plans, now displayed via an overhead projector as part of a presentation by Rodney Blake to the planning department of the Greater London Council. 'It's great virtue' he carefully explained 'was that the basic infrastructure already existed in the shape of Milehaven marina. Its existing modern sea lock would provide protection from wind and tide, being wide enough to take most sea going yachts and some commercial vessels. All that was necessary was further excavation into marsh flats beyond, to provide a series of interconnecting basins, as many as the planners felt were necessary to cope with incoming visitors, this would be the most ambitious marina scheme ever devised. When complete the name Milehaven would be dropped and the whole new complex called the London Marina'. The hour long presentation he judged, had been well received and well worth the time spent putting it altogether he thought. So much so that he took the liberty of quickly showing a short video of the work at Milehaven of the Greyhound display team. 'Thank you for your attendance this morning' he said 'If any of you fancy a short visit to the port of Grimsby on the East Coast in early September I have some complimentary tickets to the Festival of the Sea. My Greyhound team will be leading things off with their spectacular formation display. All proceeds of course to the RNLI and Coastguard Service.

Jack Delaney as the MMYC Flag Officer had also been present at the meeting this morning and was very eager to get away to give Sid a call. 'Hi Sid, I've just left old Rodney's meeting, thought I'd just check in with you.... oh not too bad mostly Rodney, full of bullshit of course, although give him his due the old fart had certainly done his homework.... Almost had me believing it might be possible, but listen he's got all us five greyhounds committed to doing our stuff up in Grimsby...four days from 20th September which could be tricky if we get the school run call.... I mean we'll have to have a good reason to say no we can't go. Either that or go straight across from there. It's only about 160 miles...No you're right best not discuss it now. Tell you what, can you meet me tonight in the wardroom bar, about eight then. .... thanks.'

'Evening Mr. Jack' beamed the Steward breathing on the glass and then polishing it 'He's waiting for you over in the corner' Sidney sat facing two chunky tumblers and slid one across by way of a greeting. Jack raised it 'Your health sir. Cheer up it might never happen' Sid took a medicinal size swallow 'That's the trouble I wish it would, it's all this hanging about that gets me. I'll be better once we're on our way. What were you saying about Grimsby? I didn't think it was a good idea to discuss things in detail on the phone'

'Oh only that Rodders has committed us to performing at the Festival of the Sea on the 20th which is a bit inconvenient cos we're on standby for the run. The only good thing is it's on the way, so to speak. Look at the chart and it's almost opposite Texel Island and the harbour approach to Amsterdam. Given the right conditions it could be just one quick dash across, due east. We could be there in just over four hours or so. But of course we shall have to play this by ear. Wait until we hear something. I'm afraid dear old Rodney will want us to motor up there together like we normally do. It's a bit like being on church parade… Spent much of your ill gotten gains yet eh?'

'Shush, keep it down. As a matter of fact not a lot. I've not got used to having so much yet. S'pose I will in time. Janet's been having a good time though, roaming around like Lady Bountiful, buying things and getting the house done up. I keep telling her to watch it, but you know her if she's got money she's got to flaunt it. That's how we got into money troubles in the first place. At least I've paid off the credit companies and the bank loans, but I've got no work coming in, the boat shed is empty. I've got to hide that fact from Janet, she thinks I'm doing so well. Got to go through the motions of going to work every day to make things look the same as usual, but I've no interests now, day to day. Do you know what, I used to take a pride in what I did. I realize now that I actually enjoyed playing around with pipes and sheets of copper metal, designing systems and putting them together. It's not the same as the old days when I had just the van and me bag of tools. Nothing to worry about. Now I'm worrying all the bloody time'

Jack took a long swig and drained his glass 'Snap out of it Sid, you're doing yourself no good, talking like this. Think positive. You're in the big time; it's the only place to be.

You're in a position to look after both women in your life. You can do what you want.   Go any place, any where, any time. You call the tune. Nobody else. It's just a phase you're going through it'll pass. Money is power Sid my friend. Power to control your destiny'

'If I live long enough to fulfil it'

'What do you mean for Gods sake?'

'Can't believe they won't catch up with me'

'Who?'

'Oh drug squad, customs, or the mob. Fenton's clients in Bayswater. He's double crossing them you know, and we're both part of it"

'Look Fenton knows what he is doing. Just leave it to him. In this game you've just got to trust the other guy to play his part and you get on with yours. Otherwise you'll compromise the safety of us all. I asked you last time if you were set to go ahead and you agreed. I know we were only going to do the one run, but it went so well and we've made so much. Just one more run and that's the finish OK!' Anyway it's too late for any of us to back out now. You've got to be confident. Don't mention any of this to Tina or Mario and sound positive if you speak with Fenton. It's just nerves mate' he slapped the drooping shoulders hard 'Lets have one more for the road, or should I say the river'

The Steward was still breathing on the glasses as he approached the bar 'Same again Mr. Jack for the both of you?'

'On the rocks thanks Ken, and just a splash of water'

'God this tunic is uncomfortable' complained Georgina running her fingers around the inside of her collar. 'In fact I'm not too keen on WPC night at all, too many complications. If I get one smart arse asking me if my truncheon is a vibrator I'll brain him with it. They always

183

have to touch it, try and unclip it while I'm serving drinks and then it gets predictably hilarious. It's all very well management having these theme nights, but it's always us that get inconvenienced. At my last job all I had to wear was a fluffy bunny tail on my bum, no hassle '

'I see you've got some of the heavy mob in tonight, table ten as usual' prompted Jenny hoping it sounded just a casual comment. 'I'm not sure your costume is very appropriate'
'Oh I see what you mean Dearie, yes I did get one of them saying he'd come along quietly. I must say they always behave very well, it's rare to see one of them drunk. They're a cool calculating bunch and that's a fact. I have quite a job ear wigging on their conversation, but I've had years of practice in the art of eavesdropping, just a case of concentration, cutting out the background noise and hearing what you want to hear really. Not that it's any of my business you understand. I'm just nosy and like to know what's going on'
'Are you hearing anything tonight then' said Jenny casually
'I'm getting there babe. Depends on how many trips I make to the table. They're arguing amongst themselves at the moment, voices are slightly raised which makes it a bit easier. It seems they buy their coke through an agent, this accountant friend of theirs, Fenny, no Fenton somebody'
'Isn't he the one I saw the other night having dinner with them'?
'Yeah I think so, seen him here a few times, but he's not here tonight'
'Which is why they're talking about him I suppose'
'I guess so, one of them said something about it being smarter to deal direct and cut the commission on the next shipment and they're arguing who should go where, Rotterdam or Amsterdam was mentioned. I suppose it would be, if they're talking cocaine'
'No I think they mean buying from the source itself that's

probably the cheapest way, you know Venezuela or Colombia. Medallin is the chief dealing centre in Colombia. It's where the refined stuff goes when it leaves the jungle factories'

Georgina looked up 'Hey you seem to be well clued up on these things, for a barmaid anyway. I'm impressed'

Jenny felt her face flush remembering that she was supposed to be a catering student and her brain raced to rectify the slip 'Who me? No it's just that I had a boyfriend who was into dealing in a small way, and talked a lot. So I know my way around the scene. He's gone now. I dumped him. God hush my mouth, I'm telling all this to the 'fuzz' You'd better go, table ten are calling you again' The sexy constable took her tray and turned away. 'Yep I'd better go investigate those villains. See what else I can pick up. Set the glasses up for the next drinks order gal' Jenny took a deep breath. 'Calm down girl' she said to herself, play it cool, 'let her set the pace. God I must remember the boyfriend I've just invented. Better call him Bruce if she asks about him again. So my face in the picture is Fenton, somebody who buys on behalf of the Bayswater Boys, well well well. Bit of double crossing going on if what Georgina overheard was correct. What a stroke of luck finding her a natural chatterbox. Long may it last, I really haven't had to work too hard to get this information'. A tray slammed down on the bar top and a tired voice ordered a string of drinks. 'Wake up, that's table six I said'

Jenny jumped 'Oh sorry I was miles away. Could you give me that order again luv' If looks could kill, thought Jenny as she quickly set up the glasses. The house lights dipped and the stage spots picked up the Three Graces who stood fully clad in what passed for classical drapes between two Roman pillars. Faith had big boobs, Hope was all bottom and Charity was showing a good deal of thigh. Things seemed to get hotted up as they proceeded to slowly strip to whistles and leers from the audience. After some time Georgina slowly sidled forth out of the gloom, lit a cigarette and cupped it between her hands. She inhaled deeply before saying 'Works quite well having these mini shows. Gives me a chance for a fag anyway. There's another order' She passed over a torn piece of paper from her pad. 'I wish some of the others would write it down like you. I've just upset Greta, because I asked her to repeat hers'

'Tell you the truth luv I'd forget if I didn't write it down. Too interested in what's going on. Table ten still arguing about their contacts, apparently everything's been left to Fenton in the past and now Charlie, that's the younger of the Nagle brothers thinks he might be creaming off too much commission. Looks as though Vic's agreed for Charlie to fly off to Colombia and sort out a direct deal or something. It's their main source of income now, bigger than prostitution or the protection racket so you can't blame them for being concerned. God help that bloke Fenton'.

'So they're big in drugs then our Bayswater Boys?'

Georgina blew smoke at turbine speed.

'Big, I should say so. Don't you be fooled by Bayswater. They're all over London, the Nagle Brothers. Most discos, and nightclub bouncers work for them. Formed a company they have. Door Security they call themselves. Means nobody gets in or out without the Nagles say so, regardless it seems of who owns the place. Indirectly you and me work for them you know. If they didn't like us or trust us we'd be out, quick smart. You should have held on to that boyfriend of yours you know. He might have made the big time by now. Drugs and clubs that's where all the dosh is these days. I intend to cut in on a bit of the action if I can. When I think of all the hours I work here with sod all to show for it, I could spit. At least you're working towards a career, though how you find the time to study I'll never know. Christ knows when you sleep. What's your secret? You must be on something'

Jenny smiled uneasily 'Secret, Oh it's just Benzedrine, black coffee and perseverance. But don't forget bar work is part of my hotel management course. I look upon this as part of my education and there's no teacher like experience is there?' Georgina waved her well-manicured finger 'So you should have learned from this experience that there's ten times more bread to be made in the leisure industry than running a hotel or restaurant'

'But what could I do around here other than being a barmaid'

'You're smart, you've got a brain; this is just like the police force. First you have to walk your beat like the rest of us in uniform. In other words become a hostess. Then you keep your eyes and ears open and your mouth shut   You shouldn't have a problem. Once you've been noticed and they trust you, then the next step's management. That's plain clothes isn't it? Then eventually into pushing and dealing and that's where the big time starts and where I aim to be'

'I'm not sure it's what I want, standing in the lavatory selling single snorts'

'You could do worse. Look at Rita over there. She reckons to get rid of ten shots a day, that's average one hundred and eighty quid on top of her wages and tips each night. Two and half grand a week or more. Couldn't make that in an hotel could you! Now if you're dealing that's even better. You can buy a kilo in London for say twenty five thousand pounds and cut, mixed and sold on the streets, that's worth around eighty thousand, nice profit eh! You've got the risk of handling it of course, and we all know what the penalties are but the biggest problem isn't being jumped upon by the drug squad it's friends like the Nagles and people like them. Greedy bastards. They want all the dealing and profit for themselves'.

'So where does that leave you, where can you buy your single kilo from?'

'Good question, from a small importer. One who's happy to sell to individual dealers like me, on the quiet. That's why I've never succeeded in getting that far. Only I think it's all

187

going to change pretty soon'
'Why's that?'
'Well some guy I used to work with rang me the other week
and asked if I was interested in taking ten kilo of the stuff. I
said I couldn't raise that amount of cash but I might for a kilo
at a time. I could be in the big time soon eh'
'Are you going to do it Georgie?'
'Yeah, I don't think I can stand this life much longer as things
are but I'll still have to be around for a bit anyway, cos this'll
be my market place. I know who's who don't I. This guy says
he's got big plans for a casino in Blackpool, says he could set
me up there, not just dealing but as principle dance director.
In charge that is...can you imagine me in show business
working in the Vegas of the North? It's something to think
about isn't it? I've danced before you know, not just at this
sort of club I was at Jack's first club in Soho that's where I
first met him. He's got several nightclubs and arcades all over
the place. He's a nice chap, not a bit Irish although you'd
think he would be with a name like Delaney'. Georgina's
voice droned on excitedly about the bright future that was
going to lift her from the dive where she'd played Barbie doll,
dressed each night for the pleasure of endless groups of seedy
perverts. But Jenny was no longer listening for the name had
stopped her mental tape. Jack Delaney, that was a jigsaw
piece that fitted into the picture. This could be what she
needed. Georgina was the link, don't stop her now, pay
attention, take in every word while she's on a roll. Poor kid if
only she knew what she was saying.
'This Jack you mention' she heard herself saying idly. 'He
sounds quite a guy, lucky you met him eh!, sounds as though
he could really set you up what with all his plans. If I were
you I'd get in there while the goings good. He's bringing the
stuff in himself is he?'
'Oh there's got to be others to put up that sort of money. It'll
be a syndicate no doubt. Like owning part of a racehorse.

We'd be talking millions here you know'

'It'll be safe will it? I mean you'll be OK supplying down here right under the noses of the Nagles after what you've just said about them!'

'Oh yes I've already sounded all the pushers out carefully. There's room for me and the Nagles, mind you I'll be cheaper, so guess who they're going to prefer most of the time. As long as I can get the stuff'

'I'm almost envious. When's all this going to happen?'

'Fairly soon I hope, apparently I missed the first shipment, that's gone, but the next is in the pipeline already so I'm down for some of that. Just got to raise the cash. Jack's going to make contact as soon as the stuff arrives in London. I wouldn't dream of asking details like where or when. It's probably safer not to know too many details. Listen everything I've said, forget it. I've already told you more than I should .I hope you keep it to yourself Jenny or we could all be in trouble. Christ! the Three Graces are getting near the end. Just time for another quick puff then it's back to the tables'. Her lighter flared and a haze of bright green smoke encased her words. Jenny nodded. 'Sure, you can trust me' adding quietly to herself 'Trust me to make the most of every morsel'

At 08.45 the next morning John Crowther answered his mobile crouched down as he was in the stern bilge section of Tradewind. He was holding tightly the rubber grip of an inspection lamp while Jock the lock keeper examined the leaking prop shaft gland. 'Crowther' he barked, banging his head on the low deck head as he sat up. 'Oh Jen it's you. This is an early call. What's up?'

'I need to see you urgently. Where are you?'

'Actually I'm down in the bilge with Jock. He's having a look

at the leak, remember'
'What this early in the morning'
'Yes he said he'd have a look before going on watch'
'So you can't talk anyway'
'Not really is there something wrong then?'
'Something urgent has come up. Will you be finished by mid morning? I could come down'
'Yes that'll be fine. I'll have the coffee pot on as usual'
'OK Bye for now'
The two men worked quietly in the darkness. 'Bastard, does' nay want to budge? It's probably been untouched for half a century'
'Try this Stilson wrench Jock, that may do it!'
'Come on...come on you so and so...come on...it's moving, that's got it.' He sat back easing his cramped muscles. 'Gee what a bastard that was'
'Thanks Jock I couldn't have tackled it on my own. I'll tighten up those nuts, that should squeeze things together a bit more firmly. If that doesn't work we'll have to repack it eh'
The Scot nodded 'Aye John that's about the size of it I'm afraid, she'll need testing again though I'm thinking'
'You're right, should have bought a newer boat, I'll see how things go for a bit. There's always something to do on an old boat like this. Not like the rest of them on these moorings, brand new engines most of them. Some never even go out you know except as far as Southend Pier to charge their batteries. Call themselves Sailors'
'True enough John. The Greyhounds that's a different matter. It's good to see them go off together. Out in all weathers. Coastguard said they spotted Sid and Jack out in a force seven the other week, just off the Dutch coast doing around thirty knots, bouncing around like corks apparently. That's keenness and no mistake. Wouldn't catch me out there in that sort of thing, not if I didn't have to. That speed is enough to shake the fillings out of your teeth I would have thought. Where

were they off to on their own? Rodney likes them to go out as a pack usually. It's good for the image you know!'

'Oh I think it was some sort of sea trial for new equipment'

Half an hour later scrubbed up, but still the lingering smell of grease on his hands, John prepared himself a late breakfast of bacon and eggs. Coffee pot was on as promised ready for Jenny's arrival. I wonder what the problem is, John thought to himself. It's not like her to phone so early and she sounded quite agitated. I hope all's well, bet I sounded a bit short on the phone. Caught me on the hop. Never at my best in a pool of dirty bilge water. 'It's alright for you Bosun lapping up your saucer of tea. Here's a bit of bacon. Now go on. Get outside for a breather. Get from under my feet; I need to wash these dishes up quickly before Jenny arrives. We always seem to be in a bit of a mess don't we boy'

Eleven thirty came. The forenoon watch on the marina. Bosun was outside and John idly wasting time waiting for Jenny to arrive. A soft drumming noise could be heard from the upper deck. Bosun's tail was beating the deck again as he recognized her approaching. John looked out of the port scuttle. Yes it was her. She stopped and looked at the silent Greyhounds moored close by and then walked back to the gangplank where John met her. 'Thought that was you, so did Bosun.'

'I was just looking at Jack's boat for a moment'

'What's wrong, you sounded frantic on the phone'

'Let's go down below shall we. I'll tell you about it'

They went below closely followed by Bosun who wanted some reassurance that she was pleased to see him. 'There's a different smell down here today. What is it?

'I should say a mixture of after shave, air freshener and just a hint of diesel oil' John laughed. 'Sorry Jock and I were working on the stern gland when you rang and now I can't seem to get rid of the damn smell. Come on now spill the beans'

'Well I'm not sure really but I think Jack's mixed up in

191

something...drugs. I believe he's part of a syndicate that's importing cocaine from Colombia'

'What Jack Delaney, our Flag Officer?'

'Yes unless there's two Jack Delaney's'

She recounted her conversation with Georgina. She lives in a seedy world of sex and drugs and he's part of it John. You said Jack was in the entertainment business didn't you, ran nightclubs and arcades. Well that's a pretty obvious connection wouldn't you say and he's agreed to supply her with a kilo of the stuff. All she's got to do is break it down and pass it on, and he's offered her a lot more if she can get the cash together. Perhaps his own clubs are a front for all this sort of thing. Then there's another piece of the puzzle to figure out. That face in the picture I took of you, you know, the one in the background shot. Well if I'm not mistaken it looks just like the man who was having dinner with the Nagle brothers the other night. Georgina called him Fenton Gesler. He's their accountant or supposed to be. Money launderer, more like. He's also the one who is buying out of Colombia. Can you remember who else was there that morning John'.

John put down two cups of coffee and scratched his head 'Well let me see, there was Jack, and Sidney Arthur. I remember them standing waving the others off from the gangway. I was up the mast and you came along with your camera, yes there were four of them. Now if that was the so called Fenton Gesler, what would he and an anonymous friend be doing on the boat of someone who you say is offering supplies of coke to a night club hostess and wants to set herself up as a dealer. 'Arranging transportation!' If Gesler is buying from Colombia the Cartel would probably ship it across to Europe. Then someone would have to bring it over to the UK. It would probably be too much for one person to bring in which means it would have to come by lorry through the channel ports, light aircraft to a small airport or by sea...on a yacht...or fast power boat'...'Like Jacks' they sang out

192

together.

'Two questions' said John. 'One, what was Sidney doing there? One boat should have been sufficient, and two, if Gesler is part of the Bayswater lot, what's he doing selling stuff to Jack? I can see why you wanted to have a look at Jacks boat now Jen. If only it could speak. What's the most likely port of arrival? Rotterdam or Amsterdam I suppose. No distance from here'

'What's your point?'

'Just that I was saying to Jock when we were working that hardly any of the boats go out to sea except to charge up their batteries and he said except the Greyhounds, going on to say the coastguard helicopter reported seeing two grey boats, Sid and Jack's by all accounts, smashing through a force seven gale at some great rate of knots in the North Sea. It seems they were on sea trials. Well perhaps they were, but they were north off the Dutch coast, and who is to say they didn't call in and collect a few parcels on the way. Perhaps I'm putting two and two together and making five, but it certainly makes your 'pieces' fit together. Mind you Jen I still find it a bit unbelievable that two of our officers from the MMYC could be involved in smuggling. I mean I know them both quite well. We've had a few drinks in the bar sometimes. They're not loud or flashy either of them. True Sid's knocking off his secretary and Jack's divorced, but who isn't these days. They just don't look the type to get involved is that sort of caper'

Jenny laughed 'You're old fashioned sometimes John. What the heck does a drug smuggler look like anyway?. I know football hooligans nearly always have shaven heads and bank robbers wear facemasks. Should they perhaps wear an eye patch and have a parrot on their shoulder. It's all in the mind'

'Or in some off shore bank account'

'You're catching on now. But don't forget, desperation can drive a normally decent bloke to crime, the motive is usually a shortage of cash. It's impossible to know what's going on in their lives. It could be just Sid or Jack, or any of the rich yacht owners on these pontoons. I mean you're here all the time amongst this wealth, but you don't know where it comes from. For all you know those gin palaces over there could have been paid for by some ill-gotten gains. Some of the most successful businessmen have got there by cheating. Honesty doesn't often yield high profits'

'You are quite cynical you know Jenny. I never realized that'

'It comes from journalism. I meet so many dodgy people, but they do make good copy. Clean living people don't inspire great headlines I'm afraid'

'So what about this situation, will it make good copy?'

'Yes it will if I can work out how to handle it. It's no problem when I'm working at arms length but this is a bit close to home if you see what I mean and that goes for both of us, you probably more so than me. Listen Georgina said she missed out on the last shipment with Jack, but the next one was in the pipeline. So obviously more action is imminent and from what we've learnt so far it could very well involve these two boats here especially as you say they have both been up to SA Marine to be worked on recently. That could mean a multitude of things. We'll just have to keep an eye open for any further activity. I'll have to sound out Georgina again. She thinks I'm interested in handling some stuff myself. I'll work on that as much as I dare without raising too much suspicion. I must say I didn't think the underworld was going to stretch out to this little backwater. You just never know what's going on, do you?'

'I hardly dare think what this would do to Rodney if it turns out to be true'

'What made you think of him?'

'Oh it's just he's worked so hard to build up this high class image of the MMYC so it can be considered as a contender for a new London marina and then of course there's the bloody Greyhounds, the Red Arrows of the English Channel.

194

Christ he'll never recover from the disgrace if it goes public'
'Yes' Jenny sighed. 'It's awful isn't it to build something up and find the foundations rot away and the whole thing falls about you'
'Still we're only discussing possibilities at the moment. Nobody's blown it yet. It's pure conjecture on our part'
'Yes, but based on known facts it's beginning to look a bit suspect'
'But not enough for you to publish yet. Can't name names Jen surely. God you've got to watch your step here. You're getting onto very dangerous ground. Even if you're sure of the facts, remember if you blow the gaff on something like a drug ring they'd probably come looking for you and it won't be with a party invitation' He held up his hands. 'OK Ok I'm not teaching you to suck eggs. I just hope you know what you're doing. I expect I've been watching too much television or something'
'Thanks for your concern John, but I'll be fine, really, I can always write under a different name as I've said, or just be the crime desk reporter. As for hurting people who are innocent bystanders like Rodney for instance, I hate doing it, but truth has to come out. It's got to and anyway what about all those lives ruined by drugs. We spoke about the addicts who rob, or murder to satisfy their craving. Other peoples lives are affected everywhere. I keep saying it, but it's true, isn't it?'
'I know facts are facts, but Sid and Jack are not just two names given in evidence as I've just said they're supposedly respectable members of this club. If you really have to expose them, I'd rather not be involved. It doesn't mean I won't help you but I don't want them to think I've been spying on them from here. Call me sensitive if you like, but it's the way I feel'
'Your sensitivity does you credit John. I'll accept whatever help you can give me and I promise to keep your name out of it because this could go national'

Sid's share of the first school run had not made him happy at all. True he'd paid off the debts, which had plagued both SA Marine and his private life. Janet was dressed in more outfits than her wardrobe could contain. She was happy with her new car and queening it with all her friends. Whilst a contented Janet with a full diary meant less inclination to question time spent with Tina, with little activity at the boathouse it was only a question of time before somebody would start to wonder where all the money was coming from. 'She hasn't said anything yet' he said to his mistress while shaving after a night spent on the boat. 'But after months of me saying watch your credit cards and now all this ready cash she must be thinking it's strange'. He turned his frothy face towards Tina. 'You know I'm not sure I wouldn't be happier working my parts off all day trying to keep pace with deadlines on production and chasing all the slow payers than this. Daft isn't it. I should love doing nothing, I've dreamt about it enough. But I don't. I hate standing around waiting for something to happen. Like now. It's the calm before the storm. God knows what's going to happen when we get our marching orders. What will be waiting for us in Amsterdam? I should have stuck to my guns and got out last time'

'Oh give over Sid do...Here hook my bra up will you. You're an old misery, you really are! The first trip went OK didn't it? No reason this one won't go the same way. All the loose ends are tied up. This one will be fine too. Once we're back home again we can be off, go and play in the sun somewhere. We could even start another business, just to keep you out of mischief.'

'Sooner the better as far as I'm concerned. I keep thinking Janet's going to turn up on the pontoon, worse still the police. I just wish we could cast off our lines right now, slip away to where nobody knows us'

'You'll feel better when Jack and Mario arrive. They'll be down here soon. We're on standby remember. Company that's what you want. We're all in the same boat figuratively speaking'

'It's alright for Jack' he replied listlessly washing the last bit of foam from his cheeks. 'He knows where he's going, that's why he's prepared to take the risks. All he talks about these days is his flaming casino. This run is just a means to an end'

'He asked us to go in with him remember? It's a huge project'

'Not my scene love at all, bright lights and tinsel. He's already in that world. Suppose I still think like a plumber. I must have a ball cock for a brain. Sorry Gal. What about you. Fancy the bright lights then?'

"No thank you, Blackpool's not my scene either. We'll just grow bananas or rather watch our workers grow them for us. Or if you prefer we could grow coca leaves on our little island and smuggle them out with the bananas'

'No thanks sweetheart, after this run I don't want to hear another word about cocaine or smuggling of any kind. I just think I'll have a little island stacked with tanks and ballcocks I can repair whenever I feel the need' They both laughed.

'You're nervous though, aren't you Sid. I always know when you make a joke of things that something's not quite right   Is it the thought of the run, or is it the decision about you and me that's going to have to be made.... at long last. You see it's always been you couldn't leave Janet and the kids because the double life was too expensive. Now we have no problems with money. There's enough to provide very nicely for your family and start up a new life somewhere with me. So what's wrong eh'

'Well it's a bit like going to the dentist, I'll be better once I'm actually in the chair, but as far as leaving Janet is concerned you're forgetting one thing'

'What's that?'

197

'Well you're assuming it's all very amicable and when I tell her I'm leaving her and going off with you, she'll accept it, just as though it's one of those things. Shake hands, take her allowance and off we go our separate ways. Well, say she turns nasty and wants half of everything and gets solicitors to look into all my assets. They just might uncover a few Fenton style surprises, and then I'm in the shit deep and nasty. That's the worry. I've got a lot to hide at the moment and my guess is she's already wondering what I'm up to, flushed with bank notes as I am. She's not the sort of person who would go looking for trouble, like use a private eye or anything of that sort. But I mustn't underestimate her. She could do a lot of damage the way things are.'

'OK well it's not as though you've led a blameless live in the past is it. She's known what you're like especially when you were a call out plumber I'm sure'

'I think she just accepted it. I always came home, sometime or another'

'Don't be too sure Sidney, silence is not always indicative of ignorance'

'Anyway I'm just a little apprehensive that's all luv, nothing for you to worry your pretty head about. Just bear with me for now and if you should speak with Jan on the phone don't forget to say we're very busy, out looking for new business. That's the line I'm taking, Entertaining prospective contract customers on the boat some evenings and weekends still. Then next week I'll announce we've landed a big contract, that'll keep her quiet for a bit longer anyway. OK?' After breakfast they studied the new memo received from Rodney Blake setting out the programme for the Greyhounds attendance at the Festival of the Sea event in Grimsby. Five days of exhibitions, demonstrations, visits of tall ships and RN Warships offshore with chandler's on the harbour side and boat sales. Milehaven's grey boat team would go through its paces each day, giving the usual polished performances they were becoming renowned for.

'At least we don't have to do the constant practices these days' commented Sid slurping the last remains of his coffee. 'We've gone through the routine so many times now it's almost second nature.'

'How long will the Greyhounds go on for?'

'Years probably, or as much as the people want them. It's certainly done wonders for old Rodney's image. He loves it. Mind you I think we've all enjoyed it. Beats cruising round aimlessly like the rest of the Milehaven members do, that's if they bother to go out at all. A lot of the boats down here are just weekend houseboats now, no more than that'

Tina nudged him 'Well we can't talk, we use this boat more as a floating flat for our little love nest. If you logged our actual sea time it wouldn't be very high would it? I bet that old wooden tub; Tradewind goes out more often than we do. I wouldn't take that as far as the sea lock let alone out to sea, not on one single engine. If that packs up you're sunk aren't you'

'No it's a motor sailor. You just put up the sail if anything should go wrong'

'I bet that sail hasn't been up for years. Anyway those motor sailors are useless, if your engine failed a little sail like that would never get you anywhere. Boats too heavy'

'And he'd probably argue that it was part of the sea and therefore safer than this skimming dish of ours'

'Anyway who's side are you on, switch the computer on so we can check the email'.

Sid's face flushed...'It's here Tina, the green light for the run. I had a feeling it might be today. He pressed the key for print and the little printer whirred into action

From Karen: Subject School Run: Class arrive 22/9 ETA 14.00 hrs Children to be collected. Pick up as before. Back of station see yellow bus. Love to Joyce and Katie

'That's it. Funnily enough I'm beginning to feel better now

199

it's come. At least we know what we're doing' In the same instant his mobile rang. 'Oh Hi Jack. Yes I have it in my hand as we speak. I was just going to ring you. Are you coming down here tonight? Good, yes OK we'll talk later. See you then'

Late that afternoon the phone rang in Jenny's flat and the answer phone cut in to receive the message.
'Hello, Jen it's me... John. Just to let you know that both our grey boats have crews on board. Two arrived about an hour ago. Two have been on board overnight. They're at the refuelling dock at present. It's 4 o'clock now. All the grey boats are due to go off to the Festival up the East Coast tomorrow. So I don't know if it's just that or something else is brewing. Let me know if you get anything out of Georgie. Speak soon'

On the pretext of taking Bosun for a walk. John saw Jack and Mario board Plumb Crazy around dinnertime. Seated around the saloon table below, their up beat company and conversation, and a few large measures of scotch soon lifted Sidney from within his veil of gloom to something more like his old self. A large crew size chilli con carne helped stoke the stomachs against the waves of whisky. By mid evening the atmosphere was 'gung ho' with Sidney convulsed with laughter at the thought of Jack being Joyce and himself known as Katie. 'You don't look a Joyce Jack, I would have said more like a Brenda and as for Justin Rosenstein being a Joan well that's just plain daft', hysterical giggles, he just has to be Ruth in my book' After strong black coffee's all round, enough sobriety was regained for some discussion as to timing and routes for the next day. It was agreed both boats would have to take their places with the greyhound team in

Grimsby but at the end of the festivities when the five left to return to Milehaven they would peel off due east towards the island of Texel, at the approaches to Amsterdam ready for the pick up on the 22nd. 'It's a piece of cake' said Jack tapping the monitor screen which displayed their track across the North Sea at that latitude. 'It's only a short hop over, shouldn't take more than a couple of hours'

'That's the easy bit' cut in Sid 'The difficult bit is what excuse to give for scooting off on our own'

'No problem' mused Jack 'You know how Rodney is dead set in us all keeping up the same high cruising speed when we're together, well I can drop back with say a problem in one of the engines, then you can stay back to cover me. Now as soon as they've pulled ahead we can change course, then later on report to old Rodney that we're doing so for emergency repairs'

'And what's the nature of our emergency' enquired the slightly slurred voice of Sidney'

'Dirt in the starboard fuel line I think. It's the most believable fault. I've had it a few times over the years. Nothing serious, easily fixed. It'll do nicely you'll see'

A mixture of adrenalin enhanced by alcohol dispelled any lingering misgivings between the two crew members. They felt only the tense exhilaration known to servicemen prior to battle. Rodney however had to be content with the command of his little fleet of display boats. He busied himself that evening preparing himself for the trip with email instructions from his flagship.

All Grey boats will secure for sea. Clearing sea lock at 07.30 Friday proceeding on course 355 degrees magnetic in vee formation. On clearing Maplin Sands Follow Waypoints set as briefing. Orders on VHF Channel 6. Open on 16 ends.
Milehaven MMYC Commodore

Rodney read it through and was pleased. They were a presentable force, his grey boats, unarmed of course but in

some ways comparable to his old navy MTB's. They should give a good account of themselves in Grimsby he was sure, and bring further distinction to Milehaven, which someday might even become the London Marina. He saw a blue plaque over the building with the words....
'Opened in the new Millennium
By its founder 'Sir Rodney Blake RN Rtd. DSO & Bar'
He would have to give careful thought to his inaugural speech at that grand opening. Still plenty of time. Can't rush these things.

Across the North Atlantic close to the Equator it was hot and very humid, causing perspiration to gather in beads along the forehead of Charlie Nagle. It ran down his bull neck to where a heavy gold medallion gleamed a message of affluence to those who faced him across the table. They were three of the cartel, one black, two off-white, all of large frame and hard of eye. This wrong footed the joint leader of the Bayswater Boys who on his first visit to what he thought of as the Colombian hillbillies expected some respect if not deference. In the event they well out stared him, forcing his eyes down to his pigskin brief case. Until the black voice broke the ice, whilst the off whites shuffled papers 'Thank you for coming over' he began in perfect Oxford English. 'Hitherto we have always dealt with your Mr. Gesler who by chance studied accountancy and finance at the same UK university as myself. From which you may gather that I act as key figure in costings and sales and these two gentlemen' he extended his arms to either side 'Have responsibilities for the actual production and transportation of our products' Charlie had as yet said nothing, just looked as mean and hard as he could manage, but kicked in with 'Yeah well that's OK but we can't leave it all to other people all the time, that's when things get slack.

So I've come out here to tighten one or two things up, know what I mean. It's gone well so far. Mr. Gesler has been looking after our books and that, for years since we were into gamblin' and call girls yer know. So when the drug scene took over in Liverpool we wanted in, but had no contacts. Well Fenton said he knew you and he'd set the deal up for us and that's the way it's been since then. We've had a very suitable arrangement up to now' Charlie spread his huge hands palms upwards on the table 'But he is taking his cut on every shipment innee and 'wif all the deals we're clocking up we reckon things could be sharper, know what I mean. It's right innit'

The white teeth flashed in the ebony setting 'Oh yes that's true, things are always sharper with smaller lines of communication. I imagine you're thinking of the cartel dealing direct with yourselves, with the prices agreed with Fenton'

'That's about the size of it yeah. You'll be dealing with me from now on which leaves Fenton to be concentrating on'...

'Cooking the books? suggested the brilliant teeth laughing loudly. 'Sounds a practical suggestion to me'. A waiter entered bearing a tray with tall glasses containing a liquid looking vaguely like Pimms.

'It's the local punch, we call it Sugar Ray, very strong. I am sorry I haven't introduced myself. I'm Sunato.' He pointed to each side of him 'Juan and Manuel and you of course will be Charles Nagle'

'Charlie', corrected the Prince of Bayswater 'That'll do' He took a long pull at the punch which at first tasted cool in its crushed ice, laced with exotic fruits. But after a second exploded like a live volcano in his throat extracting all oxygen leaving him gasping like a stranded fish.

'You like it' laughed Sunato. 'Kills off black water fever bugs and most other things as well' Charlie made to answer but managed just a rasp, nodding his head in affirmation.

'I see' continued the cartel spokesman 'That your account is paid up to date for which we thank you. But we can if you like change the current orders over to your Bayswater company direct'

'Yeah do that will you, but there's only one order not two'

'I don't think so, I'll check with Manuel, but I think it's two' Black and off-white heads inclined together over the shipping manifest for the next shipment out of Caracas. 'Yes there's one seventy five kilo consignment booked to Mr. Gesler for your company and two forty five kilo lots to Mr. Gesler again, that's his Atrium Associates batch' explained Manuel looking slightly puzzled. 'He required the shipments to be kept separate, but of course they are all on the same boat going over to Amsterdam as usual'.

'So Atrium is nothing to do with you then Charlie?' prompted Sunato.

'No but it appears to have quite a lot to do with Mr. Gesler'

'Sorry I'm not with you'

'It's Fenton Gesler who'll be sorry he's not with me' growled the Bayswater boss

'While you are our guest' beamed the black smile ignoring the threat 'I have arranged for Juan to take you to our little factory unit out in the jungle. This is where we process the coca leaves into cocaine hydrochloride powder. I think it would help you to understand the way we work'

'All I need to understand' exclaimed Charlie, eyes fixed on the fan whirring above their heads. 'Is how to ensure we get the best deal on the stuff we're buying in. I don't give a monkey's how you make it; you're the experts that's down to you. As long as it's good quality when we cut it up and dish it out to our dealers we'll be back for more, you can count on that. But from now on we ain't dealing through no one else. OK Sunato? You and me can fix the deal here and now and you can deliver as usual for us to pick up in Amsterdam'

The Cartel King looked confused. 'So everything is dropped

off at the docks and your man will take it on to London?'

'That's it stuffed in frozen turkeys as before, and loaded onto refrigerated lorries'

'And what about the Atrium consignment?'

'Drop that off as well, as per your instructions. I guess this isn't his first'

'No, Fenton dealt with the last lot his end'

'I bet he did. Leave this to us we'll sort Mr. Fenton Gesler out'

The white teeth flashed briefly, 'So you won't have time to fly out to see our little set-up then'

'No thanks, I just wanted to come over here and see what was what, here in the office, meet you face to face so to speak. I'm so glad I did. Seems like our Mr. Gesler has been looking after himself, setting up in competition by the looks of it. The low life. Been undercutting us no doubt. He's been a naughty boy, but believe me he'll soon realize he should have stuck to looking after the books.'

Detective Inspector Crossland didn't look the part. He was slight in build and slow in gait, the sort of person who might talk mowers and compost to fellow travellers on the eight thirty into Waterloo but he was sharp and knew how to use a gun if need be. The National Crime Squad were at the cutting edge of crime prevention, a million miles from speeding fines or receiving stolen goods. Their workplace was deep within the underworld of strip clubs and seedy bars, disco dives, dark alleyways and public lavatories. Drama in their days and nights was of short duration, frightening but fast. Most days would be long, cold and wet, watching, waiting on surveillance on the streets, or mixing with their targets in loud and smoky basements. They would often drink with those other hunters of the night the crime feature newshounds each

205

trying to get intelligence and information for different reasons, but with grudging respect for each other. The drug scene was of prime importance and involved inter action between many agencies, but although Crossland considered his men to be the key coordinators he would always keep an ear to the ground. Monday morning the CID's briefing room resembled a school room, blackboard, slide projector, wall maps and the noise of the fourth form on a bad day.

'OK everyone' he shouted 'Let's have a bit of hush, please! Shut up you lot. Thank you that's better couldn't hear myself think...Now, I've received a communication this morning from one of my contacts in the newspaper world. It's connected with the drug case we have in hand. This contact suspects, but can't prove at the moment that Class 'A' drugs are getting into a point on the Thames estuary out at Milehaven, possibly around the yacht club area. It is suspected that millions of pounds worth of cocaine is being smuggled in under cover of the club's blue ensign flag for which it is highly respected. Now if the press were to release some sort of story at this stage of the game it would compromise our investigations completely, forcing us to spring our trap and go in at half cock leaving us with zilch'.

'Does this mean that 'Operation Downstream' is dead in the water Gov?' said a burly constable.

'No it bloody well doesn't. It means I must get in touch immediately with my contact. Nothing must leak out to the papers until after the suspect boats make their next run across the North Sea. Remember at this point we just wait and watch. We need to know the distribution point before we move in and when we do we must have the benefit of surprise. We need them red handed to give CPS a watertight case. We track them all the way to their safe house. Any questions?'

'Just one Gov' came the educated voice of young DC Hamilton. 'This Milehaven entry point is a different one than usual, doesn't sound like the Bayswater Boys, they usually go for the channel ports. Could this be a new group on the Nagles patch?'

'Possibly Hamilton, could be a bit of double dealing, little fish getting greedy. But we do know it implicates our accountant friend, Fenton Gesler a bit more. Looks like we have the two sides of the coin and his head is on both. If we could only get the Nagle Brothers and this Milehaven lot in one swoop, but it won't be easy. As for the press people I'll thank them for the information supplied and ask them to hang fire until we pounce. Then they can have all the front page stuff they want. We owe a lot to an under cover crime reporter who came up with all this information and we'll make damn sure we put it to good effect. Don't forget this case is combined ops' Dutch Interpol, Customs and ourselves. I'll get hold of the Customs and let them know our movements. We already have an unmarked car in the area on standby. So Operation Downstream is set and ready people, all we need is the green light!'

Apart from Cowes week the Festival of the Sea was probably the most important event in any boat owner's diary, celebrating both history and high tech in the preservation of life at sea. To be taking part this year was something Rodney Blake was justly proud, having worked so hard to promote Milehaven and his Greyhound display team. This was the national event that would take Milehaven finally to the forefront of British boating and yacht centres, a worthy contender for the title of new small ship port of London - The London Marina. Grimsby was also proud to be this year's venue, a first for the East Coast and its fishing fleet. On days proceeding the event a virtual armada of little vessels converged on the little harbour from all over the country. Everything from Cornish fishing smacks, vintage ocean-going racing yachts, offshore lifeboats, to the latest luxury cruisers. Along Milehaven's pontoons the atmosphere was a cross between a village fete and the start of a world war, on departure day. Little groups of people stood watching whilst others moved purposefully between bollards with mooring lines in hand shouting to each other above the growling splutter of a group of diesels whose combined exhaust output filled the air with choking fumes, the greyhounds were on the move. The half tide level of water meant queuing to move out through the sea lock two by two, with other boats going also up to Grimsby waiting their turn, still tied up with engines ticking over. Outside on the Thames the first greyhounds clear hovered waiting until all five were through to form up and head off downstream in line astern of their leader Grey Lady.

'It's good to be off' said Tina hands on the small car-like steering wheel. All that hanging about was getting me down. It's good to have something to occupy us now'

'It's a piece of cake in this formation' replied Sid. 'All you've got to do is follow Rodney's stern and maintain a two boat length distance. He does all the navigation from now on'

The sea off the estuary was a flat grey, combined with the featureless sky and distant mud banks formed a visual vacuum in which only the darker grey of the boats and their white wakes were real. The drone of the five identical engines combined to make sounds that reverberated throughout everything, and after some thirty minutes running its hypnotic effect could make eyelids heavy and concentration begin to wane. It was almost a relief when atmospherics blasted forth from the VHF speakers followed by the metallic voice of Rodney announcing. 'Break from line astern and form the vee formation. Increase speed to thirty knots. Come on to course 030 but take stations from me...Out'

'This is where it could get a bit tricky' shouted Sid 'You OK with it sweetheart? Swing out to port, that's it now increase your speed'. Within 15 seconds the boats had taken up their vee arrowhead formation, bows rising up out of the water as their speeds increased to the instructed thirty knots.

'We'll be changing course in a few minutes or so as we follow round the Wash' explained Sid. 'At least we've got a reasonably calm day. Ever been to Grimsby before?' Tina smiled, 'No I haven't. Been to Cromer though and Sheringham, pretty places. We had some holidays there when I was a kid. Plenty of crabs and a lifeboat if I remember'

'Cromer my love is almost dead level with Texel our turning point for Amsterdam, so you'll be remembering it for more than a crab sandwich in years to come I hope'

'More likely to remember it for grey seas and sky just like today. Not like where we'll be going eh Sid. Blue sky, white beaches, hot sunshine, little bays set into the cliffs and mountains in the background. Our villa will have a beautiful stone terrace with panoramic views for miles. We can't get there by boat can we?'

'Not with this one we can't. Too far even for these engines, this is offshore not trans global. No we'll flog this, fly away and buy something more suitable once we're out there, wherever we end up. Nothing too flash, something wide and comfortable to take us island hopping till we find the one that has our villa on it. Then who knows we might even buy the island!'

The formation of grey boats roared off northwards around the bulge of the East Coast, round the Wash, passing as it did a strung out assortment of small craft making their way towards the great forgathering. Sid turned up the VHF to catch their leader making his transit report to East Coast Radio and then the harbour to confirm berthing arrangements for the boats.

'We'll be standing off' repeated Sid. 'Going to a buoy, there's too much visiting traffic for us to go alongside. Still we can go ashore for a meal if you like, mind you what restaurants there are will probably be packed out so it might be better to stay aboard with Jack and Mario then we can have a council

of war. You can rustle us up something can't you luv?'
Tina nodded 'I expect so Sidney.'

The four days that followed were the culmination of Rodney's
dream, a reality in which he could relive his former command
in the RN Coastal Forces. The Greyhounds moved as one
discipline displaying breathtaking twists and turns like a shoal
of fish darting to change directions. The people on the shore
cheered and clapped as the commentator boomed out
descriptions of their every move. Local press coverage did
Rodney proud, and his face, now sporting a standard sea-dog
beard, grinned out from front pages and local yachting
magazines. Word was that Commander Rodney Blake of
Milehaven Motor Yacht Club was to be congratulated indeed
on his excellent display team with the hope that they would be
seeing a lot more of the Milehaven Greyhounds.
'I'm afraid' said Jack throwing the local rag down on the table
and lifting a gin and tonic 'There'll be no holding him now.
God help us when we get back. Still it went alright didn't it,
although I'm still not sure how we avoided hitting one another
a couple of times'?
'More by luck than judgment' commented Sid 'Only don't
tell Rodney, leave him with his illusions, poor old sod. Thank
God the fun and games are over and it's off to work
tomorrow'
'We'll be fine' said Jack. 'Worse bit will be breaking away
from the others. I was thinking when I drop back with my so-
called problem I hope to God he doesn't reduce speed and say
he'll stay with me. We're fucked then aren't we?'
'Thing to do is drop a long way back before you signal him.
I'll be nearest to you to come to the rescue, the others won't
turn about then'
'There is a problem though, don't forget, having just left
Grimsby we shall all be line astern behind Grey Lady and we
are the first two boats so if we slow down the others will be

up our backsides'

'I hadn't thought of that, well you'll have to peel off clear of the column saying you'll tag along behind so as not to hold things up, then I'll peel off saying I'll bring up the rear to cover you We'll just have to hope for the best'.

'If there's any problem' said Mario smoking a vile smelling cigar 'Then you'll have to stop dead. That should do it; he won't want all the greyhounds to stop dead in the water. He'll be eager to get back to tell everyone about the trip so he won't want to hang about for too long anyway'

'He's right' wheezed Sid fanning the foul smoke towards the open window. 'Let's not worry about it now. Time to relax while we can'

.

Chaos reigned on a fine clear morning, as it seemed every vessel in the vicinity including the five greyhounds tried to access the refuelling dock before departing for their home ports. Congestion was such and with little room for manoeuvre the grey boats ended up in the wrong order line astern clearing the harbour entrance for the open sea with Jack and Sidney at the end of the line.

'God all that fuss last night' said Tina 'and it's sorted itself out already. Here we are tail end Charlies after all'

'It's like a football crowd leaving the stadium after the match this morning' moaned Sid. 'Watch out for that old sailing barge, looks as though he's coming straight across us,... idiot!'

The five grey boats moved slowly in single file behind their leader, their entourage of other vessels dissipating until only a scattering of little ships remained. The VHF came into life again spluttering and crackling. Sid tuned it in. 'Oh here we go again, His Masters Voice. OK, OK, I heard you the first time, increase to thirty knots, yeah yeah. Keep the channel open Tina we should hear Jack calling up Rodney soon. As soon as we get up to thirty knots he'll call and say he's in trouble then we'll cut in like the nice people we are, and say we'll drop back to give him cover. With the high jerk beneath the decks the turbo boosts cut in and they were soon spewing out mountains of white foam again at the squared off stern. They were well out now with the profile of the East Coast getting lower on the horizon. 'Come on Jack where the hell are you on this blasted radio, dammit we shall have to peel of pretty soon.' He looked back over his shoulder towards Jacks boat. 'What's he doing ...hold on I think his bow wake is smaller, yes thank God, he's dropping back' Jack's voice could be heard through the crackles of the VHF. 'Greyhound Two to Leader, I'm losing power on starboard engine. Cannot maintain speed. Will have to proceed independently. Over' Sidney quickly unhooked the mike and pressed the send button 'Greyhound Three calling Leader. Will stand by Two in case of any problems and give assistance ...over' Rodney replied immediately. 'Message understood. Hope you can maintain twelve knots. Will advise Coastguard of your later ETA. Good luck. Over and out'

'Yes, yes, yes' yelled Sidney. 'He's fallen for it. OK sweetheart we have to reduce our speed now and bring her around to make contact with Jack'

Within minutes the two boats were within loud hailing distance from each other wallowing in the long swells, engines just ticking over.

'That seemed to go off alright' shouted Jack 'But knowing Rodney he'll be tracking us on radar until we're out of range'

'Yeah' said Sid, 'but it's logical we might make for the nearest port for a swift repair job'

'OK then Sid I'll lead off towards Texel. If you want to talk, use your mobile phone when we get nearer the coast. Anything on the VHF may be picked up'. With a wave of hands Greyhounds two and three swung round to the north east. It was late afternoon and raining in the centre of

Amsterdam as the two boats glided slowly up against the outgoing stream with just a ripple from the bow wave. 'There's the Central Station again' pointed Tina. 'And the piers and there's the jetties just beyond'

'Cut your speed right down now to just steerage way so I can see where we tied up last time. We don't want to overshoot. I think I recognize that corner building over there. Keep to the right 'till I spot something familiar.' They were silent for sometime in concentration over the uneven gurgling of the boats exhaust and spurts of engine cooling system water.

Then Tina shouted 'There it is, the little yellow tanker! See it, parked up on that jetty, the one with all those tyres along side it'

'Good he's nice and early. It's a relief to see him' commented Sid. 'We've just got to swing across there now. Hold on a minute we'd better let this coaster go by. It's a bit big for us to argue with' In ten minutes both boats were tied up alongside the pontoon safely. 'Sorry about that Jack' shouted Sid

'I didn't see that coaster coming until it was right up on top of us. I had no means of warning you. It was one of those times when you wish boats had brake lights and turning indicators' They both laughed. There was no driver inside the little tanker. The two crews took a walk along the embankment mainly to stretch their legs. 'I think this is Westerdoksdijk' said Jack with some authority 'and if I'm correct we should find a Gezellia somewhere along here'

'What was that' said Tina'

'It's a Brown cafe to you' replied Jack. 'A traditional eating cafe round these parts, all dark and cosy, we missed it last time. We should be able to get a nice Dutch gin made out of molasses'

'Oh so you do know your way round here then', laughed Tina 'Anyone would think you were a native'

'No silly, it's just the tourist guide that's in our wheelhouse. I was flicking through it the other night and came across this place'

'We mustn't forget to reset our clock to local time' reminded Sid. 'The way I've worked it out we are about five hours late for our rendezvous with the tanker. So I guess our driver has gone down town for the evening. I would suggest after we've had our refreshments we get an early night in, cos' it's a long way back home tomorrow'.

If the two crews had looked about them a bit more they would have noticed the black BMW with British number plates parked behind a few other empty vehicles opposite the yellow tanker. Resting on its front console was a notebook and an SRL camera fitted with a telescopic lens.

'By the looks of that lot there's not going to be too much action tonight' remarked the front seat passenger. 'God my legs ache. You could get deep vein thrombosis doing this job. We've been sitting here for hours, not to mention the pins and needles in my buttocks'

'Shut it Kevin, you're always moaning. You should have stayed in the uniform branch. That would have kept you moving pounding the beat. Count your blessings mate. This is special duty, not traffic duty. Anyway I reckon we're safe to nip back to the hotel for a couple of hours kip and get back here early in the morning. That lot are going nowhere tonight'.

Dawn over the harbour the next morning it was brighter after the clearance of overnight rain, but still with little sign of life to take advantage of the change, other than a rusty old coaster on its way out to sea and two squat tugs en route westwards to the docks. DC Ryan and his mate in the BMW could see very little due to misting up of the windows. 'Buck up and finish that breakfast will you Kevin. This car stinks of burgers'

'But I can't stomach just rolls for me breakie, still a growing

214

lad you know'

Their long vigil was rewarded at precisely 9.45am when a man in bright green overalls with the words Sanitation Services plastered across the back approached the two tied up grey boats.

'Here Kev. Something's happening over there' Side window down and camera poised DC Kevin Taylor was able to zoom in with fully automatic action to record in close up, the faces of Jack, Sidney, Mario and Tina. Lying across the decks was the large rubber hose pulsating ninety kilo's of pure cocaine into the sewage tanks of both boats. The surveillance team stayed in place until the yellow tanker had driven off and the two grey boats had slipped their mooring lines and moved out into stream to find the refuelling barge. 'Bon Voyage my lovelies' said Ryan with a little wave of his hand. 'You've given us all we need I think, now all we've got to do is get this lot processed and we're home and dry'

'I hope the first lot in the main docks come out OK. It was a bit dark over there, pity we couldn't use flash. Most of the faces should be identifiable though, that's what really counts. Frankly I think the Gov'nor was asking a bit much for us to cover both the shipments coming in'

'We wouldn't be here if it wasn't for that reporter Jenny Sutcliffe from Syndicopy' Kevin pointed out. 'God knows how she ferreted this lot out. Who'd have thought that toffee nosed lot down at the Milehaven boat club would be mixed up in this sort thing. You wouldn't think it of them would you, but you can never tell these days. There'll be a few red faces when this lot hits the fan, mark my words'.

'How do you think she got in the know of what was happening down there?'

'Apparently she was down at Milehaven covering a story on some old bloke about to go single handed around the world, and when some shot she'd taken at the time was processed it showed up some folk in the background getting off one of the grey boats. She recognized one of them as Fenton Gesler, our suspect working with the Nagle Brothers. We've suspected his involvement with drugs for some time now. By all accounts he's got greedy and is double-dealing. Tempting I suppose when you've already got the contacts. Anyway our little news girl has been doing some undercover work herself, put two and two together seeing a known drug importer visiting what seems to be an ideal smugglers boat. The boat in question has just gone out. It belongs to a Mr. Jack Delaney, nightclub owner, no criminal record as yet but his clubs are well known for associated drug dealing and prostitution. Never proved. Not yet anyway. Delaney's got big ideas, recruited by Gesler no doubt!'

'Another greedy bastard, What about the second grey boat?' Any form?'

'No he's clean. Heavily into debt though. Some of it to Delaney I expect. Probably thought it would be easy money and a bit of excitement. Think of all those rich pigs down at Milehaven, most of them bored out of their skulls. Fed up with cruising around, pouring vast quantities of gin and tonics down their throats and shagging someone on the side. Believe me Kevin you don't want to know how the other lives, you're better off being a policeman just like me, gives you a sense of purpose'.

'I think I'd rather have the money'

DC Taylor, you're hopeless, quite hopeless. You'd better get out and stretch your deep vein legs before we head off for the ferry'

The Dutch coastline was now a smudge on the horizon. 'Next stop Milehaven Skipper, turning now to come on to course one seven nine degrees magnetic, speed fifteen knots'

'Thanks Tina, you're getting expert at this. Increase to thirty knots when you're ready. I'll just check with Jack on the

VHF'

'Jack we're clear now, sea states reasonable, going to increase to thirty knots. OK with you? Have you heard anything from old Rodney? I'd forgotten about him in the excitement'

'Yeah I called him up on the RT just now, he's at home now. I told him we had to divert to Amsterdam overnight as I'd virtually lost all power on one engine. I told him it turned out to be dirt in the fuel line and an engineer cleared it this morning and we are now on our way back'

'Sounds good to me Jack...over and out'

He put his mouth to Tina's ear against the roar of the engines. 'I'll take over now luv. You can check the waypoints on the console in a moment 'Have we got any thing to drink with us?'

'Nothing in the flask I'm afraid and we're leaping about too much to put the kettle on. All I can suggest is pre-mixed gin and tonic and a shared chocolate bar. Bit unconventional for elevenses'.

'That'll do nicely, I think we deserve a proper drink don't you'

So they supped their G & T's straight out of the airline type mixer bottles, holding on tightly to the grab rail whenever a wave became too heavy. They skimmed from wave top to wave top, sometimes almost completely clear of the surface, twin propellers screaming for seconds clear of all resistance before plunging once more to exert their bite into the grey green substance of the sea. The routine observed at sea was usually one at the helm maintaining course and speed and the other at the navigation table checking the display screens. There was much to do in constant checking the echo sounder for depth, engine instruments for temperatures and oil working pressures. The radar screen on a larger vessel would be constantly checked by its operator but by Sid only when and where he thought fit. Quite by accident Sid noticed a blip up on the screen 'It's up on the outer ring' he shouted 'Could only have been there a short time. It's not been that long since I last checked it. Any visual check Tina?'

'No but the cloud base is quite low now'

'It's gaining on us' shouted Sid again, now bent over the green glow of the screen where the sweeping arm blipped at the point where it passed over the object. 'Must be doing some fifty knots to gain on us so quickly, can't be a surface vessel, must be a low flying aircraft or helicopter'

'Could be our Coastguard boys in the Sikorsky' shouted Tina back 'You know they often fly over for a chat. I bet that's it'

'No they usually come over and circle us this thing is coming up fast then hanging back as if it's shadowing us'

'That sounds rather sinister Sid'

'Yes it does, the only thing we can do is slow down a bit and wait and see if it catches up. I wonder if Jack's got his radar on. I'd better call him up and let him know what we are doing'

Sid reached for the VHF 'Use the mobile' shouted Tina' You never know who's listening in'

'You're right thanks Tina, how stupid of me'

'What did Jack say then? I couldn't hear with all this noise going on'

'He's in agreement we'll drop down speed to ten knots, just enough to give us steerage way.' The two throttles were pulled back and the bow dropped instantly as they came off the plane settling down into the water causing the boat to pitch and roll in a most uncomfortable way. 'Now let's see what they're up to'

The blip has slowed down too it's matching our speed, dammit, they're shadowing us alright, just keeping us within range on their radar. I'll go outside and see if I can hear anything while our engines are fairly quiet' He opened the wheelhouse door and stepped out into the wind and spray. 'Can't hear anything at the moment, the winds a bit noisy. Let's resume speed; this motion is making me feel pretty

218

queasy. Take her back up to thirty knots, Jack will follow alright'

The grey boats sped like the wind towards the home coast. Sid kept checking the radar screen and the blip remained with them. 'Who the hell is it? This is putting the wind up me' Sid looked back at Jacks' boat plunging up and down. Behind him the skies were clearing from the north. 'Perhaps our little friend will show up visually now the weather is improving' he said to himself. The latter part of the run off Lowestoft, Harwich and Southend was in fine weather over moderate seas resulting in a much more comfortable ride. It was easier to move around the boat now. 'Won't be long now Babe. I'll take over now, give your arms a rest' Tina moved away from the wheel 'God that's better, my shoulders are beginning to ache' She opened the wheelhouse door slightly stepping out onto the afterdeck where a mountain of water churned by the twin props roared skyward before collapsing into a patchwork of foam racing astern to merge into obscurity. Staring with tired eyes hands clasping the wet stern rail her mind was racing. Could this new life with Sid ever become reality or was it like the horizon always in sight but never any closer. So far so good with the run though. That couldn't be denied. Sid and Jack seemed to know what they were doing and left nothing to chance, but the realization that it wasn't just a game was beginning to infiltrate her brain. It was exciting, they had all felt that, but a strange blend of both fear and elation that made the pulse race, a little chill of uncertainty or perhaps it was conscience. The little voice from time to time saying what am I doing here with somebody else's husband drug running of all things. Drugs that cause so much pain and suffering to others but give us the chance of money and a new life together. What if the police were waiting for us when we get back? What if Rodney suspects something. No this is stupid. Nothing is going to go wrong, and as for the pain and suffering of other people, they have control surely to some

219

extent, don't they. Get a grip Tina, It's going to be alright. Get a lungful of that fresh sea air and get back to that wheel again. She took a deep breath and held her head high looking towards the northern sky. Low down on the horizon was a small black dot like a bird without wings. Head on, it hardly seemed to be moving. She slammed the door tight shutting out the roar of tortured water. 'There Sid on the horizon' she shouted in his ear 'Look there. I'll take over you go and have a good look'

'It's definitely a helicopter' said Sid using his binoculars. I can just about make it out. It's difficult with all this movement. It's not the Sikorsky, looks a bit smaller. It's got big floats underneath or they could be long-range fuel tanks. We're definitely being shadowed, but I wouldn't like to say by who at this stage'

'Could it be the police'?

'I'm not too sure but I think we should split up and see what happens'.

Jack responded smartly to the call saying he too had been watching the stalker astern. Action agreed the two boats split up, putting an area of sea between them.

"He's still on my tail' shouted Sid through his mobile. 'I'll keep you informed' Approaching the Thames Estuary the two closed back into line ahead. The screen and sky were clear.

'No sign of the chopper now' reported Jack. 'I'll get in touch with Jock and tell him we are heading for home'

'So there you are at last' shouted Jock catching their lines as they finally edged their way into the lock.

'Yeah made it at last' responded Jack. 'Got a bit of trouble with one of the engines. Had to drop back and put into the nearest port and get it seen to. Thank God for twin engines eh. Thanks also to old Sidney here. It was good of him to standby just in case. I expect you've already heard all this from the others'

'Aye we did, but it's nice to see you two gentlemen

back again'.

It was happy hour as the two grey boats edged their way back onto their moorings. The club bar was full of boaters sipping cocktails. Tina with lines in hand and fenders ready, gave a nervous quick look around the environment for anything unusual, but it all looked normal. No police, plain vans or dark saloons. Only the little yellow tanker was on the bank side, watching and waiting. Sanitation Services Sewage Disposal, the words standing out to welcome them in. 'He's here' she shouted to Sid 'Straight from the shuttle. Can't ask for better service can you'

'What happened to the helicopter' said Jack to Sid in the Wardroom. 'Put the wind up me I don't mind telling you'

'It slipped off the scope as fast as it came' said Sid. 'Thank God it didn't come any closer. Now let's see if we can find old Rodney. He's bound to want an explanation on what's been going on. Just remember what we rehearsed' Luckily Rodney was far too busy talking excitedly about the Grimsby event and the explanation of the breakdown and overnight stop in Amsterdam didn't have to be put to the test. Back at the boats Mario was overseeing the yellow tanker pumping out the little chain of pods ready for transportation to Jack's warehouse on the canal. The crew members watched in silence the yellow tanker backing out of the marina gates. 'Thank God' said Sidney. 'That's another stage done and dusted'

'Had he but known the significance of the old Ford Escort that followed Sanitation Services out of the main gate, he might not have been so hasty in offering up his thanks, for its base-ball capped driver was DC Taylor. 'Car one' in a series of four unmarked police vehicles now tracking the yellow tanker from Milehaven to the school runs safe house. Their coordination in this five-section relay chase was in the hands of police helicopter Whisky Tango Five. Minus long range fuel tanks and now rigged for land with skids instead of floats. The tanker driver would never see the same car following for longer than an average of twenty minutes and hopefully never become suspicious or spooked into heading the pursuers off into a wild goose chase.

'Control this is bird, target heading off south west towards London on A228. Yellow Tanker marked Sewage Disposal, car one in tow, listening out'

Some ten miles inland on the A228 a twelve seater social services bus driven by WPC Lockhart sat on a lay-by, engine running, her radio receiving. 'Bird to car two, target approaching one mile standby' She pulled out behind the Escort and adjusted her speed to maintain distance until it indicated and turned left, leaving her free to close up on the target. In the Control Room DC Crossland bit hard on his pipe then waved it at the wall map of London. 'So far so good, but I expect that worse is yet to come. If these guys in the cars happen to lose him in the traffic, bird should be able to stay in visual contact'

'Couldn't we have just left it to the chopper sir, not involving the cars' suggested a voice behind him.

The pipe flared and enveloped the speaker in acrid smoke.

'If you were driving for a couple of hours and you had a helicopter overhead for company, wouldn't you be just a tiny bit suspicious Hayter? Doing it this way, bird can stand off and not appear too obvious. We also need eyes on the ground to pinpoint house numbers, road names etc. Little details Hayter, little details'

The radio crackled 'Bird to control' target has turned into service area followed by car two, both now in car park area. Could be just a toilet stop. Standing by'

A few minutes later the tanker driver, ignoring the Happy Eater, pulled out again quickly followed by the 12 seater bus. By the A13 in London and approaching the north circular, the bus had become a Ford Mondeo. Now merging into heavy traffic with traffic lights and constant intersections, the tail would often be two or three cars behind and need directions from above to keep station. But after a couple of hours the last tailing car, a tatty Metro, kept its distance from the yellow tanker as it turned and turned again around the back streets of Brentford to where the dingy warehouse backed on to the canal. 'It's a backwater with a few narrow boats moored up. There's one or two out buildings and a parking area, all contained within high walls on the street side. It couldn't be rushed from the street. The yellow tanker has gone inside. Leaving area now, Bird to control. Over and out'

At crime squad headquarters, room 401 that afternoon, hands were shaken, backs were slapped and toasts raised in machine coffee. 'Hush up lads' shouted DC Crossland 'Let's have a bit of quiet here. Now we've got our objective in sight and I believe we've retained the element of surprise. What we haven't got is too much time in hand. We need to catch them red handed. Thanks to our stake out teams we now have hard photographic evidence from the point of importation in Amsterdam, back to Milehaven and now as far as their safe house on the canal site at Brentford. Before nicking them we need evidence of their distribution network so we can track down the stuff and the pushers. If things go true to plan our friends will be cutting up the stuff, processing the bulk cocaine into small easily managed packages, possibly doing a bit of blending. Depends what their customers want. My guess is this will be done at the warehouse within the next couple of days. We need to hit them at the right time and when we strike it must be fast and clean. Can't afford cock-ups at this stage. Now the usual approach in cars is no good as there seems to be a ten foot wall around the place and razor wire to contend with, which knocks out any element of surprise, but as this canal shot from the chopper shows'. He pointed to an enlarged black and white photograph on the blackboard, 'They are vulnerable from the canal at the back. Here, see there's a wooden jetty. Now the first place we could access the canal is about half a mile away where there is a railway bridge and a small basin with a few boats. Unfortunately the towpath from there no longer exists so we can't walk to the warehouse, but we could use a narrow boat. Only problem is noise, it's very quiet along there and the sound of a boats engine could carry and easily give the game away. If we could approach by narrow boat from higher up the canal where this basin is, we'd have to motor along until some distance off, then we could cut the engine and drift the last couple of hundred yards completely in silence. The rear entrance is only about twenty feet from the jetty so we would be able to jump them nicely from there. Any questions?'

A hand was raised. 'Will firearms be issued sir? Just in case they are carrying shooters'

'I think if four of us are armed that should do the trick'

Another hand was raised. 'This narrow boat sir, can we get someone to handle it as none of us would be capable of doing it...quietly anyway!'

'Good point; we'll organize the boat and a couple of crew. As you say any noise could jeopardize our approach'. DC Crossland looked well pleased. 'Thanks everyone. I think that covers everything. DC Ryan's in charge of this operation. He'll tie up all the loose ends and confirm timings. Good luck, come back with a result and don't get seasick on that boat!'

On Sid's boat that night there was a sense of relief that the north sea part of things was done with and could now be set aside. Things were going so well. A sense of comradeship existed between the four of them, borne out of the risks they had shared. There was still a bit of work to do out at Brentford, but they'd done it before, so this time it should be easier. 'No need for you to come along Tina' insisted Sid. 'With Jack, Mario and I, plus the two others at the warehouse, we should be able to cope. I'd rather you get back to normal and spend some time up at SA Marine. There's bound to be some mail and a few phone calls on the answer phone to deal with. I've got to be careful. It's still my legitimate business. I can't just let it go'

'Anyone for a drink' said Jack 'It's nearly happy hour. By the way Fenton rang, says congratulations are in order for the successful run. OK then, the three of us will go up to the warehouse tomorrow and get stuck into the toilet rolls. I'd better check there's enough stock to deal with the demands. Fenton said he'd made another contact, another club that's interested in taking stuff from us, so it looks as though this shipment won't be hanging around for long'

'You sure you won't need me at the warehouse' said Tina almost disappointedly. 'It's another pair of hands'

'No we're fine sweetheart, we'll doss down there overnight, few cans and some pizza, that'll keep us going. Be a bit like a stag do'

'Can't think of anything better me old lad' commented Jack 'If it takes us two nights well so much the better'

'Here Jack, talking of toilet rolls. I saw Rodney on the pontoon and he was going on about our sewage problem. He says he couldn't understand why we have to have our tanks pumped out so often the amount of times the boats get used. He seemed quite bothered about the fact.'

'How did you get round it then'

'I said we had both fitted half size tanks to allow us to carry a bit more fuel and increase our cruising range. I said we could get away with small tanks because our crews were not large and we didn't carry herds of people like he did. It was as simple as that'

Jack laughed. 'You clever old sod. What gave you the idea'

'Probably old Rodney himself. Always full of shit, so he'd

225

need a king size tank'

The news that school run two had been successful should have pleased Fenton greatly as the pick up in Amsterdam was the most dangerous. Yet something felt not quite right. Little bells were ringing. What was Charlie Nagle doing out in Colombia. He'd never been out there before, always leaving the dealing to him. Just a social occasion visiting the factory they had said when he rang, but he knew Charlie had no interest in how the stuff was made, only how much he was going to make on the deal. So he was at a meeting in Medallin discussing what!! It could only have been the current shipment. A sickening thought struck him. Suppose Juan, that smooth talking local pratt had let it slip he'd been dealing on the side. If he'd done that, the bastard, no surely not, after all the kickbacks he'd received over the years. Surely he'd be a bit more loyal. But this could be disastrous. If Nagle is aware, God help me!. He walked across to the window, gazing unseeingly at the muddy Thames water swirling underneath grimy black arches. 'God no, please, God no' He rested his head against his clenched fist placed hard against the glass of the window as if to squeeze out images that spiked his consciousness. How could I have trusted that little toad? Christ, he might have even told Charlie how much commission I've been extracting. What the bloody hell do I do now? Think man, think. Charlie hasn't said anything yet, hasn't phoned to bawl me out, not a word... He walked across to his cocktail cabinet and poured himself a large slug of whisky and drank it down in one gulp 'No news is good news I suppose. But when the Nagles go silent they're dangerous. I'll have to find out what's going on before I meet up with any of them. It doesn't look as though I'll get a lot out of Juan or the others in Medallin, that's for sure. Not if Charlie Nagle himself is involved now. His finger drummed incessantly on the bar top. Who to turn to for information, an

opinion he could trust. Justin of course. The oracle of finance. He might have heard something. Christ, where's my mobile..., answer phone, damn..., 'Oh Justin, it's Fenton can we talk... I need your help.... I'm at home for at least an hour...ring me when you can. It's urgent...bye'... Damnit!. He's always tied up in a meeting, not around when you bloody well need him. God I'm getting paranoid. Calm down. Fenton. Have another drink, the mails just come, let's just check that... He took the pile of leaflets and letters over to the window seat. Double-glazing, insurance, personal loans. A group of seagulls were drifting backwards in the swirling tide that was too strong for them, helpless other than in flight. The phone rang. Fenton leaped up 'Oh Jack', his voice was flat, 'Yes that's fine. Yes I've got another outlet possibility; it's a new club, the Peccadillo in Soho, up market venue, mixed membership. The perfect market for our stuff I would say. Yes I've had a chat with the boss man and they're good for two kilo's straight stuff, they've got a little surgery on the premises. They'll do their own mixing...No as far as I know no other mob is involved...we are in on the ground floor.... Doorman? He didn't say whose pay roll they were on, but that's his problem, we're only passing the stuff on.... Look Jack I'm sorry I've got to go. Expecting a call from Justin...yes, I'll pass on your regards...Sure we'll meet up as soon as the distribution is complete. Thanks for ringing'
The phone hit the cradle with a clatter and Fenton's fingers resumed the drumming on the tabletop. When the phone rang again, he picked it up instantaneously.
'Were you sitting on the phone?' enquired a gravel voice
'No just passing' Fenton lied. 'Thanks for ringing back. I just wanted your advice. Have you heard anything from Charlie lately?'
'You mean Charlie Nagle, one of your clients isn't he? Nasty piece of work by all accounts. I'd like to get my hands on some of their investments. Rumour has it they own a good bit

of Southern Spain, Costa del Nagle it's called isn't it'

'Never mind all that, have you heard from him?. I think I'm persona non grata in their camp at the moment, which is why I rang you. You always seem to have your ear to the ground, but you haven't heard anything of him then'

'Not likely my friend. We don't walk the same path he and I'

'What I meant was he knows you and I work closely together, and he might just have started asking questions about me'

'I don't think so, that gentleman probably knows all the answers already. Anyway if you think you've offended him best thing to do is ring him up and ask if all's well. Direct approach that's the best way in the long run'

'I can't do that, firstly I'm not certain anything is bothering him and I don't want to put ideas in his head and secondly, how can I put it, I just can't say.Look Charlie, have you heard through the Colombian lot that I've been hiving off some of your profits and done a bit of double dealing on the last two shipments, now can I'

'Oh I see your little problem now. You've been a naughty boy as far as they're concerned. Best thing is keep your head down for a bit and see what happens. Anyway he's not asked me what you've been up to with the Bayswater funds, so you can rest easy on that one. Tell you who has been on the phone though. Our Jack. Dead keen on this casino. . Must say he's done his homework. Knows how much it's going to cost. I said I could inject half a million. He says you're interested. Could keep us busy in the future. But let's concentrate on laundering this next lot from the school run. That's what you and I are good at. You keep a low profile from the Nagles for a bit until the dust settles. I'll give you a bell next week and we'll grab a bite to eat somewhere'. Fenton replaced the receiver, gently this time. Perhaps Justin was right and nothing is wrong. After all I'm only surmising that Juan had mouthed off to Charlie. He doesn't need my permission to fly off out there. His meeting could have been quite legit. Fenton was feeling a little better about himself. He was glad Justin had put his mind at ease. He would take his friends advice and chill out, drift like the seagulls with the tide.

Four floors down, parked up outside Fenton's block of flats was a large white laundry van. Inside were two shirt-sleeved police officers sitting at an array of high tech audio equipment. PC Taylor eased off his headphones and switched off the tape recorder. 'I think that's it Tony, all nicely taped loud and clear. Care for half a doughnut?'

The gatekeeper inside the rusting wrought iron gates had a clear view along the approach road and was ready when the car drew up and flashed its headlights. He swung them open swiftly causing the board sign Sanitation Services to slip lopsidedly as he did so. He touched his cap 'Evening Mr. Jack, if you park over by the garage the car will be out of sight. I'll lock up after you'. Sid and Mario disappeared and Jack strolled round to the canal-side loading jetty. It was by most standards a drab and squalid place but had tranquillity. Perfect reflections of mellow brickwork and brambles where the towpath had once been, hung mirror-like, unspoilt by the slightest ripple, except where carpet weed covered whole sections of stagnant water, broken only by the intrusion of domestic rubbish. Even inside the building there lingered the smell of decay peculiar to old buildings. Only in the kitchen where fresh sandwiches and cans of beer were laid out was there a welcome, an oasis of activity in three floors of disuse. 'Thanks Ticker, you've done us proud. Is everything ready in the outhouse? The old man nodded 'Yep Mr. Jack the trestle tables are up and we're stocked up on toilet rolls and packing materials again. Vans round the back ready for loading. I've unlocked the cupboards ready for storing the packages waiting for delivery.'

'Nobody knows about our activities here do they Ticker. We can't afford any slip-ups now.'

'Good Lord No Mr. Jack You can trust me. I know when to keep me trap shut'

'Good man. We'll start as soon as we've polished this lot off and then work on until we're bushed. We can bunk down in the annex for a bit then carry on in the morning if necessary. The less time this stuff is around here the better. OK Lads?'

'Just one thing' said Sid. 'The cupboards in the outhouse, bit obvious for storing aren't they. This place is so full of your old furniture, why can't we hide it in some of the old desks or the filing cabinets?'

Jack smiled 'I hope the stuff won't be here long enough to worry about it'.

Whilst the boys enjoyed their sandwiches and beer they recalled the highlights of their north sea trip.

'Remember when the water police waved as we passed. I could have shit a brick at the time' said Sid. Jack turned to Ticker. 'We thought for a moment they were waving us down and going to bring us in'

'But' said Sid 'The strangest thing was that blip on the radar, it was weird, following us like that for hours'

'What was it' asked the caretaker 'A ship'

'No' said Sid 'It wasn't a ship. I spotted it well above the horizon with my binoculars. It was definitely a helicopter, but thankfully it disappeared when we got nearly home'

'OK' announced Jack, 'Enough's enough. Bring the radio Ticker. We'll have a bit of music while we work. Let's get out and on with the job'

High above in the night sky a flashing light winked unseen, and engine unheard by those inside. 'Control this is Bird. Am in position over canal target, in sight by infrared. One light in main building. Outhouse well lit. Condition slight overcast, intermittent moonlight. Listening out, Bird over'

The pilot pointed above his head. 'We'd better back off and gain a little height. If they hear us hovering it could spook them a bit and screw up everything for the others'. The police helicopter climbed steadily away from the conspirators in their kitchen, to where its lights merged with the stars and any engine noise dissipated into the night. At this height the canal became a silvery ribbon where moonlight touched water in this sleepy backwater. Half a mile away along its banks a narrow boat lay nestled under a railway arch. Dark figures were moving on the 'Camden Rose' One by one they disappeared down below. 'Last one in shut the hatch and doors. We don't want to disturb the neighbours, if there are any around here. It seems a bit of an urban desert'

'Gather round' said the leader. 'Now you've all been briefed, but we'll go through a few points again. Our object is to gain entry to the storage warehouse along here where intelligence indicates it's being used as a safe house by a drugs ring. We anticipate finding three or four suspects inside, We need a nice clean bust! Access from the road is very difficult so we have to go in from this canal. Approach from the rear is ideal, but only possible by boat. Hence our presence on Camden Rose,... this gentlemen' DS Ryan indicated with his hand a scruffy old man with a teenager by his side, 'is Mr. Jenkins and his son. They own this boat and have been kind enough to help us out tonight. They are going to transport us along this canal, gaining sufficient momentum to be able to cut the engine before the warehouse and glide silently to our target, where we will nick our suspects, hopefully red handed and in possession. Simple really. That's the plan. Now the bad news. Boats have no brakes and with a heavy steel boat like this the only way to stop is to go into reverse and rev up the engine. But we can't do this cos we'll be heard by all and sundry. So Mr. Jenkins is going to judge the right moment to cut the engine and hopefully we shall drift right up to the warehouse jetty. Not before it, as we don't want to get wet. Now we're not exactly sure where the villains will be, in the main building or the outhouse. Our eye in the sky has reported both buildings well lit. So once on the jetty we'll divide into two groups and tackle both entrances at once. Remember no shooting, unless threatened, nor the gas grenades unless I give the word. Once in position, don't nobody move a muscle until you hear the whistle, then with these axes, we smash the locks if necessary. OK? Anybody who drops any gear in the canal is in big trouble.

Poor Mr. Jenkins, when asked to hire out his narrow boat that night, he was expecting a TV crew shooting the boys in blue for a television drama production. Even thought he and his son might be film extras. Instead they were confronted by the stark reality of sinister figures dressed in black with hooded faces, and armed for combat. The Jenkins mouths opened in concern growing swiftly into fear as Smith and Wesson automatics were unholstered and checked for ammunition. 'OK let's go' shouted the leader. 'No noise from now on. You lot keep silent'.

Neither of the Jenkins moved, their feet rooted to the spot at the prospect of the unscheduled active service. 'When you're ready Mr. Jenkins. Turn the engine over and we can get this show on the road'

Dom, dom dom, spluttered the ancient Bollinger engine, smoke belching out of the boat funnel. Her bow edged out gingerly clear from the bank side. Jenkins son pushed the back end away and jumped aboard with ease. Displacing surface slime and scraping gently against a rusty shopping trolley gradually Camden Rose increased speed. Jenkins senior peered ahead through the night shadows, one arm on the tiller. He whispered to his son standing beside him. 'The laundry chimney is about half way, that's where we'll cut the engine and try and drift down from there. We should just about get to the jetty. You look out and make sure nothing's in the water to stop us. And let me know when we're about level. You'll have to go down the front'. Jenkins junior jumped up onto the roof and made his way along the seventy feet of boat towards the front mumbling 'Jesus it's the real thing this is, better than the telly'

The sky had cleared of overcast as the four walked across the yard to the outhouse, waiting as Ticker unlocked the door. 'Lovely night' remarked Jack looking up at the night sky.

'There we are Gents' croaked the old caretaker standing aside to let the trio in. 'I'll lock you in then I'll get back to the kitchen and make up some thermos jugs of coffee for later' He waved and ambled towards the landing stage. A first quarter moon wobbled weakly in the black water at his feet as he cupped his hands to relight a dog end, then tapped hard on his hearing aid... Damn thing was making a dom.dom noise now. Never been the same since he'd dropped it in the pub and someone had stepped on it... He left the kitchen door on the latch ready to empty the waste bin and went inside.

'It's coming up Dad' hissed Jenkins Junior...Fifty yards.... level.... now!' With a resigned cough the vintage engine cut, leaving a silence which was nothing short of eerie. Just a swish of water flowing past and a barking dog somewhere in the distance. Everyone on board felt the slowing down of the boat. Junior gave two flashes on his torch indicating that he could see the warehouse and jetty ahead. A patch of rather nasty weed slowed the boat right down till it was hardly moving forward at all. 'Come on you stupid cow' said old Jenkins to himself. 'Don't let me down now. Just a few more yards'. Junior standing on the front end with mooring rope in hand expertly slung the loop over an old rusty bollard on the end of the jetty and hung on with all his life. The back end swung round. Jenkins Senior got hold of the back rope and jumped onto the greasy jetty. Camden Rose was dead in the water now and her sinister passengers would soon be gone into the shadows of the night. 'Thank God' he said to himself. 'What a night'

At the thump of old Jenkins feet and the judder as the old iron hull ground into the side of the jetty the squad steadied themselves and one by one shifted forward, emerging silently as instructed out into the night air and away into the shadows. Father and son watched mutely still wondering if all this had happened to them or was a dream. A dark figure hissed at old Jenkins 'Well done, thanks. Don't start up the engine, smoke or show a light. Stay put till I tell you OK'

Jenkins nodded in the dark.

Ryan led the pack until they were in the yard area, then beckoning with his hand got them altogether in a huddle. 'Right stay low I'll do a recce. They neither saw nor heard him in the next few minutes as he flitted in short cat like hops from corner to corner until he re-emerged behind them.

'OK there's only three of them in that building over there. Bloody place is full of toilet rolls. Hope we're not being led up the garden path here. There's a light in what looks like a bit of an old kitchen. I can only just see in because the curtains are half drawn. Right, four of us will take the outhouse building, two the kitchen. Johnson you stand by the van and the main gate just in case someone makes a break for it that way. Right you three with me. Try the doors first before you break in they may be unlocked. OK on my signal then'

The huddle broke away.

Back on the Camden Rose, Jenkins Senior hissed at his son who had remained on the landing stage. 'Get down here you pillock before any shooting starts. You heard what the man said. Let's make ourselves scarce till he comes back'

'Oh I'll miss all the fun Dad' he wined. 'They won't shoot us. Not when we've been working with them'

'You don't know if there'll be any stray bullets flying around son. Or one of them criminals rushes out here and takes us hostage or hi-jacks the boat'

'Oh very likely Dad, They'd only get about five feet on Rosy and that's if we could manage to start the engine!

In the harshness of the strip light glare in the outhouse two trestle tables end to end were covered with toilet rolls in various stages of preparation. Ends carefully prized open to receive the exotic and expensive additives, that slid neatly into the cardboard tubes. 'It's as quick as loading bullets into a gun' shouted Mario above the noise of the radio.

'Trust you to make that comparison' said Sid. 'But I must say it's'... He never finished his sentence. No one had noticed the lock being quietly tried until a heavy blow smashed it open. Within seconds the room was of full of black figures, faces covered with gas masks, guns in hands. One pushed his mask up and shouted 'Against the wall. Hands up, legs spread, all of you. Now!' Don't move a muscle, don't even fucking breathe'. Immediately hands were frisking them for weapons. 'This ones got a shooter Guv' said a black figure taking a 38 revolver from Mario's leg holster. 'Rest are clean'

'Right then, bracelets on' snapped Ryan 'Good nice clean job lads, no mess that's the way we like it'

Another figure materialized in the doorway shouting 'Old guy in the kitchen passed out when I broke in, conscious now, but he doesn't look too good. Seems he's a caretaker of sorts round here. I think he may need medical attention I've called an ambulance. No one else around. Johnson's opened the main gate and our van is here with the uniform lads. They'll secure the premises, Bloody hell! There's a lot going on here sir. Bog rolls everywhere, looks like national shit house week!' Ryan nodded. 'Release the boat people now, tell them they can go home and someone better stay with the caretaker till the paramedics get here. Now then you lot' he turned towards the three men pinned up against the wall 'What have we got here then. Think I'd better read you your rights. Get them down the Nick lads. It's going to be a long night'

By midnight the toilet rolls now destined never to reach the bright lights of London sat secure in police custody together with their cocaine content, and the caretaker overtaken by a brief life of crime lay on a trolley in A & E recovering from shock. Down at the station in separate cells three members of the school run were in detention. Around the warehouse everything was quiet. Only from the canal could any sound be heard, the distant dom dom of the engine as Camden Rose returned slowly through the darkness to her mooring beneath the bridge.

'Shine your torch over to the left a bit more' shouted Jenkins to his son who was sitting cross-legged on the cabin roof. 'I can't see where I'm going. You realize we've been breaking the law tonight navigatin' without lights. Serious offence that. Amazing what the fuzz get away with. Perhaps we should add danger money to the hire fee'

When Syndicopy was given clearance to release the story of the school run and its connections with Milehaven marina, bells were to ring in many places. Rodney Blake was to receive a letter from the planning committee stating that Milehaven marina was no longer seen as a viable location, in the light of recent events connected to the smuggling of drugs. In this instance a venue further into the city was found to be more pleasing for planners and potential backers.

Rodney studied his letter, His eyes moist. 'What a total disgrace, How could those two bastards Delaney and Arthur do this to him? How dare they destroy the reputation of the club and all it stood for? Two trusted committee members who actually flew the Blue Ensign flag abroad while smuggling drugs right under the noses of the membership and both with the greyhound boats at that. God's teeth it didn't bear thinking about. He'd have to resign now as Commodore, there was no other course. He was responsible for the actions of his crews. It was the way of the sea, always had been, so unfair to those in command. I must fall on my sword just because of the vile greed of a couple of low life villains. Why didn't I see it coming? All those trips to Amsterdam.... all too late now...the damage was done. Milehaven and my name tainted as far as society is concerned. The letter must go off today with a suitable press release'. He stood for some time hands covering his face, trying to shut out what had happened then with a roar of anguish, like a wounded lion, swung his arm across his huge inlaid leather desk sending everything flying. The photograph of Liz and he, taken at the Investiture joined an oval silver tray and crystal port decanter smashed together on the marble floor. His globe atlas bounced into the corner of the room ending India upwards in an ornamental fern.

The Nagle Brothers were taking breakfast on the balcony of their luxurious apartment in Marbella when the phone rang in the hall. 'Get that Sophie will you' growled Charlie. Take a message if you have to, we're eating'
'It's Slim' she squawked 'says it's very urgent, 'ee needs to talk' The addressed stood up, mouth full of black pudding. 'This better be werf it'
He returned some moments later and relit the remaining half of his cigar before announcing. 'The drug squad, they've nabbed the family that call themselves the School Run'
'Ooh' said his brother picking his teeth with the end of a business card.

237

'Their cover was Sanitation Services you know'
'Well that's their hard luck. No big deal for us though eh!'
'I'm not too sure, that's the mob our Fenton got himself involved wif'
'Ooh 'as 'ee naw'
'Yeah when I was out with the cartel they dropped a clanger by letting it slip that our Fenton might be double dealing. Buying for someone else. Well it's this lot. Now if the police get their hands on Fenton and arrest him. He might go Queen's evidence. That'll drop us in it, good and proper. The blokes too smooth by arf' just the sort for a bit of plea-bargaining if push came to shove. I've had me worries over Fenton before. We've given him too much rope in the past'
'And you think it's time to hang 'im then'
'Let's say we can't afford for him to get into the enemies hands. I'll give Slim another ring and get the matter put in hand. OK with you Brov' He turned to the two girls sat on the loungers soaking up the sun. Right you girls, here's a wad, go on down to Malaga and buy something pretty for yourselves. Vic and I have a bit of business to do'

Janet Arthur looked a bit of a mess; she had hardly stopped crying since Sid's phone call saying he'd been remanded in custody until he came up before the magistrates. She was in the middle of sorting out the washing when the doorbell rang and in no mood to talk to anyone, but the caller persisted.
'Oh Tina' she said half looking through the glass of the front door. Undoing the chain she let her in saying 'Oh please don't take any notice of the mess. I'm all behind this morning. I can't stop thinking about Sid. What do you know about it all?'
'Only that he's been held in police cells with Jack and Mario, following some sort of police raid in Brentford'. Janet motioned her into the kitchen and put the kettle on. Something

238

she did as a reflex action when she felt threatened by life.

'The dreadful thing is Tina; I don't know what's going on. It's something to do with drugs. The police have been here and gone through this place with a fine toothcomb. But drugs, that's evil, and Sid's not that sort of man. I told the police. It must be a case of mistaken identity. They've got the wrong man locked up'

Tina hesitated for a minute, swallowed hard and said 'Actually Janet, you're right in one way Sid doesn't take drugs, he's not an addict, it's something far worse. He's been smuggling them in. He's a dealer!'

Janet's mouth dropped open 'What do you mean he's a dealer, someone who hangs around pubs?'

'Not exactly, he's brought stuff into the country on his boat and taken part in the distribution of it'

Janet swung round in defence of her husband. 'But how do you know all this, how can you be sure.'

'Because Janet I've been part of it too. That's why `I'm here to tell you before you read it in the papers'

Janet shook her head in disbelief.

'So you're telling me that you and my husband have taken the boat and smuggled drugs without me guessing anything'

'I'm afraid so'.

'I suppose you two have been having an affair as well'

Tina lowered her head. 'I'm so sorry, believe me I never meant things to...!'

'So it's true, I often wondered about the nights he spent on that boat. You bitch, you scheming little bitch. You wormed your way into our marriage, our business, our boat, and now you've dragged my Sid into the underworld. Well madam, I hope you're satisfied with what you've done. So tell me then, all this extra money that we've had just lately isn't because my husband has been working so hard down at SA Marine, it's dirty money, drug money. I should have known. No wonder we've been swimming in used ten and twenty pound notes. I really thought he'd being doing jobs on the quiet and had been paid in cash. It's like him to try and avoid the taxman from time to time. But no, I can see it now. Well if he goes to prison at least I'll have the satisfaction of you not being with him. It'll be better to think of him shut away in a cell rather than sun-bathing on some beach with you... Get out of my house before I tell the police where to find you...you scheming witch you'...she screamed dissolving into sobs.

A red light glowed on the tape machine as the record button was depressed.

'Interview of suspect commenced at 0905. Present, DS Ryan and DC Taylor. 'So you deny knowledge of others involved in the drug ring known as the School Run?'

'No comment'

'And neither you or Jack Delaney have any connection with the Nagle Brothers and the so called Bayswater Boys?'

Sidney shifted awkwardly in his chair. 'No comment'

Detective Ryan stared hard at the accused who seemed to lack the arrogance of a seasoned professional and he judged shouldn't be too much of a problem to break down, given time and patience.

'For the purpose of the tape I am showing Mr. Arthur two photographs. One of Mr. Fenton Gesler standing on a pontoon at Milehaven with Mr. Arthur and the other is of Mr. Arthur standing at the doorway of Mr.Gesler's flat. Do you agree these two meetings took place?'

'He's just a friend, that's all. I've met him once or twice with Jack. Some joint business. He's Jack Delaney's accountant that's all'

'Did you know this man is known for his connection in Colombian drugs, the handling and transfer of large sums of doubtful money into offshore accounts?... I am stopping the tape as Mr. Arthur's solicitor has just entered the room...

Resuming interview at 10.22am. Now come on Sid, make it easier for yourself. You and Jack did the running, while Fenton paid the bills and did the business side with Colombia, right?'

'You don't have to answer that' warned the solicitor.

'He might as well' pressed Ryan. 'We've photographic evidence of both boats being loaded with the cocaine in Amsterdam and forensics have found traces of cocaine round concealed compartments on both Arthur's and Delaney's boats. Also you were found in possession of the stuff in the warehouse. Look Sidney you're going down for a long time unless you help us with our inquiries. We need the low down on the others in this set up. Why protect them. They're the ones who stood to make all the money while you and Jack did all the dirty work. Now he's the smart one Jack is. He's told us nearly all we need to know. All we need is for you to confirm a few things'

'You don't have to Sidney. He's probably bluffing. It's the oldest trick in the book' warned the legal eagle.

Ryan's voice cut in. 'He can make up his own mind can't he. He knows we have the proof. He also knows how much the others have used him. It's like the warehouse man Ticker isn't it. He knew something was going on, but chose to turn the other way. Now look at him, in hospital wondering what hit him. Do you know what'll hit you Sidney I bet you do, and it'll get worse unless you help yourself' He leant forward across the desk and whispered 'You see Sidney there are others who want to talk to you. In fact we are doing you a favour by keeping you locked up. But then you've never heard of the Nagle Brothers and the Bayswater Boys have you Sid. But their little patch is what you and Jack have been muscling in on. I'm surprised at you Sid, no form, never been inside, having the bottle to take on those lads. They're not nice to know, dear me no, evil things they do to families of those who double cross them'

241

Sid's bottom lip started to tremble, hands clenched, signs well known to interviewers and lawyers everywhere. Ryan sat back. The solicitor put his hand on Sid's arm... 'I think my client should...' but it was too late. Sid's emotional boiler burst and clutching his head in both hands he blurted out in between sobs 'But I didn't want all the money. Just enough to clear my debts. God help me that's all I wanted. I've done nothing to these Bayswater Boys' He dissolved into a sobbing heap; head down almost on the table. The distraught suspect was beyond restraint or calculated response, exactly what Ryan had hoped for, the veritas of uncontrolled emotion. He checked to see the spool on the tape machine was still revolving just as Sid's tear stained face came up from the table 'It's Fenton they should be looking for. I've done nothing to the Nagles. He's the one whose been double dealing. People like him and Justin Rosenstein, they deal in money for the sake of it'. Sobs again from Sid. Ryan reached across to the tape machine. 'Interview stopped at 11.31 am. I don't think we'll get much further today we'll continue tomorrow. See Sidney gets a cup of tea Kevin will you?'

The little group stood up and Sid was escorted back to his cell. 'That was emotional persecution Ryan and well you know it' hissed the solicitor 'And I was given no chance to restrain my client given the state he was in' 'Worked brilliantly didn't it. He'll be alright tomorrow, and a bit of luck we shall have pulled in Fenton by then. Sid needed to get it off his chest'

Two long polished corridors and a grotty lift later they were back in Ryan's office, a jumble of computer monitors, keyboards and printers strewn with pink memo's, note books and half drunk plastic cups of coffee. 'Gesler is the key to getting at the Bayswater Boys I am sure of that. If we can pull him in, on suspicion of the school run charge, that's Sanitation Services of course, perhaps we can lean on him a bit and blow the whistle on the mob, offer a bit of a blind eye in return for helping us with our inquiries. Then of course there is this Justin Rosenstein, our Sidney has just mentioned. Listen Kevin, see what you can turn up on this Justin guy and I'll get the boys to bring in Fenton. I'll get this transcript written up. I'll tell you one thing, Gesler won't be a push over like our Sid, probably won't say a thing until his lawyer is present. I hate interviews with smooth talking accountants'

Fenton's coffee had long gone cold. His toast hardly touched as he sat at the breakfast table whisky tumbler in his hand. There was no panic. The police raid at Brentford was a nasty turn of events and had shaken him badly, but there was nothing to connect his name to the school run, nothing on paper anyway. He had always been so careful not to keep anything in writing relating to these matters. So if the others kept silent he and Justin could stay in the clear, which is what he'd told him on the phone. Nevertheless it did make sense to go to ground for a bit and take up Justin's offer of a holiday on an island in the Indian Ocean. That would be far enough away until things cooled down this end. After all there was nothing he could do for them. He couldn't give evidence could he now! Keep a low profile, far away, that's it. This deathly silence was becoming wearing. He would normally be working on the Bayswater books now, but since Charlie's trip to Colombia, things had gone very quiet and he still hadn't taken Justin's advice by ringing him. He also had avoided dining out in the club just incase he should bump into one of the boys. Well he'd soon be in another world, sitting in the sun, sipping something exotic...His suitcase was packed, checked everything was turned off, that'll be it... He glanced at his watch twenty minutes till the taxi came. Right, time to get the cases down into the hall. The door phone rang and a bright voice came through the metallic box. 'Yellow pages for Mr. Gesler'
'Leave it in the hallway. I'll pick it up in a minute'

With the cases stood to one side of him in the lobby he opened the textured glass front door, bending down to bring in the yellow pages volume, noticing as he did so the black van parked in the road outside. The last thing Fenton Gesler ever saw was a flash before the first high velocity bullet struck him in the chest just below the collarbone; the second went in his forehead. There was no cry or violent flailing of arms. He simply fell back still in his crouched position to land amongst the cases. Five or six minutes later the taxi drew up. The driver got out of his cab and went to push the doorbell. The door was half open with Fenton's foot obstructing it. He pushed the door harder. Inside he found Fenton arms outspread across two matching suitcases, head blasted back almost out of sight. The taxi driver clutched his head and shouted loudly for help but such was the anonymity of London flats that no one came. Having established the victim was dead the driver staggered back out to his cab and summoned the emergency services via his control. Within minutes medics and police were on hand. Identification was soon established from the luggage labels and his wallet. DS Ryan had to report to his boss that their prime suspect for the school run, and any chance of nailing the Bayswater Boys as part of this bust had been severely damaged and as he wryly put it there, was no prize for guessing who had so neatly taken him out before he had time to point the finger.

The next day Justin Rosenstein would sit alone on his balcony with its panoramic views over mountains and the sea hearing Fenton's suave voice saying… 'I can't come to the phone at the moment so if you'd care to leave a message after the tone 'I'll get back to you on my return'

Late Autumn sunlight filtered through vertical blinds in the Wardroom bar, casting shafts of light across rows of optic bottles on glass shelves, causing Steward Ken Miles to squint as an early drinker stood before him.

'Morning Sir, can't see for looking. It's a bright one isn't it, what'll it be?' The young man smiled, touching one of the four brass beer pump handles 'I'll take a pint of this I think, you're a free house I see.'

'Yes the members like it that way, better than being tied to one brewery, good drop of bitter this, real cask conditioned ale'

They both watched as Ken's practised hands eased the beer frothing into the glass. 'Tell me' asked the stranger 'What time does the Chandlery next-door open. I imagine that's where the Brokers Office is?'

'The yacht brokerage, that's right, Bob Jensen, he handles that side of things. Should be anytime now. Is he expecting you?'

'Yes I rang him yesterday, he's handling the sale of the Grey Lady I believe'

'Rodney Blake's boat, yes that's right, sad business. He loved that boat you know. Broke his heart when all the smuggling business came out. Sent him over the top, poor devil, took an overdose. He's been in a clinic ever since. You've probably read about it in the papers. He used to be our Commodore here at Milehaven. None of us could hardly believe it I can tell you, what with two of our committee involved, our club secretary and our flag officer as well. Couldn't have been worse really.

'Sidney Arthur and Jack Delaney you mean'

'That's right. D'you know them?'

'Not personally but I've heard them mentioned'

Ken shook his head sadly 'Well they'll be out of circulation for a long time it seems, about fifteen years. It's caused some changes around here. We've had to elect new officers as you can imagine. John Crowther is Commodore now. He's a nice bloke, real Gent. Ex Merchant Navy Captain. Retired of course now. Lost his wife a couple of years back. He's been living on that old motor sailor down there on the pontoon. Just him and his dog Bosun. He planned to take it on a single-handed global cruise but of course he ended up taking over here and living with the journalist who was largely responsible for the police solving the case as quickly as they did'.

'Who was that?'

'Sutcliffe, I think her name is, Jenny, that's it, a crime reporter. She'd been around the drug scene for some time in London and by chance recognized one of the people involved visiting Jacks boat down here, and sort of took it from there you might say. You interested in boats then? Oh you must be or you wouldn't be down here would you'

The young man took a long pull on his pint, wiping the froth from his lips before replying. 'In that boat in particular, yes because it's different. It looks purposeful, unlike the others down here, which are all, well pretty playthings I suppose. But this place itself has got a lot going for it. Not as your Rodney Blake saw it, a new London marina, wasn't it? But certainly it could be extended to accommodate more berths, luxury housing and sophisticated entertainment for visiting foreign yachtsmen. Who knows, may be even a quayside casino'

Ken eyebrows raised 'My goodness that would certainly do wonders for takings here in this bar. You sound like someone with an eye to the future sir, if you don't mind my saying so'

'Comes naturally I suppose, you see I'm a surveyor specializing in development projects. Have been ever since I qualified. I handle all property purchases and interests for my Father and Uncle and I hope Milehaven could be one of them'

The Steward smiled 'Same again Mr.? Sorry I didn't catch your name'

'Oh it's Nagle, David Victor Nagle'

246

About the Author

Bob Gondolo left art school to enter the London advertising scene as a fashion art director. But, having enjoyed location photography with top models in society's chosen high spots around the globe, a chance idea had him signed up to write a weekly cartoon strip in a TV magazine. An increasing interest in words rather than pictures, coupled with experience on a seagoing motor yacht (and, latterly, his own boat in the south of France), provided the background for *The School Run*. He has held three Art Fellowships, with membership of the Cartoonist Club of Great Britain, and is now well into writing his next novel, working in an 18th-century stone cottage in Leicestershire with Maggie (his wife), a runaway church cat, and a garden fit for goats.